On the Rocks

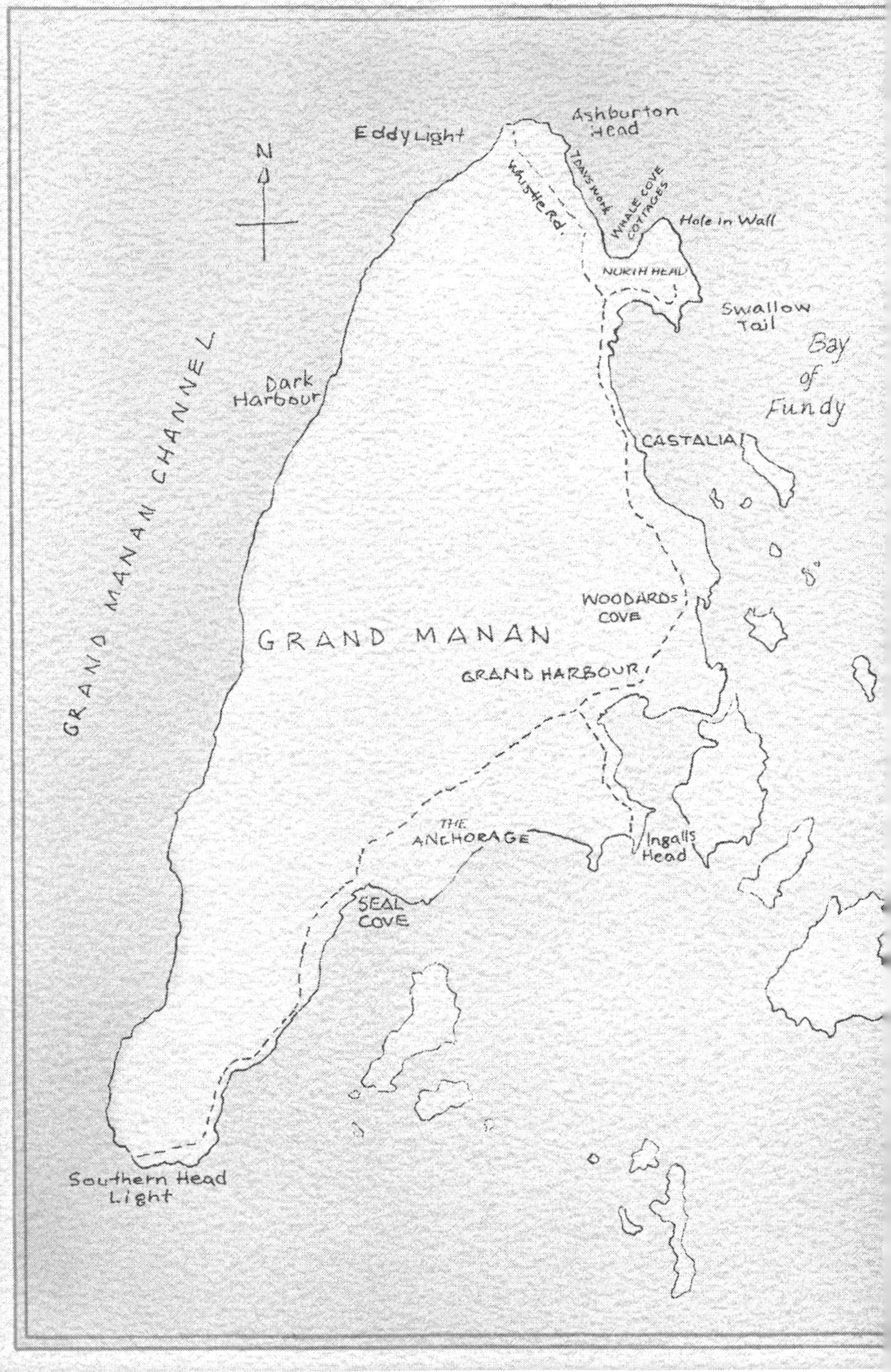
Eddy Light
Ashburton Head
N
7 DAYS WORK
Whistle Rd.
WHALE COVE COTTAGES
Hole in Wall
NORTH HEAD
Swallow Tail
Bay of Fundy
Dark Harbour
GRAND MANAN CHANNEL
CASTALIA
WOODARDS COVE
GRAND MANAN
GRAND HARBOUR
THE ANCHORAGE
Ingalls Head
SEAL COVE
Southern Head Light

On the Rocks

A Willa Cather and Edith Lewis Mystery

Sue Hallgarth

ARBOR FARM PRESS
Albuquerque

afp

ARBOR FARM PRESS

P.O. Box 56783, Albuquerque, New Mexico 87187

arborfarmpress.com

Printed by BookMobile, Minneapolis, Minnesota USA bookmobile.com

Distributed by Itasca Books, Minneapolis, Minnesota USA itascabooks.com

Cover design by Ann Weinstock

Interior design, photo illustration, and typesetting by Sara DeHaan

Photo and illustration credits: Window frame (front cover) copyright ©
Csaba Molnar/Vetta/Getty Images; Willa Cather and Edith Lewis 1920
passport photos (front cover) courtesy of the National Archives and Records
Administration; *Grand Manan Map* (frontispiece), *From the Red Trail* (p. 143),
Facing the Bay (p. 199) by Jake Page; *Grand Manan Ferry 1927* (p. 9), *Tourist
Brochure 1927* (p. 116) courtesy of the Grand Manan Archives, Grand Manan
Museum; *Hole in the Wall* (p. 28), *Herring Weir* (p. 49), *Eel Brook* (p. 65), *Low Tide
Seven Days Work* (p.171), *Naughty Spruce* (p. 215) by Sue Hallgarth; *Whale Cove
Inn Living Room* (p. 84) courtesy of Laura Buckley; *Rock Wall with Herbs*
(p. 107) by Sara DeHaan; *Their Circles Widen* (p. 244) by Cliff Romig.

This book was set in Bembo with Bodoni titling,
using Adobe Creative Suite 5.5 software.

Library of Congress Control Number: 2012938786

ISBN 978-0-9855200-0-7

To the late Kathleen Buckley
and the "Cottage Girls"

I

EDITH LEWIS GOT out her easel and watercolors and set them up near the edge of the bluff in front of their cottage on Whale Cove. Most of the previous afternoon Edith had spent trying to catch the rough beauty of the rocks just where the water cascaded over for a long, leisurely dive to the darker rocks below, then joined the chill, salt water of the Bay of Fundy. From this angle she could just hear the faint sound of its rush.

Actually two waterfalls occupied this section of the cliffs between Whale Cove and Ashburton Head known as Seven Days Work, where rock layer upon discernible layer rose well over two hundred feet to tower above the beach below. The height of the cliff in front of the cottage she and Willa had built four years before was breathtaking, but these cliffs just to the north were even more dramatic, dwarfing the fifty foot tides that regularly rose and fell in this part of the world, so that except for the long rattle of shingle with each tide's withdrawal, the waves seemed almost usual.

The afternoon light was perfect for another try, Edith decided, fastening the paper so the slight breeze coming off the water would not disturb her work. A pair of gulls circling just off to the right caught her attention, and she paused to watch as one of them, nearer the water, pumped her wings and rose to the same level as her mate, then reached out to re-embrace the air. Floating opposite each other in the same lazy circle, the pair rode effortlessly, graceful, chattering occasionally, almost inconsequentially, Edith surmised, about the prospect of fish offered by the solitary rower in the dory below. He was, Edith knew and she thought the gulls probably did too, heading out to check the herring weir staked well out in the water below their bluff. A lone boatman inspecting nets at high tide would supply few fish for the gulls. They must know that too, Edith thought. Perhaps they were riding scout just to be sure or, it was such a lovely day, maybe they thought it would be a shame not to tag along for the flight.

Flying seemed such joy compared to bobbing about on the sea. Edith never reached Grand Manan without nausea and had only once dared to go out with the others to see how the local fishermen worked their nets. Willa went out at least once every season, but Edith preferred the solidity of earth. Such rolling about was the same as living with an inner ear disturbance, Edith declared every time they made the crossing between Eastport and North Head. Humans weren't intended to imitate fish, and only dead fish float like boats.

But flying might be different, Edith thought now, turning back to her preparations. At least soaring would be, like those gulls. Lindbergh made flight look easy. Willa and Edith had followed closely the news of Lindbergh's flight. When he landed in Paris, it was as though he had reached the moon, Edith chuckled to herself, people were that excited. Of course, now he had to learn to live with fame, Edith took a moment to massage the bristles on her brushes. And fame was much less glamorous than most people guessed. Lindbergh still seemed to be having fun, even with all the row about his wedding and new wife. But they were young, Edith smiled, plunging her brush into water. They should have fun. Plenty of time for the rest.

With the afternoon sun on the other side of the island, shadows cast the rocks near the two waterfalls into sharp relief. Edith hoped today she could manage exactly the right touch, fanning her brush to keep the deeper shades firmly on the outer edge of the bristles. It was difficult to capture the jagged recesses of the ledge just where the waterfall flung itself over. Once she had that, she thought a few strokes of the darker hues topped by some touches of green to suggest the wind-tossed evergreens above, and it would be finished.

A flash of red caught Edith's attention, and she stared at a stand of scrubby trees less than thirty feet from the nearest waterfall. Nothing red reappeared. The weathered spruce where the flash had been reminded Edith of nothing so much as naughty children digging in their heels and leaning back vigorously, as though they wanted to touch the land beneath with their whole bodies, refusing even to look at the sea beyond.

Someone must have scurried away from the edge, Edith guessed. The old sheep trails everyone used could get much too close for comfort along Seven Days Work. Inexperienced hikers were often afraid, especially when they found themselves sharing a trail with the sheep that still grazed loose among the rocks.

Then a sound came, muffled, something like a shout. Edith strained to hear, but it was gone. Nothing followed. Just water falling and the waves. Gulls still chattered near the weir. Edith touched her brush to the paper, fanned it slightly, and then pulled the stroke down. This would work, yes, she decided. She reached for the ocher and glanced again at the cliff.

Soundless this time, motion. The back of a red shirt straightened. An arm shot out. Then a body appeared to fling itself over the edge, head first as though diving. It was a man, dressed in what looked from this distance like a business suit, but tilted oddly, sideways, as though he had decided to face Edith throughout his decline. After the first rushed impulse, the body seemed to slow precipitously and momentarily to drift, then pick up speed again as it neared the waves, Edith realized with a shock, receding from the rocks below.

EDITH alone had seen the body plummet. Eric Dawson, the solitary rower, glimpsed only the end of its fall, his attention directed by Edith's horrified shout and frantic gestures. He laid to the oars and watched Edith spin away, running first toward the cliffs at Seven Days Work, then back toward the cottages at Whale Cove. Before he reached the spot where he thought the body landed, just south of the waterfalls, he saw the cliff by the cottages fill up with women, first the one they called Cather, then several more. Cottage Girls. He could tell by their clothes. None of the local women wore men's horse-riding pants or dresses that looked like sacks with no waists at all. They were holding onto each other and pointing, running back and forth, arms flailing. A dog leapt from one to another, almost spinning in air, then charged a few sheep making their way toward the cove. White dots disappeared into the trees. Eric could hear only his own breath, the quick creak of the oars, and the waves washing him in.

When he reached the beach, Eric could see no body, just a few boulders poking through the foam. Instead of leaping out of the dory and running to rescue the man as he expected, Eric had to climb onto the seat of his dory to get a vantage point. He put his hand to his forehead, shading his eyes as though that might help him find the man. Then he noticed reddened foam sliding from one of the boulders, and just beyond a dark suit rose and fell, slapping gently against the rocks nearby.

II

"STRAIGHT UP. THAT'S how I take mine," Sabra Jane accepted the cup Edith had offered earlier that afternoon. "I'm not a fussy person. Never have been."

The day had been typical on Grand Manan, a small island in New Brunswick, located just above Campobello in the Bay of Fundy. Populated by fishing villages and invaded each spring by a few tourists and colonies of summer residents, Grand Manan spent most mornings cloaked in fog, then the sky would clear and the day would remain peaceful, quiet, and generally uneventful.

Edith smiled, appreciating Sabra Jane's directness. It matched her sensible habits of dress, the tailored red shirt with sleeves rolled to the elbows revealing the strong hands and wrists of a potter. Locally, Sabra Jane was famous for her clothes and long, loping stride. People thought it was nice that she could also make pots.

Edith bent to offer the second cup to Willa, turning the tray slightly so Willa could reach the milk and sugar easily.

"Just a touch of milk and sugar. That's all I ever take," Willa settled back in the Adirondack chair, placing her heels on the low wicker table that did double duty as their hassock outdoors. "And I like my tea hot," she sipped. "Hot and strong, so I can taste it. Just the way I like coffee. It's the taste I'm after, and the heat. Sets me up as if it had a lot of caffeine but without the aftereffects." They had been talking earlier that afternoon, as they prepared the soil for planting herbs, about homeopathy and Willa's preference for Sanka, one of the special supplies they brought with them every summer to Whale Cove. The caffeine in coffee worked against homeopathic remedies.

"I'm afraid I'm almost British when it comes to things like tea," Edith felt momentarily stuffy but smiled again, this time at herself, pleased to have gotten the whole sentence out without the halting half-stutter that sometimes made her blush. She took the chair between Willa and Sabra Jane and almost without thinking rested her feet next to Willa's on the low wicker table. Their canvas shoes nearly touched. Sabra Jane certainly wouldn't mind, and it felt good to stretch her legs after so much strenuous labor. Building a rock garden was not a simple matter. "I want my tea well brewed, and I add plenty of everything," Edith reached for the sugar.

"Sounds like Twenty-Seventh Street to me," Willa's grin was infectious, her teasing gentle. "You can take the kid out of Nebraska," Willa added by way of explanation, "but you can't take Nebraska out of the kid."

"Or the kid out of the adult, presumably," Edith teased back. "You have smudge on your nose."

Willa rubbed the side of her nose with the loose, flowing end of her sleeve, still unbuttoned and turned at the cuff from her earlier effort to recivilize herself, as she called it, with the wash basin at the back stoop, where there was plenty of soap and water but no mirror.

WILLA and Edith, with the help of Sabra Jane Briggs, had spent several hours grubbing in the bank behind their cottage. Earlier that morning, Roy Sharkey and a nice young man named James had delivered a load of stones from the creek bed below Ashburton Head and stayed long enough to loosen the soil for them. Dense fog still blanketed their end of the island, and the morning was so cool the men stayed wrapped in their jackets and so foggy Edith wondered how they managed to find their way through the woods on the unmarked portion of the trail from the road to their cottage. So many twists and turns and, as customary on these mornings, except for reassuring, rhythmic moans from the fog horn at The

Whistle, just above Ashburton Head on the northern tip of the island, so much silence.

While the men worked, Edith remained indoors reading, periodically building up the fire in the living room fireplace, knowing Willa would share the heat from its chimney. Willa spent mornings in the attic room above, working at the small desk she kept there. Spare, almost spartan, as Willa's workrooms always were, this one was also comforting. Pungent cedar shakes served as both roof and ceiling, and windows in the gable ends brought glimpses of the cliff and sounds from the sea below. Willa filled the shelves around the perimeter of the large, open room with books from Quebec and Paris, and they covered large parts of the unfinished wood flooring with some of the rich earth-toned rugs they brought with them from Santa Fe and Taos.

The fog lifted just after lunch when Sabra Jane arrived, as promised, to provide expert advice. She had just finished a rock wall behind one of her cottages on the south end of the island and promised to show them how to build one that would last. The rest of the afternoon they spaded fertilizer into the soil, then began placing rock upon rock in rising tiers on the freshly turned earth. Progress was amazingly slow, but the bank reached over five feet high and the rocks were to span a twenty-foot stretch. The rock wall with herbs interspersed would take most of the summer. It would be their marker for 1929.

NEVER at ease among large numbers of people, Rob Feeney liked it best the way it was now. Only two passengers he didn't know were making the crossing with him from Eastport back to Grand Manan. One of them, a young woman, was probably going to The Anchorage or Whale Cove. She had an air of confidence in her stride. The other one, Rob couldn't quite tell. The man was a loner, like a porcupine with its quills out. The only person who drew even a flicker from this fellow was Burt Isaacs, a loner himself and surly enough. Rough customer, Rob thought, could be doing anything on the American side, even bootlegging, which Rob knew was illegal there. He wanted nothing to do with Burt Isaacs. Rob wondered briefly whether Isaacs knew the other loner, but Isaacs spent the crossing in the galley by himself. The others stayed on deck. Rob eyed the other fellow standing off by himself, pressed against the ship's rail where the breeze pulled at his jacket. Something pinched and mean about the eyes, Rob thought, and the man was oddly overdressed. No one ever came to Grand Manan with eyes like those. Certainly no one in pin stripes with wing-tipped shoes.

Grand Manan suited Rob for exactly that reason. The island had no real strangers or dress-up occasions. Gatherings and celebrations, maybe, but no crowds or calls for starched collars beyond office hours. Rob actually enjoyed events like yesterday's Canada Day parade in the village of North Head, but he was still happier spending the holiday quietly on the American side, though it did mean he would be out of his office until the S. S. Grand Manan docked this afternoon. But Rob had always loved the hours on board, despite the fumes belching from the ship's smokestack, settling soot on his collar and cuffs. Nothing new in that, though it might be to the pin stripes. Rob glanced at the man again. He seemed unconcerned. It was a problem Rob dealt with on a regular basis, since it was his job as the company's shipping line agent to check the passengers and lists of lading as they came into dock at North Head. Rob was often on board this and every other ship that came into Grand Manan, whether he actually went anywhere or not. And Rob had loved going places ever since the war. He had hated being in the service but loved the life, transporting troops to and from Southampton and later Le Havre.

Grand Manan Ferry 1927

That's where he had seen eyes like those, Rob paused in mid-thought to glance again at the pin stripes. Vacant eyes, empty eyes. Eyes that had seen death and didn't care. Rob had seen men with eyes like those sometimes on returning transports and occasionally, very occasionally, on the streets of Le Havre. Pinched, mean. Eyes that were hard at the center, hard at the edges. It was as though, Rob finally decided, when some men get the hang of death, they hold onto it. Mercifully few came away from the trenches of that bloody war with eyes like that. Eyes that cared about nothing, nothing at all.

WHEN Sabra Jane left, Willa retrieved the story she had worked on that morning and settled back down in the Adirondack chair. Whenever the weather permitted, they used the early afternoon to hike along the bluffs or work on projects like the rock garden, but Willa generally took some portion of the afternoon to edit her day's progress. Tea had extended the visit far longer than any of them planned, and Sabra Jane drove off lamenting the fact that she was completely off schedule and still had to stop in North Head

9

for supplies. But she was as pleased as they were with the job they had done, and she left promising to advise Roy Sharkey about additional sources for stones. They would need several more loads.

Sabra Jane Briggs, Edith mused, putting away the few things she had gotten out for their tea. Finally, a chance to get to know this young Amazon the island had been buzzing about for years. They began hearing about Sabra Jane the moment she first stepped off the steamer and checked into The Swallowtail Inn. Red hair, everyone marveled, blazing red hair. And jodhpurs, the islanders gossiped, always jodhpurs. And she whistled and strode about with a free air. Sabra Jane surprised more than one islander cutting cross-lots or bursting out of the woods wearing a backpack and carrying her own water. She's an artist, off-islanders would shrug and flicker a sharp look, from Greenwich Village.

The second summer Sabra Jane brought a friend with her, a young woman named Marjorie. They leased the old Ingersoll place in North Head and started an inn of their own. They called it The Anchorage, a place to grab hold. Sabra Jane's lungs would no longer tolerate New York. Foul air, she explained. Her doctors advised a coastal cure. The third summer, she brought a Reo with a rumble seat. It had to be craned on deck in a net. With cars still rare on the island, Sabra Jane's patent black Reo was the cat's meow. A Flying Cloud it was called. Everyone wanted a ride in the rumble and got it. Even Willa succumbed. Islanders, off-islanders, the Reo never went anywhere without passengers. It helped attract lodgers, though business at The Anchorage was never as brisk as it was at Rose Cottage, The Marathon, or Swallowtail Inn, the three other places in North Head that catered to summer tourists. Or as dependable as at their own Whale Cove.

The fourth summer Marjorie stayed in New York and Sabra Jane began a series of long conversations with Sallie Jacobus, who had been taking care of lodgers at Whale Cove for more than twenty years. Cobus, the islanders called her. Cobus, Coney, and Felix. People said the names as if they were one. Between 1900 and 1902, Sallie Jacobus and Sally Adams, two young graduates from the Boston Normal School of Gymnastics, and Marie Felix, recently graduated from the Boston Cooking School, purchased twenty acres with a few outbuildings and immediately invited their friends to join them while they fixed the place up. Alice "Peter" Coney, a classmate of Sallie Jacobus, was first to take them up on the offer, and when Sally Adams decided to marry a young medical student, Coney bought her out.

Each summer the number of friends who returned for the season increased. Cobus, Coney, and Felix bought adjacent cottages. They added bedrooms. They hired more kitchen help and enlarged the communal dining room in the main house until it served twenty-four at one sitting. Finally in 1926, several of the Cottage Girls, including Willa and Edith, bought adjoining land and built their own cottages but continued to use communal facilities and services. Whale Cove had become a cooperative, with Cobus in command. Sallie Jacobus had plenty of advice for Sabra Jane Briggs.

By the fifth summer, Sabra Jane had given up the lease in North Head to start a new Anchorage twenty kilometers south, on land that had a farmhouse, one barn, two ponds, and a wooded ridge. She would repeat the Whale Cove experiment on the other end of Grand Manan, right down to the concept of central lodgings with a communal dining room surrounded by private cottages. Whale Cove had a full house. Sabra Jane was certain she could fill The Anchorage with her own younger clientele of single, professional women who wanted good company, good food, maid service, and a place away.

The new Anchorage prospered so quickly during the next two summers that Sabra Jane hired several women from Seal Cove to help out while she and the Reo maintained a constant crawl up and down the island, hauling young women from New York, New Jersey, and as far west as Ohio to and from the docks at North Head. During the eighth summer, when Ray Gilmore and his brother Claude agreed to extend their one-car taxi service down island, Sabra Jane finally began to relax and even to take time away.

Edith thought it generous of Sabra Jane to lend them a hand with a project as taxing as a rock wall, but everyone on the island was charitable that way. Distinct lines existed between islanders and ✓ off-islanders: off-islanders usually paid for the help they required—but everyone was available to assist everyone on Grand Manan. The whole island turned out in a storm, and because island time followed the tides, the same periods of high and low activity were built into everyone's daily schedule.

Rob Feeney's office had been in shade for several hours when he finally arrived from the S. S. Grand Manan, carrying a satchel of papers to file. The doorknob felt cool and firm against his hand. He liked its feel, the well-worn brass smooth to the center of his palm, and the quiet click of its latch. The door swung open, almost of its own volition, and Rob inhaled the odor of polished wood. He liked to keep everything about him well preserved.

Pin stripes in front of the bakery caught Rob's attention, and he paused for a moment, remembering those eyes. Then despite the afternoon's warmth, he felt a chill and put the satchel down to button the jacket of his uniform. Just then, Sabra Jane Briggs exited the bakery, and Rob found himself witnessing an event he thought more promising of fireworks than any Canada Day parade—the Encounter of the Amazon and the Pin Stripes. Sabra Jane Briggs tolerated no fools, especially male fools, and Rob could only guess what the Pin Stripes might make of Sabra Jane. But the Encounter proved disappointing. The Pin Stripes' eyes widened and then narrowed and grew hard at the center, hard at the edges. His mouth moved briefly, lips tightening over his teeth and curling into a sneer. But Sabra Jane merely glanced at her wrist and responded with something brief. Even from the rear it was clear she barely had noticed the man.

Of course, Sabra Jane Briggs rarely did notice men, Rob chuckled to himself. But like most women more attentive to other women, she generally got on well with men. An affable, brotherly, sisterly, companionable getting-on, the words ran through Rob's mind. A getting-on easier and less strained than what often passed for friendship or love between the sexes . . . or between men. Rob finished his musing and curved his right hand around the satchel's leather handle. The encounter between Sabra Jane and the Pin Stripes had passed without the slightest pop of a firecracker, but even on such slim observation, Rob felt certain he knew few men who hated women the way this one did.

III

"I DON'T RIGHTLY know what I think." For the second time in the last hour, Mark Daggett tamped down the tobacco in the bowl of his pipe and lit it with a wooden match. Daggett carried the matches in a tin case tucked away in his jacket pocket.

"Did he jump. Was he pushed. Or did someone throw him over the edge," Daggett retraced the possibilities, leaning against the back of his chair until it began to rock on its hind legs. His feet had disappeared under the table.

It was often difficult on the island to get anything lit. Lamps, firewood. Tobacco was the least of it. Sea air dampened everything, and fog made it worse. Matches were often at a premium. Edith appreciated the forethought of Constable Daggett's little tin case. Jacobus and the others didn't seem to notice. No one spoke.

Several of the chairs in the dining room were still occupied. A few of the women, including Willa, had gone on to bed. Nothing they could do now, and it was a strange vigil for a man they didn't know and a death Edith had witnessed but none of them could explain.

"THE registry down at Swallowtail says he's John T. Brown. From New York," Daggett paused to draw on his pipe, "but he hadn't anything on him that would say if that's right. Pockets were empty except for twelve American dollars. Tag in his suit says Boston."

Daggett had joined the women at Whale Cove just as they were finishing a very late dinner, delayed by all the excitement of the afternoon. He was returning to bring them up to date, he said, but immediately confessed that he had very little new information. Of more apparent interest were the plates of stew and baking powder biscuits Coney rescued for him from the kitchen. While he ate, he asked each of them to recount in detail her afternoon. Perhaps one of them had seen or heard something that by itself now seemed meaningless but later might solve the puzzle. This point in any investigation, he explained, was like finding and turning all the jigsaw pieces right side up. Once he had done that, he could begin sorting and matching them one to one. Edith, who genuinely disliked being the center of attention, spoke last. She began with the rock garden. Her statement was the longest and, despite occasional hesitations, the most vivid. Daggett paused often to take notes.

When Edith finished, Daggett shook his head at Jacobus, who was offering refills. "I'll have another piece of that carrot cake, though, if it's handy. Worked up an appetite out there on the trail."

The phone call from Jacobus had come shortly after five-thirty. It took Daggett a good thirty minutes to get out the Chevrolet and drive to Whale Cove from North Head. Then he was preoccupied about seeing to the body. Eric Dawson brought the body as far as Whale Cove, where the ladies helped him take it out of his boat and lay it on the dock. They covered it with a tarpaulin.

When Daggett arrived, Jacobus pointed him toward the tarpaulin. Eric Dawson sat slumped on the ground near the dock facing the Bay, his head between his knees. The women were scattered around him, the one called Cather sitting next to him. "Nonsense," she was lecturing Eric, "women have been doing this for centuries. And we've none of us lived in the city so long we haven't had to take care of our own."

"That's right," Jacobus turned toward them. "It's men that have trouble with death. My father could never even clean his own game."

Daggett wondered momentarily if Jacobus would mind taking

over this part of his job. He had seen very few bodies since he had been sent home wounded from Ypres, all but one an accidental drowning. And from what Jacobus described on the phone, he wasn't anxious to look at this one. The island had occasional hurricanes to deal with and fishing vessels lost at sea, but no violent crimes to speak of. A fist fight now and then and occasionally some men roughed up their wives. Daggett just called in the minister and left them alone.

Off-islanders rarely did more than get lost. This one seemed to have done that and more, but the body told Daggett little more than he already knew. The man had gone over the cliff. Not much of the left side of the head remained. No apparent gunshot or stab wounds. Several broken bones. A mangled left hand. A series of tears in the left side of his suit, pockets torn inside and out, rips in the sleeves and pants legs. That was about it, all Daggett could see from what was left of him.

Daggett jotted his notes. What was odd was the suit, he tapped the end of his pencil against his note pad. And dress shoes. The expensive kind, leather with scrolled tops. What on earth was a man doing on Seven Days Work in a pin-striped suit wearing wing-tipped shoes.

Daggett deputized Little John Winslow, who pulled up with a team and wagon within a few minutes of Daggett's own arrival. Little John could haul the body to Doc Macaulay's at Castalia, the only doctor on the island. He would check it over and do what was needed for the time being. The island had plenty of cemeteries but no coroner and no undertaker, though this man would eventually be shipped back to the United States for burial. Later this evening, Daggett would drive down to Castalia to take an imprint of his right hand for finger prints, but right now he wanted to have a look at the trail on the edge of Seven Days Work. From what Miss Lewis told him, someone in a red shirt might still be running toward The Whistle for help or lying there hurt.

Miss Lewis, Miss Cather, Cobus, and Felix went along to help him locate the spot where the man had gone off the cliff. They saw no sign of a red shirt anywhere. In fact, they saw no signs of anything on the trail. Nothing let them know the exact place of the man's fall. A few scuff marks here and there on the hard-packed earth and small patches of scattered stones in the open areas among the trees, but nothing unusual. They went as far as the place where the brook from Rocky Corner turned into a waterfall, then Cobus and Felix volunteered to cover the rest of the distance to The Whistle while Daggett and the others headed back to Whale Cove. There was just enough time before the sun went down for Eric Dawson to row him to the beach below.

With the tide running out, Eric was uncertain about exactly which boulder caught the man's fall, and they found nothing further to guide them. They reached the dock at Whale Cove just as Cobus and Felix returned to report that they had been alone on the trail, and no one at The Whistle remembered seeing anyone or hearing anything unusual that whole afternoon.

By the time Daggett reached North Head, every villager readily directed his attention to The Swallowtail Inn. The stories about the dead stranger were already beginning to build. He had arrived only that morning on the S. S. Grand Manan. He came by himself and asked directions to The Swallowtail Inn. To the best of anyone's knowledge, he had never before been on Grand Manan. He had eaten lunch at Rose Cottage and purchased three biscuits at the bakery. He had not yet fully unpacked his luggage. He had been seen on the docks and strolling through the village. Every person in North Head claimed to have exchanged words with him but no one remembered hearing his name. He had expressed interest in the island's numerous trails.

Were it not for Miss Lewis, Daggett would at that point have gone home for the evening satisfied that this unknown off-islander was unnecessarily hasty about hiking and had taken an incautious

17

step in his wing-tipped shoes. But the red shirt had somehow to be explained. When it was, maybe then Daggett would understand how a man in a pin-striped suit could wind up on the rocks below Seven Days Work.

DESPITE all the hard work Sabra Jane and Willa and Edith had put in on the wall, tea that afternoon had been intended more as an opportunity for conversation than a revival for tired bodies, though Edith had hoped it would serve both purposes. Now, her body thoroughly exhausted with the day's events, Edith settled deeper into the mattress and chose to rest her mind in the pleasantness of that earlier conversation, hoping sleep would soon follow.

Sabra Jane had been coming to Grand Manan for at least as long as they had, but she was still relatively unfamiliar to them. They always said hello when they saw each other in North Head, the main village on Grand Manan, within easy walking distance of Whale Cove, but Sabra Jane was not part of their Whale Cove enclave and so they had little occasion to get to know each other.

"I grew up on Twenty-Seventh Street," Edith found herself responding to Sabra Jane's puzzled eyes during their conversation over tea. "In Lincoln, Nebraska, not New York."

"Of course, I should have realized. Twenty-Seventh Street just didn't make sense with everything else you've said about living in New York," Sabra Jane's eyes, brown-flecked with gold, crinkled with her smile. She seemed unconcerned about crow's feet and made no attempt to cover her freckles with powder or her head with a hat. Edith liked that about her. She was quite certain Willa did too.

"Willa did not enjoy Twenty-Seventh Street or Lincoln as much as she might have," Edith arched her right eyebrow, the only one that would arch. "I believe she felt somewhat constrained by Lincoln's attention to good manners."

"As did you," Willa reminded her. "Dancing lessons, drawing lessons, piano lessons," Willa shifted to an exaggerated drawl, "and club meetings, club meetings, club meetings."

Sabra Jane giggled, "Ogdensburg, too. Didn't matter that we lived on a farm. It took ten years in Greenwich Village to unlearn those lessons and get on with the real ones." Sabra Jane retrieved two oatmeal cookies from the plate Edith passed and placed them on the napkin in her lap. Then ignoring the cookies, she began an elaborate flourish. "Living on Grand Manan," Sabra Jane's hand swept from the woods behind their white trimmed cottage, to the terraced lawn where they sat, to the open sea beyond, "living on Grand Manan means I take only what I want from those lessons." She leaned back and added her feet to the wicker, crossing one booted ankle over the other, "The rest I ignore."

"And here I had been thinking you were just young enough to have missed the white gloves and drawing rooms altogether," Edith plucked at a raisin on the edge of a cookie. "I lived through those lessons," she glanced at Willa, "but apparently I haven't yet managed to live them down."

Willa grinned in reply.

"Nonetheless, those were heady times for the New Woman, and my Aunt Mary was an important personage," Edith hesitated, glancing again at Willa, then chose to go on, "important to me and to Lincoln. She started the art league and was very active in founding the General Federation . . . "

"Your aunt, my hat," Willa emptied her cup.

Edith half rose to flick away a bee, sending it back to the purple foxgloves near the cottage. When she sank back into her chair, Willa was well into her argument.

"Admit it, Edith, it wasn't just your aunt." Settling her cup in her lap, Willa began ticking her right index finger against the fingers on her left hand, "It was your cousins, your brother, your sisters, your mother, your father." She ran out of fingers and pointed directly at Edith, "And you." Then she spread both hands in the air and stiffened her arms as though she were holding a banner to exclaim, "The Civic-Minded Lewises."

They all laughed.

"You can't deny it," Willa shook her head at Edith and helped herself to a cookie. "One of Lincoln's most promising and prominent men, her father was," Willa turned back to Sabra Jane, "He was a banker. Her cousin, too. Good friends with Charlie Dawes. Helped him win the Vice Presidency. He's a bank president in Boston now," Willa took a firm bite of the cookie. "Her cousin Dan," she crunched, "not Dawes, of course."

"I had heard you were both from the Plains, but I didn't realize you grew up in the same town."

"We didn't," Edith assured Sabra Jane. "We didn't even know each other. Willa's a little older and grew up about a hundred miles west, in a small town called Red Cloud, but she came to Lincoln for the university." Explanation over, Edith reverted to teasing. "Willa went to parties with my cousins and knew everyone my parents did, but she always insists she wasn't part of that crowd."

"I wasn't. And you left before you were old enough to feel the politics of that place." Willa took a deep breath and turned to Sabra Jane, "Edith graduated from Smith," then back at Edith, softening her tone, "but you were just a starry-eyed youngster back then, gazing off into the firmament," she paused, "and into the eyes of others."

"Now, now, now, remember who it was who was bewitched in those days," Edith chided, grinning back at the twinkle in Willa's eyes, slate blue today like her blouse. "Willa caused a bit of a scandal at the university because of the way she chose to wear her hair. Short," Edith raised her hand and separated her fingers less than an inch, making it clear by contrast that her own bobbed and graying locks were much longer than Willa's auburn hair had been. "I mean really short," she restated, "and often as not, she called herself William."

"Ha! My family always called me Willie," Willa squared her shoulders to sit taller in the Adirondack, but her eyes still laughed and the dimples in her cheeks deepened.

"And she had a smash, that's what we used to call it, on a brilliant young classmate and tennis champion," Edith lowered her lids, sliding her eyes sideways toward Willa, "by the name of Louise Pound." Edith's voice eased down and held the last consonant with a hint of breathiness.

"Who now teaches literature at the university and whose brother is head of Harvard Law School," Willa cut in, "and a member of President Hoover's newly appointed Commission on Law Enforcement."

"Red hair and high jinks, that's what Louise was. But now you are name-dropping. First my cousin and now Roscoe Pound."

Willa laughed, "Roscoe the Ridiculous, he was. Pompous prig. He took offense when he realized I was more interested in his sister than I was in him. I retaliated by lampooning him in the university magazine. That was the end of that. But it was also the end of Louise," Willa adopted a rueful tone, "and of the world, as far as I was concerned then."

"The end," Edith dead-panned.

"Ah, youth! Ah, propriety!" Willa refused to be finished. Her hand fluttered to her forehead. Finally, she added, "How silly we all were."

Sabra Jane was laughing so hard her tea cup rattled in its saucer. Her face had turned a lighter shade of the reds in her shirt and hair. "I know the man," she finally wheezed out. "Met him in New York. He was buying antiques. I'm an interior decorator. Specialize in antiques," she caught her breath and began to speak more fluidly. "He never stopped being a prig, you know. Wears bow ties," she giggled, "but then, what do you expect from Harvard Law."

"Exactly," Willa punctuated the point and rose to offer more tea.

"Those years in Lincoln were wonderful times," Edith heard her own voice turn wistful. "So full of the future, of looking forward to great things. Especially for women," Edith raised her cup toward Willa, "and, I suppose, especially for women from Nebraska. We could go to college. We could have careers. We could live in Greenwich Village. We could do anything, we thought."

"And we did. We did all of it," Willa sat down again and reached over to pat Edith's hand. "It just wasn't as easy as we expected. Or as well appreciated."

"The Great War changed everything," Edith nodded but found her glance resting on the steamer, the S. S. Grand Manan, crossing just beyond the entrance to Whale Cove at the start of its return voyage to the mainland. It was somehow soothing to have one's eye surprised by the familiar passage. With Whale Cove fogged in that morning, Edith had missed its arrival. She paused now to follow its progress before picking up the strand of their conversation again.

"The Great War, yes," Willa repeated, her voice dropping. "It certainly changed our lives . . . "

"Our expectations, our sense of ourselves," Edith returned her attention to the women before her and picked up Willa's thoughts, "our sense of each other . . . "

"Our freedom," Willa joined in, "to live as we chose . . . and with whom. But it was hard on men. It remapped their world," she paused, "and ours, too."

"It still dominates the world," Sabra Jane's voice was firm, her nod grave. "Heroes, debts, reparations. That's about all there is in the news these days."

"Along with rum runners, sensuality, and every imaginable machine. Radios, motor boats, airplanes, Zeppelins," Edith agreed, "but the war years must have been difficult for you, too," she turned to Sabra Jane.

"They were and being on the farm didn't help. I was already living in New York by then, but I went home every weekend and most of the summers. Everything we raised went for the war effort. My sister and I helped in the fields and knit socks and rolled bandages. And right along with everyone else, we waited for news about the boys from Ogdensburg."

Sabra Jane raised her cup in both hands and held it for a moment before taking a sip, "I wanted to go over and drive an ambulance, but my dad wouldn't hear of it. My mother never stopped being afraid, and we, just none of us, ever talked about the future." Sabra Jane's eyes returned with her cup to the saucer still balanced in her lap. "Thank God my brother came home with only a slight limp. Shrapnel lodged in his knee. Two of his friends died of influenza on the ship over and a third fell at the Marne."

She glanced at Willa, and her eyes crinkled again, "I've read *One of Ours,* and I'd say you got it right, even for upstate New York. My brother liked it too, though he had a hard time when David died and then Claude."

"Thank you," Willa was grateful for that kind of praise, especially when it came for the novel she privately called Claude's story. It let her know she had been honest.

Very few people besides Edith realized that Claude was actually Willa's cousin, G. P., who fell at Cantigny less than a year after he shipped out. He died a hero's death, which no one, least of all G. P., ever expected. And he died happy, happier than he had ever been in his life. No one expected that either, certainly not his mother, Willa's Aunt Franc. She had been surprised by the final intensity of his life and devastated by his death.

Claude's story won Willa the Pulitzer, but it was heavily attacked in the press. The vehemence of the critics caught even Edith off guard. Women and veterans loved the novel, but the more it sold, the shriller the critics' voices became. No woman, and especially not Willa Cather who wrote so well about the past and Nebraska, should ever take on what women can never experience or understand, the critics, all male, assured each other and the world. Miss Cather, they declared, should return to Nebraska.

Bemused, Willa and Edith guessed that what really rankled was the subtle sureness of Willa's bead on men. Men with women, men without women, men with men, men at peace, men at war, and men at sex. Especially men at sex. Men and sex, Willa and Edith knew the critics would never admit, were taboo for women writers, restricted to men who simply said the same thing over and over again and called it truth. Comstock had nothing to do with this. Lewdness was a side issue, though not everyone realized the difference. The offense by women writers was even worse when the men women wrote about were not very successful at sex. Willa regularly brushed up against that one. In *O Pioneers!* she drove Frank Shabata to murder and Emil Bergson to a suicidal tryst, she ridiculed Wick Cutter in *My Antonia* and toyed with Fred Ottenburg in *The Song of the Lark,* and she dared to suggest in her stories that mortal men might be terrified by an Aphrodite or Medusa. Then she not only unmanned Claude Wheeler in *One of Ours,* she turned him into Parsifal, a sacrificial savior.

Perhaps Parsifal was a bit too gentle for modern heroics, Edith pointed out, and Willa's subtlety lost on men enamored by Mars, however much they might hate war. That young Hemingway, for instance, they heard through Isabelle and Jan Hambourg, had been telling wicked jokes among their friends in Paris, claiming that Willa's war experience came from watching *Birth of a Nation.* Willa and Edith had laughed when they read Isabelle's letter, but they felt the ground tremble. They knew the herd was sniffing the air and starting to paw, maybe even beginning to circle. Unless Willa

24

was very, very careful, there would be a stampede. Women should write about women, men were saying without saying, their undertone muted, serious, deadly. Women should write about what they know. Love. Children. Young animals. Beneficent nature. Women might pretend to write through men's eyes, as Willa had done in *My Antonia,* but their subject had better stay female, and their eyes must never stray into the real world, the world of men's experience.

Willa and Edith knew the rules. They had grown up with them, like catechism. And when the fuss came, they rather enjoyed it. Willa never minded outright criticism. She had been a critic herself in her younger days and knew the game. What she hated, and said so, were the gushers, the I-just-loved-your-last-book dreamy-eyed wonders. Edith long ago learned to run interference, to hold that type of admiration at bay. Not because Willa could—and consistently would—be rude, but because people like that threw her too far off balance. Willa might be depressed for days. Twice she even tore up manuscript pages, vowing never to write another word if only gushers read them. Willa and Edith spent hours piecing the pages back together.

IV

BREAKFAST THE NEXT morning brought continued speculation among the women at Whale Cove. Willa and Edith donned their Wellingtons, slickers, and hats for the quarter-mile trek from their cottage to the main dining room. Dew-proofing, they considered their morning attire. Neither of them was the least bit particular about clothes. Not like Winifred Bromhall, the lean Britisher who occasionally joined them at their table and, everyone said, looked just like Greta Garbo. Even less like Eloise Derby, whose several trunks arrived every summer from Paris weeks before she did. Eloise would unpack an outfit a day. Blue, all of them blue, the same color she insisted on for her room. But Winifred and Eloise were exceptions. That was one of the reasons Willa and Edith so loved Grand Manan. They could leave their own office and evening wear hanging in their New York closets, not even tempted, as they sometimes were for visits to Lincoln and Red Cloud, to drag their more stylish garments along for show.

Soon after their usual fare—Willa's standard breakfast consisted of cereal, sliced oranges, four strips of perfectly done bacon, toast, jam, and Sanka; Edith's was a repeat, but she liked her bacon crisp and some days added an egg—Willa retreated to the attic room, and Edith walked into North Head. She wanted to hear the gossip first hand.

THE previous summer Willa and Edith transported as much from their beloved Greenwich Village apartment as their cottage would hold. Construction on the Seventh Avenue subway had made Bank

Street untenable and with housing still tight after the War, especially in the Village, they had not yet found another place they wanted to call home. For the time being, The Grosvenor, a well-appointed hotel near Washington Square where they secured a two-bedroom apartment, served as their temporary city residence. But Whale Cove was now their grounding place.

In truth, neither of them ever missed New York in July, when sun-drenched buildings and heavy humidity carried the heat from one day right through to the next. By early spring every year, the sheer volume of New York—its numbers, its noise, its pace—increased at least tenfold. People poured out of doors and into the streets. As much as they both loved the city, Willa and Edith were always ready to flee by mid-May.

For some years they had been undecided about where to spend their summers, the months Willa used and so desperately needed for her work. Circumstances in New York, even on Bank Street, had been barely tolerable in the summers before Willa became famous. After she won the Pulitzer, they simply had to get away— from business, from the city, from the public, from everything and everyone they knew. It was all just too much, too distracting. Willa needed room to ruminate. To roam, to feel free, to be playful, to engage in conversations and activities that did not drain but revived a tired mind, and at the same time to be deeply serious but never so serious that she lost perspective about herself or her writing.

They considered joining Jan and Isabelle Hambourg, old friends from Willa's years in Pittsburgh, in their villa on the outskirts of Paris, and they talked briefly about building a small place in New Hampshire with views of Mt. Monadnock or an adobe near Mabel and Tony Luhan's in Taos. Those places and the people stirred them deeply, but they chose Grand Manan because it took them away from the world without putting them into a circle of temperamental, expatriated, or self-involved artists. That crowd might be pleasant for short dips, but they both felt the strength of its undertow. They wanted instead to be able to float leisurely or stroke as they pleased, and the women at Whale Cove granted them that.

THIS morning, as Edith picked her way over the rocky shore on her way to Church Lane, the sky was absolutely glorious. Earlier they had seen the sun leap from the sea with great fanfare, feathering wisps of clouds a multitude of rose and gold. Now Sol sat lemon-crisp and satisfied, the sky around him clear, open, blue. Edith breathed deeply. She loved the fresh salt air. And except for the difficulty of navigating the huge expanse of well-worn rocks and shingle that made up the beach at Whale Cove, she enjoyed the walk to North Head. She preferred crossing the beach to Church Lane, which cut through the woods and delivered her into the village just below the Anglican church.

Often Willa and Edith, instead of turning right onto Church Lane turned left, taking the path along the cliffs that brought them out of the trees at a formation called Hole in the Wall. Well known among picnickers and hikers, this leaning tower of rocks rose out of the cove to attach itself to Grand Manan through an arch spanning

Hole in the Wall

more than twice the length of several tall men. It was one of Willa's favorite picnic spots. From there they looked back across the cove at the cottages or, with a glance to the right, took in the grandeur of Seven Days Work where volcanic rock had been pushed apart by igneous intrusions during the Triassic period to form the well-defined layers that gave the cliffs their name. From the top of Hole in the Wall, they could also look out to the open sea. Often after a leisurely lunch, they stayed for several hours watching for seals or whales swimming in the clear, green depths nearby. They were closer to the water here than at the cottage, and the outer ledges of Hole in the Wall provided comfortable bleachers for viewing. Edith wondered if anyone had been sitting there the previous afternoon and witnessed, as she had, Mr. Brown's precipitous descent.

WHEN Edith reached the North Head Bank, she turned in, hoping for a long chat with Mr. Enderby. He was a safe bet for news. Men claimed never to gossip, but Edith knew better. People always trusted bankers, and Mr. Enderby was a good listener. Edith considered him almost a friend. She was often in the bank transferring money or arranging for bills to be paid in the States. She handled all of their personal business, and by now Mr. Enderby knew what that was about as well as she did.

Edith waited while Mr. Enderby counted the fistful of change Janey Dawson had stretched her full height to deposit in a small pile on his side of the teller's cage.

"My," Mr. Enderby nodded approval, "you carried this a long way and kept it very safe. I'm proud of you." His glance at Edith shared his amusement. "The coins are still warm from her hand," he paused to fill out the deposit slip, "and a bit sticky as well."

Mr. Enderby's smile was a special treat. He was a genial man. Janey was radiant in return, and after a slight curtsy and "Thank you" and "Good day, Miss Lewis," to which Edith replied in kind,

Janey opened the clasp of the little patent leather purse she carried draped on her arm and tucked the deposit slip inside. The purse, it seemed, was for paper, not coins. Then Janey ran out the door, forgetting all about manners and matters of finance, to join Jocko Winslow, just passing by with his black-and-white puppy.

"Eric and Mary Dawson have got themselves a fine young one there," Mr. Enderby observed after his own "Good day, Miss Lewis."

"Indeed they do. And well they might. Eric Dawson seems to be a fine young man himself."

"That's certain, he is. Got himself an education and keeps up with the world. He loves the island, but he would do well anywhere and so will his daughter," Mr. Enderby concluded his observations and turned back to Edith. "I understand you had occasion to make his acquaintance yesterday."

With no one else in the bank, Mr. Enderby was clearly prepared to spend whatever time necessary to hear the whole of Edith's version of the previous afternoon. She began with Eric Dawson and moved backwards, then forwards again to bring him to the point where she could ask what more he had heard in North Head.

Mr. Enderby cleared his throat. He approached every opportunity to impart knowledge with a gravity Edith relished. He reminded her of her father, an investment banker as familiar with a three-piece suit and watch fob as Mr. Enderby. Edith long ago learned to be patient with the need for authority and understood the terms of exchange. She had given Mr. Enderby her story. He would take the time he needed for his.

"I understand you saw someone in a red shirt," Mr. Enderby observed now, leaning against the polished wooden shelf at the rear of the cage, his left hand cushioning his back. His right hand reached forward to straighten the knot in his tie. He was waiting for Edith to answer.

"Only his back," Edith nodded.

"Yes," Mr. Enderby glanced down. His right hand brushed the front of his jacket. "Can you be certain it was a him?" Mr. Enderby's words came slowly, each one distinct. He returned his attention to Edith's face, his eyes echoing his inquiry.

Edith paused. "I saw only a back. And an arm. The right arm shot out in the air." She made the gesture herself, bringing her arm quickly up from her side. Her hand passed in an arc across her midsection before flinging itself straight out, fingers extended. She looked at her hand and took a moment to feel the way her body had arranged itself, then she sought Mr. Enderby's reaction.

Behind his rimless glasses, Mr. Enderby's gray eyes were squinted slightly and seemed a little out of focus. He was seeing Edith and the figure on the cliff at the same time, Edith guessed. She was working on that inner vision herself, trying to attach gender to the shirt. It was difficult. The distance had been so great. Had there been a hat? She couldn't tell. Did the person wear pants? She thought so, dark pants, perhaps. She could not say for sure.

It was as though her memory was playing tricks. She could surround that red shirt with a variety of costumes. All of them seemed possible. Her eyes must have been so attracted by the red they saw nothing else. And it happened so fast. When the man went over the cliff, she saw nothing else until he landed. No, that wasn't true. She could distinctly remember shouting to Eric Dawson and waving to catch his attention. So fast it all happened, yet hours seemed to pass between the moment the man went off the cliff and the second he landed on the rocks below. She remembered his body slowing and seeming briefly to drift. Surely an illusion.

"I thought it was a man," was all Edith could affirm. "There seemed to be some sort of scuffle beforehand. I heard a shout."

Mr. Enderby took a step forward and placed both hands on the counter, then leaned against them. "Constable Daggett drove off for Seal Cove about half an hour ago. Said he wanted to talk to Sabra

31

Jane Briggs. She's the only person anyone remembered seeing in a red shirt yesterday." Mr. Enderby pushed back to rock on his heels, then leaned forward again to add punctuation, "And Little John Winslow saw her standing outside the bakery talking to that man not more than two hours before he died."

When Edith left the bank with twenty brand-new Canadian dollars in her purse, she headed straight for Newton's Bakery, though in the usual course of events she would have stopped by Rose Cottage first for a cup of tea. The rest of Mr. Enderby's story had included the full roster of Mr. Brown sightings from the day before, but none of them were as urgent as the one connecting Sabra Jane to the man in the pin stripes and wing-tipped shoes. That morning the women at Whale Cove puzzled over the man's attire as much as Constable Daggett had. Willa even suggested that if Edith hadn't been there, the man's death would have been presumed a suicide or a tourist's mistake. Now it seemed Edith was also to be responsible for the accusations beginning to swirl around Sabra Jane Briggs. Edith wanted to know more about Sabra Jane's encounter with this Mr. John T. Brown outside the bakery. And fast.

THE trouble was, Edith thought, stirring fresh milk into her tea, the flowers on the teal green wallpaper at Rose Cottage her only company for the moment, no one in the bakery saw Sabra Jane Briggs talking with Mr. Brown. Both Emma Parker and Jesse Martin remembered Sabra Jane in the red shirt. She had purchased two loaves of St. John's bread. And they remembered Mr. Brown. He purchased three biscuits. They recalled seeing several other people as well, Little John Winslow among them, but no two together and no one at all in the company of Mr. Brown.

"He was alone," Emma Parker's nod was decisive, her gray curls bounced once.

"He didn't seem a bit nervous or anything. Not like he was thinking of dying," Jesse Martin interrupted. "And then there were the three biscuits. Whatever happened to them? I heard they weren't in his room at The Swallowtail."

"Not nervous," Emma Parker agreed. "But he wasn't friendly, either. Sort of pinched he was around the eyes and nose," she pursed her mouth and squinched her eyes, trying to catch his look. "I can't say as I liked him. Jesse neither."

"Well, I didn't dislike him exactly. I didn't know the man," Jesse Martin demurred, her blue eyes widening. "But I didn't like him, that's true. He seemed not quite nice, if you know what I mean. All tight and sort of beaky," she opened and closed the fingers on her right hand, pulling them toward and away from her face, trying in another way to convey his expression. "And maybe a bit mean-spirited." Her voice was thoughtful. "It didn't bother him a whit to break off some scone and stand there nibbling, then choose the biscuits. Not a may I, not a thank you, not a nothing."

"I'd have called him persnickety if he were a woman," Emma Parker giggled. Emma Parker never giggled. "But he was no woman. Not that one," her voice returned to its usual deadpan. "He had a leer about him. I don't mean he liked women. I didn't get the feeling he did. Just that he had nastiness in his eyes."

EDITH sipped her tea, investigated the roses on the wallpaper, and thought about the men they knew. Not one of them was mean-spirited, nor did they wear pin-striped suits or wing-tipped shoes. They didn't know many men on Grand Manan except for the village doctor, who was learned and sympathetic and helpful, especially to Willa during those painful periods when from some undiagnosed malady she could not write and had to keep her hand in a splint. Among Edith's colleagues at J. Walter Thompson, the advertising agency that continued to consume at least six to eight months of every one of her years, even the most competitive men were generally pleasant to work with, mannerly and well intentioned. The men they counted among their friends—Alfred Knopf, Bruce Barton,

Sam McClure, John Phillips, Edith began parading them through in a mental review—were without exception honest and accessible. They met her approval. Some, a few, Edith considered actually wise.

Rudolph Ruzicka and Earl Brewster at the very least aspired toward wisdom, Edith smiled to herself. Twenty years ago, during their early studio days on Washington Square, Rudolph and Earl had been among Willa and Edith's closest friends. Both were artists, Rudolph an engraver, Earl a painter. And, oh, such energy, Edith grinned at her tea cup. After a full day at *McClure's,* where Willa and Edith both worked as editors, they would come home to argue half the night with Rudolph and Earl. Long, meandering arguments. And silly, since all of them fundamentally agreed, but the talk itself was exciting.

"Creative genius be damned," Rudolph would declare, his voice firm. Rudolph was a quiet, gentle man, but passionate about his art. Later Willa would ask that he illustrate *My Antonia,* but these long evenings were early in their friendship. "Craftsmanship, that's what counts. Craftsmanship and honest sympathy with the subject. Not genius, not schools, not *art*-ificiality," Rudolph would pause after the first syllable to make his meaning clear. "Craft and sympathy. Those make the artist." Earl or Willa and sometimes Edith would respond. Then for hours upon hours they would dissect individual artists and their works, Burne-Jones, Chase, Sloan, one of the upstarts like Matisse, or examine writers like Hawthorne, Howells, James, and the young radicals hanging around Dreiser.

Back then Willa felt increasingly desperate for time to practice her own craft, but she also had a great deal to contribute to their conversations. Edith sometimes caught echoes from Willa's early commentary in the Lincoln newspapers where she labeled Oscar Wilde the leader of insincerity and his "epigrammatic school" of aesthetics dangerous in its assumption that society could improve upon nature.

During those long argumentative evenings, Willa's voice would remain steady but her words were urgent. "If the choice were only between aesthetics and genius, I'd have to choose genius every time. Genuine genius," her hands moving as though they were conducting a choir building toward crescendo, "untrained, elemental, primitive, sensuous, amoral, perhaps. But genius. Genius as full of the joy of life as the old barbarians. Genius like Whitman's, whose reckless rhapsodies in *Song of Myself*," she'd smile at the superfluity of alliteration, "might very well have been written by a joyous elephant who just happened to break into song."

Edith distinctly remembered Rudolph's laughter and her own giddy vision of an enormous gray beast in crushed hat, flowing scarf, and rumpled suit cavorting among fields of flowers and rising on powerful hind legs only to toss his head and trumpet glad-hearted lyrics to the open blue sky.

"No Barnum and Bailey for a gay blade like Whitman, eh?" Rudolph's laughter had filled the room then and again when Willa opened fire on writers who fell victim to America's appetite for stars.

"Of course it happens elsewhere. It happened to Wilde and even to Whitman," Willa contended. "George Sand, too, a little, but probably not until she became George," Willa smiled at the aside, then let her voice rise, "and they let it happen, all of them, like Faust."

"And what about Marguerite," Rudolph began to tease but Willa ignored him. She had been through too many discussions comparing the aspirations of women artists to their relative worth as muses for men to get sidetracked by false issues like Faust's Marguerite.

"Well, audiences do demand that artists be bigger and better than life, but the artists don't have to deliver," Rudolph admonished with a sharp intake of breath.

No one responded until Willa leaned forward, "Audiences demand sentimentality from women artists," her right index finger tapped hard against the surface of the table, "but the best don't give in. George Sand never did, George Eliot either. The two Georges," she mused, "and Sappho, the greatest of women writers," then added her own teaser, "but somehow men seem to find it harder to resist fame than women do the sentimentality men complain so much about."

"Sympathy's okay, not sentiment," Rudolph insisted.

They all nodded. Edith remembered how straight the lines of their mouths had been fixed at that moment.

Finally Earl snatched Willa's bait, "Why resist fame?"

Willa settled deeper into her chair and hooked both heels on the rung below before answering. "You've noticed, I'm sure, that men do say a great deal about women and sentimentality," she paused to look him in the eye, "but almost nothing about men and fame?"

"Yes," Earl drawled it out, stalling while he figured the loopholes and consequences of his admission. Earl might be a gentle man and generous, but he did not like to be wrong.

"Oh," Willa broke in to concede with a sweep of her arm, "men used to talk about fame a great deal. 'That last infirmity of a noble mind,' Milton called it. And before Milton and before the Renaissance, men talked about fame all the time. With great anxiety. Hardly talked about anything else. Considered it part of Pride, the worst of the Seven Deadly Sins. It got in the way of absolutely everything, they said. The farther back you go, the more anxiety you'll find about it. People refused to sign names to what they did," Willa brushed one hand against the other as if she were erasing records. "Names weren't important. Homer got attached to the *Iliad,* but we don't know who Homer was any more than we know who painted pictographs or the symbols in caves."

Both men lit up with the reference to visual art. "Well, names are important now," Earl pointed out. "All you hear about is the artist, not his paintings. One painting often stands for all he's done."

"Exactly my point," Willa laughed. "And in case you haven't noticed, for all we know, all painters are male. Those we consider important, anyway," Willa paused. "Now men pursue fame. Fame's certainly no problem any more. For men, that is. Women who pursue it come off as silly. But men are important, men can be famous. It's so American," she finally sighed, "and so wrong headed."

"American, yes, but wrong headed?" Rudolph challenged.

"Wrong headed, yes. Why carry on so about individuals," Willa demanded. "And why get the myth of creative genius all mixed up with stories about artists' personal lives? Or better yet, why let journalists get them all mixed up? It's what we do that matters, not who we are. Deeds. Actions. Art. Not individuals or personalities."

Earl cleared his throat. "That sounds pretty old fashioned," he finally said, "almost old-time religious."

"Well, old time stays in fashion sometimes," Edith finally entered the argument. "Milton and Spenser and those other Renaissance fellows did think a certain kind of personality important. But they called it character, the kind Everyman should have. Milton himself said it took a good man to produce great art."

"Good character, great art, yes," Willa agreed, "but what I am talking about is older fashioned than Milton. Maybe even pre-church religious," she paused to grin at Earl. "Just think about it. All this genius talk and personal gossip just puffs men up beyond the limits of sense and human gravity. Enlarged heads are only the beginning," she chuckled. "Once started, their reputations swell them up altogether and carry them off like the hot air balloons at Coney Island. First they bloat and start to look distended," Willa puffed up her cheeks and shoved her belly out until it pushed against the table, "and then they preen and dance and swagger through the air."

Edith giggled again at the image, remembering how Willa rose to whirl about the room like an awkward, pregnant Isadora Duncan. "Readers no longer see writers' works, only those floating

Kewpie doll figures filled with their own hot air," Willa's words came slowly, each following a swirl. When she sat back down, her expression turned serious and intense, "How the Great Man as Artist or, for that matter, a Silly Woman Writer can expect readers to achieve empathetic identification with what's going on in their novels when they refuse to get out of the way of their pages is beyond me," and she thumped her hand hard upon the table. Willa had been so forceful, so adamant, her whole body so involved in her words, that at that moment the legs collapsed from under her chair.

Earl, springing forward to bring her back to her feet, laughed, "Well, that certainly fell flat, didn't it?"

But it hadn't, of course, and now Willa's collapse served to punctuate Edith's memory. Edith also remembered Rudolph's surprise at the questions that followed about why it was all so much worse when the Great Man was female. Edith had guessed that it was because of the different standards people used to judge the personal lives of men and women. Willa had said it amounted to three little words, all of them capitalized, Women Should Not.

Rudolph and Earl had come a long way toward wisdom since then, and Willa claimed that those long nights of talk with Rudolph at the helm were the some of most decisive moments in her career. That's when, she said, she moved from pretending to be in Bohemia to being there. They also learned a great deal from Earl about painting and religion and, more recently, about meditation. He was already wise enough then to marry Edith's college roommate, Edith smiled to herself, though why Earl had to cart Achsah off half way around the world, Edith would never fully understand or approve. She wanted them closer. As painters, Earl and Achsah loved the light on Capri, but now Earl was translating the writings of Buddha, and they were talking about moving to India. Achsah's letters were full of the plan. They expected D. H. Lawrence and Frieda, two of their closest friends, to go along. And they wanted Edith and Willa to join them.

Well, Lawrence might go, Edith refilled her cup, but she knew Willa would desist. Edith replaced the pot and glanced out the window, her eyes settling momentarily on Rob Feeney, whose uniformed back was just then entering the bank. Edith's inner eye glimpsed the passage of the S. S. Grand Manan as it crossed the mouth of Whale Cove. Feeney was a nice fellow, always teasing Edith about seasickness at the same time he tried to make her passage as comfortable as possible.

When they built the cottage on Grand Manan, Willa declared that twenty miles off the tip of Maine was as far from the United States as she wanted to be for any extended period. And not just because of Edith's regular bouts of seasickness. They had already tried France. After all, with Earl and Achsah and Jan and Isabelle within a day's journey of each other and the cost of living so much less abroad, moving to France or Italy seemed sensible. Especially once Willa's own fame took hold. But after only a few months, they began to feel disconnected. From themselves, not just from the country or the people they knew. Insulation from crowds and hectic schedules, yes, they both needed that. But they also needed immersion. It was important for them and especially for Willa to hear the nuances and feel the pace of their own country. It was a writer's life blood, Willa finally had determined. Her life blood. Not to experience the language and cadence of America, Willa guessed, meant that she would become a different writer or perhaps no writer at all. That was a price neither of them chose to pay.

But men, Edith realized she had digressed into woolgathering. Nice men. Mean men. Men had nothing to do with their decision. One man in particular, however, might have a great deal to do with Sabra Jane's ability to make any decisions at all from now on. Surely there was a mistake here.

EDITH tried again to see what surrounded the red shirt that had so centrally occupied her mind's eye. This was like working a motion picture film. Edith tried slowing the reel of her memory to inspect the image with the shirt frame by frame. But her eye fixed the scene in considerably less detail than a camera might have. Or perhaps the problem was focus. She had been too far away to catch the sharp features necessary for distinguishing the sex or identity of the person in the shirt. She was sure it was the person's back, though she couldn't say exactly why. The pattern of the movements, she guessed, told her that. The way the arm flung itself out, perhaps that was it. The legs, she recalled, seemed to be spread. Yes, the person wore pants. Black pants, brown pants, blue, she couldn't tell. But dark, darker than the blaze of red above or the rocks below. Boots, shoes. She couldn't say. She looked again toward the head. Dark, darker than a face would be, Edith thought. But she caught no hint of color or length of hair. Probably short, she guessed, unless the person was wearing a close hat, something knitted, perhaps. Not likely, the way the day had warmed up.

What was there, Edith wondered, among the things she could remember about this shirted figure to separate it from Sabra Jane Briggs. Sabra Jane wore her hair bobbed and shingled in the back, so that was no help, and its color didn't matter. The color of the shirt could easily have been the red Sabra Jane wore, and the person seemed to have a waist, the shirt tucked in just as Sabra Jane's had been. Her jodhpurs had been a mahogany brown that day and her boots the tall lace-ups she customarily wore. Could the person have been wearing those boots? Maybe. Maybe not. All Edith could say for certain was that the legs had been spread, the figure's final pose like a ballet dancer's or the flourish of a star who wants the audience to recognize with applause the rest of the cast. Why had the arm flung itself out? Edith had no idea.

"AND then, you know, he never took the time to unpack." Edith's thought was interrupted by the jangle of a bell and voices from the next room, where the entrance to Rose Cottage was located. "He just opened one bag and left it there."

"And left his bird book on the bed," another voice, this one male, interjected before greeting Mary, the young waitress Edith and Willa so much enjoyed. The voice asked for a table for four. They wanted an early luncheon, it said, because they were planning an afternoon at Hole in the Wall.

Mary appeared, leading two couples into the dining room. They crossed to a table on the wall opposite. The young men were wearing the white pants, sweaters, and canvas shoes of tennis players. The women wore jodhpurs and short boots. The brunette was in the process of removing a smart pork-pie hat. She and the blond settled into chairs their husbands held for them. One of the men smiled in Edith's direction. Edith looked out the window toward the dock to inspect the fishing boats tied up there. Too many gushers tried to get an introduction to Willa through her. Edith had learned to discourage strangers even when Willa was not present.

"What I don't understand," continued the first voice, now attached to the pork-pie hat, "is why they don't know more about him. At The Swallowtail, I mean. I realize it is too soon to hear anything from the wire the constable sent to St. John, but this what's-his-name, Mr. Brown, must have written The Swallowtail for reservations. Wouldn't you think they would have his address? Know where he came from? What he did for a living?"

The woman interrupted herself, reaching across the table to select a Lucky Strike from the opened silver case resting in her husband's hand. Edith recognized the brand even at this distance. It was Willa's. Wouldn't that scandalize Willa's readers, to know that she smoked cigarettes? So many people still thought women like this one in the pork-pie hat racy and immoral, and those who thought that assumed Willa was just like they were. Well, let them think what they like, Edith smiled and looked away again.

"The people at The Swallowtail certainly seemed to know everything about us," the woman leaned forward again. Edith heard the woman's chair creak and her husband strike a match. She noticed the top of his forehead had been pinkened by the sun.

"Not exactly, dear," the husband finally spoke. "I mean, they didn't exactly know what business I was in," he shook the match until the flame went out. "Now, what shall we order," he turned with raised eyebrows back to their friends. Edith glanced out the window again.

That young man who had helped Roy Sharkey deliver the load of stones for the rock garden was just then swinging from a ladder attached to the dock onto a blue and white fishing boat. It had an engine, Edith noticed. Earlier that spring, one of the fellows in the office next to hers at J. Walter Thompson asked the women's department whether they thought a woman could handle an Evinrude. The result was an advertisement showing a woman at the tiller in house dress and heels, Edith snorted.

A lobster boat this was, she guessed. The Barbara Ann, it said on the stern. Edith was never sure which boats were which, and now she couldn't remember the young man's name. James, that was it. Nice young fellow. Strong, too, and a worker. Edith hadn't caught his last name. He had said *ma'am* three times. She made a mental note to ask Roy Sharkey when he planned to bring the next load of rocks. If young James had found work on one of the fishing boats, it might be a good while. He could be out at sea for several days, and Roy Sharkey was not known for ambition or hard work. His wagon and time on his hands had made his reputation.

But the immediate concern, Edith reminded herself, was learning more about what happened on Seven Days Work and more, too, about Sabra Jane Briggs. Edith thought she might stop by Constable Daggett's on her way back to Whale Cove. She could not believe

Sabra Jane had been part of that tragic event. Someone else must also have been wearing a red shirt the previous afternoon. Why hadn't anyone noticed?

V

CONSTABLE DAGGETT RETURNED from The Anchorage well over an hour ago, his wife told Edith. And he was already off again, this time in the direction of The Whistle. No, she did not know when he would return or what he had learned. Perhaps Miss Lewis could inquire later by telephone. Elizabeth Daggett was rather firm in suggesting that Edith inquire by phone. She did not open the screen door of the trim yellow house, nor did she invite Edith to step in.

Edith supposed she would have been similarly firm. Willa even more so. Willa increasingly had taken to practicing what she called her Medusa stare, calculated to induce terror in the hardiest of gushers. She had learned the effectiveness of the Medusa from Olive Fremstad and went to some length in *The Song of the Lark,* much of which she based on Fremstad's career, explaining how once Fremstad reached the Metropolitan Opera, she used the Medusa to protect her inner, artistic life. It had occurred to none of them at the time that Willa would ever need the diva's mask for herself. But that was before Edith shifted to advertising and Willa met Alfred Knopf. Without Alfred, Edith thought, Willa might still be buried among the genteel ladies and sentimental authoresses on Houghton Mifflin's list. Willa thought so, too. And now, though not everyone might agree, she was outdistancing even Edith Wharton. In fact, Edith guessed, no other American writer, with the possible exception of Harriet Beecher Stowe, ever laid such claim to a diva's fame.

It was silly, Edith supposed, to compare the actions of a constable's wife to their own awkward attempts to deal with Willa's fans.

Not only had Willa and Edith worked very hard to create the situation in which they now found themselves, the reason Willa adopted the Medusa and used other devices to keep people at bay was as much to maintain the illusion in Willa's fiction as it was to protect their privacy. Willa meant to evade both puffs, the Silly Woman and the Great Artist. She planned, in fact, to stay so far out of sight, her readers would never be quite certain who or where she was, especially in her novels. She was always experimenting, anyway, with different ways to tell a story and different stories to tell. I want to be a character actor, not a star, Willa declared. No typecasting, please. Or, she would say, I'm a wild turkey, I'll scramble to find new feeding grounds whenever anyone sets foot on mine. And off she would go, up the stairs to start her morning's work, Gabble, Gobble, Gabble, Gobble, arms akimbo, working up and down like wings.

Elizabeth Daggett had no such motivation to explain her behavior. Or sense of humor, it seemed. Either she was very sour by nature or she too had some reason to master the fine art of polite distance. Edith did not like to think Mrs. Daggett was sour by nature, for that would mean Mr. Daggett had chosen unwisely. Edith preferred to think that marriage to the local constable brought with it the trials of being a partner to a certain kind of renown, where people felt free to ask questions whenever they pleased and freer still to offer their advice. Whatever reason Mrs. Daggett had for putting her off, Edith chose to believe it was positive.

More important than worrying about Elizabeth Daggett was finding out what her husband was up to. Edith fairly trotted along Church Lane and picked her way as fast as she could over the rocks at Whale Cove. Perhaps Mr. Daggett had stopped at the cottage. Edith didn't want to miss him, and she hoped Willa was ready to reappear. That was how she thought of it, Edith realized with a smile. Each morning Willa disappeared into her manuscript and remained there until it was time to come out. Well, Edith needed

45

Willa to make her reappearance now. She wanted to talk over what was happening on Grand Manan, just as they always discussed what was happening in the worlds Willa created.

Edith could already hear Willa saying they needed to do more homework. Then Edith would suggest that they walk to Seven Days Work to get a fuller sense of the circumstances, and as they set out they would consider what they knew of the characters, of Mr. Brown, the red shirt, and Sabra Jane Briggs. Only then could they speculate about who else might belong in the cast.

WHEN Edith reached the cottage she found Willa in the Adirondack reviewing her manuscript and wearing the brown leather boots and twill pants she liked to use for hiking the more difficult trails on the island. Constable Daggett had indeed stopped by, Willa told Edith, but he had said nothing at all about Sabra Jane Briggs. He had, however, reluctantly agreed that it would be a good idea for the two of them to go back to Seven Days Work. He wanted Edith to help him determine the exact location the man had gone off the cliff. Daggett had already hiked back over the section of the trail they decided yesterday was most likely, but once again he had found nothing to give away the exact spot. He would rather be with them when they went, he said, to be sure they did not destroy evidence, but he also needed to go into North Head to continue to locate people who noticed Mr. Brown walking about. No one he talked to so far had seen Mr. Brown leave the village.

Thirty minutes later they found a handwritten note pinned to a single strand of white cotton rope draped across the trail on Seven Days Work, just where the trail broke out of the woods and onto the open cliffs. The note said "Crime Scene, Do Not Enter."

"Busy man, our constable."

"Busy man," Willa agreed, "who seems to have read too many

dime novels." She eyed the note before raising the cotton rope for Edith to duck under. "Possible Crime Scene is what he should have written," Willa suggested. "All we really know is that two people were present when one of them went off the cliff. Isn't that right?"

"And that the other one failed to go for help," Edith tossed back over her shoulder.

"Do we actually know that?" Willa paused to consider. "What did you see the red shirt do after Mr. Brown went off the cliff?"

"Nothing," Edith stopped to reconstruct the scene once more in her mind. "I mean, I did not seen him do anything," she heard her own words come slow, deliberate. "I was not looking at him. I saw Mr. Brown fall, and I shouted to Eric Dawson, and you came, and then I ran for help." Edith fast forwarded the motion picture film in her mind, then with a shrug she spoke more quickly, "The red shirt was there, and then it wasn't."

Willa appeared to be contemplating Edith's shrug, "And Eric Dawson never saw the red shirt and only saw Mr. Brown just before he landed."

Edith nodded and glanced out toward the weir, trying to imagine just what Eric Dawson had seen. But Eric Dawson had been rowing from the direction of Whale Cove. That meant his back was turned toward Seven Days Work. He must have seen Mr. Brown only because her shout drew his attention.

"Maybe if we look at the weir and the cottage from different angles on the trail, that would help us pick the spot," Willa suggested and Edith agreed. It was a sensible idea.

The trail narrowed the minute it broke free of the woods, then ran for a good thirty or forty yards along the edge of the cliff, jutting in and out in sharp, irregular patterns, occasionally cutting back into the trees. Just beyond they could hear the two waterfalls. Here and there a solitary spruce gripped the rocks, its outer boughs bare,

47

its tip thrown back from the sea. Years of living with the wind did that, Edith caught again a glimpse of naughty children leaning with their whole bodies to touch the ground.

Edith called Willa's attention to two places in the trail where the spruce were more numerous. "Let's try there," she pointed to the first one about thirty feet ahead.

When they reached the spot where the cliff jutted forward, sporting enough soil to hold a few wisps of grass and three scrub spruce, Edith took a pair of binoculars out of the small case she carried loosely strapped around her neck. She aimed the binoculars first toward the weir and then toward the cottage. The weir was clearly visible, its round configuration slightly elongated from this angle into an oval. Unique to Grand Manan, herring weirs reminded Edith of the tadpoles crowding the fishbowl on the dining room sidetable of her childhood, their large heads and bulging eyes dragging bodies as narrow as banners listing in a slight breeze.

Only weirs weren't as numerous as pollywogs and the Bay of Fundy was hardly a fishbowl. From this angle, Edith thought, the weir Eric Dawson had been heading for looked more like a modified Cupid's arrow pointed out to sea. Originally devised by the Passamaquoddy Indians and built just beyond low water, herring weirs consisted of a fence made of nets strung on poles that ran several hundred feet out from the shore in a line straight as an arrow's shaft. At the arrow's haft, the poles and nets swung into the rounded top of an enormous valentine not quite joined at the center, luring the herring into its snare. But instead of coming to a point, this heart-shaped arrowhead took on the snub-nosed appearance of a giant mallet, its tip worn and smoothed by generations of resistance to incoming waves.

Edith admired common sense and ingenuity, and she paused for a moment to regard this passive form of fishing. Weirs trapped thou-

Herring Weir

sands of fish each year. Herring came inshore at night and dropped along the shore on the high water and ebb. Edith and Willa often heard fishermen talking about how they could tell when herring were playing in the area by their sweetish smell. When herring encountered a weir fence, they were forced to work offshore until they came to the opening at the haft and swam dead ahead, probably imagining themselves free, Edith guessed, until they met the mallet shaped head of nets at the tip and slipped into a continual swirl. Each weir, they had been told, held several tons of herring. Fishermen simply let the weir do its work until the owner negotiated a sale with a processor and a team of fishermen came to seine the weir and transport the fish to the smokehouses at Seal Cove.

The only weir Edith had heard about before coming to Grand Manan was the one that drowned Eustacia Vye. But Thomas Hardy had never been to Grand Manan. Herring weirs worked just like cattle pens at the stock yards, Edith grinned at the thought, and fish farmers had about as much time as ranchers to negotiate a price for their perishable stock. Grand Manan, Edith and Willa had learned shortly before they arrived for their first visit in 1922, had been a major supplier of smoked herring since the 1880s, when the island's weirs provided the world with more than 20,000 tons of herring a year. By now, Edith guessed, it must be more like 100,000 tons.

"I wonder what Eric Dawson was doing out there," Edith interrupted her own thoughts.

"He told me he was going out to check the nets and see whether herring had begun to work their way in," Willa stepped back several paces toward the woods and sat down on a rock. "Jason Logan smelled them in the cove the night before last."

Edith remained on the ledge. It felt like the right place, precipitous, precarious. If someone were to rush from behind or give even the slightest nudge, well. The red-shirted arm again flung out in her mind and the man in the suit seemed to leap once more into his sideways dive. Edith took a step back. She could not see their cottage with her naked eye, only that portion of the cliff that swung out to form their lawn. It also held the small stand of pines that grew below their cottage, shielding it from the others in their conclave.

That was where she had stood the previous afternoon, she was sure. Just there, a few feet north and west of the first pine. Right on the edge, she had been, but probably not noticeable to anyone standing on Seven Days Work. Underbrush and tall grass camouflaged the edge. Behind, the evergreens on their cliff, nestled well into Whale Cove, stood tall, their limber boughs heavy and deeply green. Looking at them through binoculars, Edith also saw them for a moment in her mind. So still the pines were and erect, shading the moss-covered ground beneath, redecorated each year with fresh blankets of pine needles and cones. Edith knew those arms swung sometimes violently in high winds and hurricanes, but compared to the few stalwart spruce that braved the constant assault of salt winds off the sea at Seven Days Work, their pines, it seemed to Edith, lolled like overfed gods.

"WELL, what do you think?" Willa's patience was wearing thin.

"Oh," Edith hadn't noticed how far she had slipped into her own thoughts, "I was just thinking how deceptive this spot would be to someone who didn't know the island."

Willa's eyes formed the question before she raised it. "Deceptive?"

"Standing here I could believe there were no cottages on this side at all," Edith raised her binoculars to look at the shoreline on the other side of Whale Cove, "and if I didn't know from having been there, it would never occur to me that across the cove was the trail to Hole in the Wall."

"I doubt that anyone could see from there without binoculars," Willa raised her hand to shade her own eyes.

Edith contemplated the shoreline, then swung the glasses back toward their cottage. For pinpointing the spot where the man had gone off the cliff, it was not important that all she could see were the pine trees and not their cottage. What mattered was where she had been, not where the cottage stood. Edith wished briefly that before they left, they had gotten out her easel and repositioned it in the spot she had been the previous afternoon. But had she done that, Edith guessed, they probably would not have been able to see the easel from this distance, even with binoculars. After all, she had barely been able to make out the red shirt and the business suit, and she supposed her body would have been pretty well camouflaged by tall grass and underbrush. The easel too.

"It could have happened here," Willa broke in again. "Both the weir and our cliff would have direct views. And if Mr. Brown had been talking to the red shirt from where I am," Willa spoke from her rock, "you would not have been able to see him, would you?"

THE second outcropping of spruce, about ten yards further on, turned out to be less promising. Standing in the open area there they found themselves more likely to face toward Ashburton Head than Whale Cove. Willa tried but found no comfortable spot for sitting and no easy access to the woods behind.

"Let's go back to the first place for another look," Willa suggested. "That must be the spot."

Twice more they retraced their steps, then settled together on the first site. Besides the three spruce and a few patches of grass, the area totaled probably less than a hundred square feet of almost solid rock, its bit of surface dirt packed tight. The trail ran in varying degrees near the edge for twelve feet or so then swung back in again toward the woods behind. They were approximately twenty feet south of the waterfalls.

With the site determined, they separated to comb the area carefully. They could hear the waterfall and the waves below and an occasional cry from a gull off shore. They had no idea what to look for. Scuff marks, perhaps, a drop of blood, a fallen pen knife, a gun. Nothing appeared to give them a clue.

Twenty minutes later, Edith broke their silence. "I do believe this is the right place," she stood at the edge of the cliff, her hands on her hips, looking down to determine the trajectory of Mr. Brown's fall and the site of his landing, "but I do not understand why we are finding no sign of their being here."

"It seems likely that neither Mr. Brown nor the person in the red shirt took time to tidy up."

Edith smiled at Willa's joke. It was a very long way down, and even at full tide, Edith guessed, the larger rocks along the base of the cliff would signal their danger, their formidable heads rising well above the incoming waves. Edith couldn't imagine anyone being careless enough to stand as close to the edge as she was now, certainly not someone in city shoes. But then Mr. Brown hadn't stood near the edge, had he. He had come from somewhere behind, suddenly and fast. Edith turned her head to look back. Why?

Rob Feeney retrieved a paper clip from the top drawer of his desk and attached the passenger list to the names of the crew members who had made the crossing the day before with Mr. John T. Brown. Then he drew out a pen and added his own name to those of the crew. So few passengers and no strangers among the crew, but Mark Daggett eventually would want to know who they all were, Rob was sure of that. Daggett was a thorough man. He was probably already busy finding out who on the island knew Mr. John T. Brown and why he had been on the cliff at Seven Days Work. Rob would have the lists ready when Daggett came by, whenever that might be.

Later that afternoon, Rob thought, he would drop by for a visit with Miss Edith. What a frightening experience she had just had witnessing Mr. Brown's demise. Rob caught an inner glimpse of the ashen face he often saw arriving on the S. S. Grand Manan and smiled at the set of its lips. Tough lady, Rob heard himself saying and realized that Miss Edith didn't need sympathy. And, he reminded himself, Miss Willa didn't like interruptions. Privacy, he mused, placing his papers with their lists of names above the blotter on his desk and pushing back in his chair. He was already late for lunch. A writer's indulgence, privacy. He decided not to intrude.

"What do you say we try the woods," Willa headed in that direction. Several old sheep trails, as well as those maintained by wildlife, meandered everywhere on the island. Inexperienced hikers often found themselves fooled. Once a year in late spring, islanders would take a day to mark the trails, painting slashes of colors on trees and rocks at strategic points. Red, blue, orange. Different colors to denote the different trails. Seven Days Work was on the Red Trail. "We don't know which way they came," Willa pointed out. "Maybe they didn't come on the main trail at all."

"That's true. They might have come through the woods," Edith scrambled behind, "but why?"

"When we know the answer to that," Willa moved further into the trees, "we'll probably understand the rest of it."

Willa turned north toward the brook that bubbled out over the cliff.

Edith followed.

VI

"YOU MUST BE joking," Little John Winslow waxed eloquent before a small crowd of three adults, two children, and a puppy standing outside Tinsley's Pharmacy. "She's a witch."

Mark Daggett, just exiting the bank, heard Little John all the way across the street.

"I've known there was something wrong about that woman since she first set foot in North Head. Her and her red hair and fancy car. She could have done it."

Daggett smiled despite his annoyance. No stopping Little John in the best of times, and no reason to think that deputizing him would ensure his silence. It didn't matter what Little John swore to uphold.

"She could have done it easy," Little John, driving his point home, shook a finger in the direction of Daisy Edwards.

Little John's voice always carried well, though mostly he was restricted to writing letters to the editor or delivering speeches at village meetings. People otherwise walked away. Maybe it had been a mistake to involve Little John. Gives him too much importance. But he had been the only one to arrive with a wagon, and Daggett had had a fleeting notion that deputizing Little John might bring him more into line. That clearly was wrong.

"Got the strength of a bull, she does. And anyway, you've heard of levitation," Little John's voice and hands became more agitated. "Witches do that. She could have levitated him right off over the edge." Little John raised his hands, palms down, fingers extended. They floated horizontally off to the right, then shook once sharply as if they were shedding rain from their tips.

Daggett reached the group just as Janey Dawson's eyes were growing wide and Daisy Edwards exchanged glances with Jason Tinsley. Eva McDaniels was nodding and working her mouth, a sure sign that she was about to add to Little John's newly discovered wisdom.

"Excuse us," Daggett brushed past Eva's paisley pink shoulder to take hold of Little John's arm, "we have business to do. Little John, I need your help."

Mistake number two. Little John's chest puffed out, and Janey's eyes grew wider. Leaving Eva McDaniels speechless would also be short lived, Daggett realized too late. Eva published a bi-weekly rag called the *Recipe Exchange* and had the best gossip network in the village. Daggett swore silently to himself and jerked Little John's sleeve more firmly than he intended. Little John's feet finally joined with his body, and they moved off in the direction of The Swallowtail Inn.

Daggett didn't speak, and Little John contented himself with matching Daggett's stride. Little John's head had snapped up, eyes forward, mustache following the upswing at the outer edges of his lips. Little John was grinning. Immensely irritated, Daggett lengthened his stride.

"You shouldn't spread rumors, you know," Daggett waited until Jackson's Drygoods to break his silence. They had only a short block to go along North Head's single business street. The wharf took up most of the opposite side, along with the dock where the S. S. Grand Manan delivered her passengers once every second day. The Swallowtail Inn stood off by itself, facing away from the village toward Petit's Cove and The Swallowtail Light.

By the time they reached the front steps to The Swallowtail Inn, Little John had ended his protestations and twice promised he would stay mum on the subject of Sabra Jane Briggs. He thumped his chest and crossed his heart, but Daggett was hardly mollified.

"You do have to admit, now, she's a different one," Little John finally concluded, his eyes conveying luminous certainty, "that she is."

Daggett had never before noticed how the droop of Little John's mustache concealed the fleshy fullness of his lips.

At Daggett's insistence, Little John considered the duty of walking the kilometer or so out to the lighthouse, asking at cottages along the way whether Mr. Brown had passed by the previous afternoon. Daggett readily agreed that it was probably a fool's errand.

"That's the wrong direction entirely," Little John's voice began to rise again.

"Routine police work," Daggett patted him on the shoulder. "Part of the process of elimination," Daggett lowered his voice to suggest confidentiality. "Has to be done, and you could save us a lot of time doing it."

With Little John's shrug, Daggett spun up the steps to The Swallowtail Inn. Daggett was pleased he had thought to say "us." Little John was always difficult. An odd combination of ignorance and intelligence, Little John generally favored superstition and prejudice. But if at times he was unpredictable, he was consistently stubborn. It was devilishly hard to talk Little John into doing anything, especially if it involved walking. Little John hated walking, and Daggett knew it.

"Wasn't anyone here wearing a red shirt, I can tell you that," Harvey Andrews' finger ran down the list of names on The Swallowtail register. His finger pressed so hard when it came to the last name two thirds of the way down the page that the skin under its nail turned a combination of white and bright pink. "Only but two of these people aren't regular guests. This here Jackson Knoll, a large fellow, kind of swaggery, you know," Harvey's voice rose to a question mark before he cleared his throat, "says he's from Toronto." The finger stabbed higher on the page, "and Miss Anna Driscoll," the finger ran back down, "says here she's from New York. Has a friend up at Whale Cove, I believe she said. Or maybe it was The Anchorage."

Daggett cleared his throat and jotted in his notebook.

"Oh, and those two young couples from Boston," Harvey glanced up, then narrowed his eyes. "But they wouldn't know anything. They were down birdwatching at Castalia all day yesterday."

Daggett looked above the finger to catch the spellings upside down of all the names on the page. Jameson, Johnson, Ainsworth, McKinney, Blackall, Reimer, Hart. Anglo-Saxon names most of them, from New York or Massachusetts. One from New Jersey and two Canadians, one from St. Stephen, the other from Montreal. Jackson Knoll had a heavy hand. The pen had spread wide to accommodate him. Miss Driscoll's signature was neat, with scrolls.

Harvey finally relaxed his finger, and Daggett turned the registry around for a better look. John T. Brown was second to last, only Driscoll followed. Mr. Brown's hand was light, his letters precise and erect. Had there been any *i*'s, Daggett guessed, little round dots would appear directly above them. A vertical sort of man, this Mr. Brown.

"Did Mr. Brown give any indication of knowing any one of the others? Regular guests or otherwise?" Daggett always hoped the answers might change. He had already been through this with Harvey and his wife Geneva the night before.

"Like we said, we didn't notice him talking to anyone."

"And as far as you know, only Miss Driscoll came over on the same passage with him?"

Harvey's nod was short, "Might be someone checked in other places but not here. You ask around?"

Daggett smiled, "Haven't checked with the agent yet, but the captain telegraphed three passengers boarded in Eastport. I've been able to find only these two."

"You been down toward Southern Head? Miss Briggs, she takes in quite a crew," Harvey began sucking air between two teeth on the left side of his mouth.

"This was a man," Daggett wished he had a toothpick to hand Harvey. "The captain said two men and a woman."

"Could have been an islander," Harvey pointed out. "Did you try Isabelle Ericson? She sometimes takes boarders, but that's generally for overflow." Harvey used a finger to probe the inside of his mouth. "We're not full yet," the finger reappeared, "not by a long shot. Been too cool for July." He rested both hands on the counter. The sucking sound resumed.

"No one called for Mr. Brown? You didn't see him leave with anyone? A man?" Daggett paused, "Or a woman?"

"No, like I told you."

"And he left for a walk about half an hour after returning from lunch at two?"

"Like I told you."

"And neither of you saw him return or heard anything unusual?"

MR. BROWN'S room was virtually untouched. He apparently had not even sat down on the bed, though a copy of *Audubon* appeared to have been casually dropped on the yellow chenille bedspread next to an open suitcase. Audubon come home to roost, Geneva Andrews had ventured after showing Constable Daggett up to Mr. Brown's room the previous evening. Audubon was one of the principle reasons people came to Grand Manan. He had visited the island in 1833 and sketched many of the 330 bird species that used Grand Manan as their sanctuary. Geneva was the principle reason the people who came stayed at The Swallowtail Inn. She had a pleasant sense of humor and provided ample meals.

Daggett had already been through Mr. Brown's room once the night before, when he had set the large brown leather suitcase on the luggage rack and pried its lock. The smaller case still lay open on the bed where Mr. Brown had placed it. There were no name tags and neither bag was packed full.

Daggett went through them again, beginning with the smaller case, taking everything out just as he found it. One copy of the book all the tourists were reading this season, *All Quiet on the Western Front*. One black leather notebook, its blue-lined pages entirely clean, a freshly sharpened pencil tucked into a pencil fastener inside. A small case containing shaving equipment and toiletries with nothing unusual. No prescription drugs, no wrist watch, no rings, either here or on the body. Daggett had recovered an Elgin pocket watch, a pair of gold cuff links, and a black leather belt from the body, all without peculiarity. Two garters and four pairs of socks, two black, two navy blue. One pair of cream colored pajamas. Four pairs of cotton underwear, one bow tie, and two linen handkerchiefs with *JBT* embroidered in the corner.

The larger case held one maroon bathrobe of good quality silk. One pair of leather slippers, their tan doeskin uncreased, heels unworn. Three starched shirts, white with French cuffs, still in their wrappings from Chin's Chinese Laundry, 148 W. 13th Street, New Bedford, Massachusetts. One light wool plaid shirt and one sweater, a navy blue pullover, both from Abercrombie and Fitch in New York City. One pair of navy blue knickers. And one three-piece suit, a fine light gabardine, also navy blue, with Marvin Gates, Boston's Finest Tailor, For *JBT*, embroidered on the label.

Daggett had already jotted down the numbers and names on the labels and laundry wrappers the night before and sent telegrams to the police in New York City, Boston, and New Bedford, asking for help in tracking down information about John T. Brown. Now he ran his hands over each piece of clothing to make sure he was missing nothing and then felt carefully around the inside of each bag, making small slits in their bottoms to check the linings. Nothing he hadn't already seen made itself evident.

The room, too, was empty of new clues. Daggett shook his head. He'd gotten various descriptions of Mr. Brown, ranging from blue eyed and tall to green eyed and medium height, but Daggett had never seen the man, only his mutilated body. The body carried no pictures or identification. What had happened to the personal effects on Mr. Brown's body, Daggett wondered and reached for his pipe. The key to his suitcase, for instance. And if Mr. Brown's death had involved robbery, why hadn't the killer taken the twelve American dollars from Mr. Brown's pocket?

Nothing about this case made sense. Daggett tamped tobacco into his pipe and sat down in the room's solitary chair, a hickory rocker with a yellow quilted cushion. The rocker was deep and made a pleasant creak with each forward roll. Daggett rested his head against its tall back. So far, the only hints that this was a murder case were the lack of identification on Mr. Brown's body and the red-shirted figure that Miss Lewis had seen. Of course, Brown's identification could have been lost in his fall. And so far, the red shirt implicated only one person, Sabra Jane Briggs.

Daggett closed his eyes. The bowl of his pipe felt smooth against his palm. He cradled it there. As soon as he asked Miss Briggs about the red shirt, she told him to make himself comfortable while she went to get it. Most of her lodgers were off for a day's hike to Hay Point, but there were still five women in the sitting room, four playing bridge, the fifth reading a rumpled copy of *The New York Times*.

"It's like avoiding the bends," Dottie Voorhees grinned, introducing herself. Miss Voorhees had deep dimples and eyes that laughed with her lips. "Have to come up slow. Takes at least a week for your head to leave New York and a good week more before you can give up the *Times*."

When Daggett noticed a button missing from the left sleeve of Miss Briggs' shirt, she said, yes, it had come off while she was hauling rocks around the previous afternoon. She had not been able to find the button and had worn the shirt with her sleeves rolled up. She offered to send the shirt back with Daggett if that would be helpful. After a moment's hesitation he told her he thought that would not be necessary. But he also asked her not to sew on another button just yet.

It had taken several promptings before Miss Briggs recalled speaking with Mr. Brown. At first she protested she never met the man. But as she recounted her activities of the previous afternoon, at Daggett's request, she recalled greeting a stranger in a pin-striped suit. Oh, she said, yes. A well-groomed man with hazel eyes and an odd manner of glancing off to the side when he spoke. Yes, she remembered she had given him the time of day. Literally. He had pulled a watch out of his pocket and set it.

It was 3:48, that's what it was. Miss Briggs' eyes focused somewhere beyond Daggett, her brow furrowed. Yes, she remembered she had been just about to put her parcels in the Reo and start home. She had spent the earlier part of the afternoon at Whale Cove with Miss Cather and Miss Lewis. They were building an herb rock garden behind their cottage. And before Daggett could express interest, she took him by the arm and led him out the back door of the big house to show him the rock garden she built for herself. Daggett didn't mind. The farm that was now The Anchorage had once belonged to his uncle Jerome, and Daggett was curious to see the improvements Miss Briggs had made.

Before Daggett left, Miss Voorhees ran out after them to issue a special invitation to their theatricals the following Saturday evening. Miss Briggs was to play Brunnhilde, Miss Voorhees announced and clapped her on the back. And Miss Voorhees was to play a Valkyrie. Call me Voorhees the Viking, Miss Voorhees roared, and rolling her shoulders forward and placing a fist on each hip she began to swagger around the apple tree in front of the big house. Daggett drove off promising nothing.

The Cottage Girls gave theatricals, too. Daggett's wife had been once, his daughter twice. It was something to do and preferable, Daggett thought, to the moving picture shows at the Happy Hour Theatre. The movies had been installed, like the tennis courts and motor boat rides, to entertain the tourists, but they dazzled islanders, too. None more than his daughter until she saw the Cottage Girls perform *Jane Eyre*. Jennifer thought their costumes were lovely and said so for days. Miss Bromhall was beautiful and Miss Cobus so handsome, Jennifer's eyes sparkled. Elizabeth said she thought perhaps the Cottage Girls were not the best influence on their daughter, but Jennifer and her best friend Alice Bright had gone on to play *Jane Eyre* for months until finally they read the book and announced that Rochester wasn't so wonderful after all. Daggett wasn't sure what they played now. They spent much of their time out of doors in the summer.

Daggett stopped the rocker. This was no help. He couldn't even keep his mind on the crime. The room was quiet and orderly, its pale yellows restful, but something very disorderly had happened to its occupant, and it was up to Daggett to figure out just what that was and who was responsible. He hadn't a clue.

What did he know about murder and murderers in any event? The rocker creaked again. He could never understand why some people chose to steal from other people, or drink more than they should, or hit one another. It's God's will, some people said, like war or pestilence. Other people said it was part of man's nature. But what did that mean, for heaven's sake? Daggett had sworn to keep the peace. His duty was to maintain law and order. That meant keeping people out of trouble. Well, he had failed. Or they had.

VII

WILLA TOOK EDITH'S hand to help her over a large fallen log, then held it for a moment, drawing her attention to their surroundings.

"Can this be the way they came, do you think?"

It was doubtful, Edith thought, but still possible. The log made negotiating the trail difficult, and once they were on the other side, the trail seemed to disappear altogether. Of course, this sort of thing happened all the time in the woods. Storms and high winds often rearranged the trees, fooling even hikers who knew the trails well. Willa and Edith long ago developed a routine for these occasions, the one behind stopping at the point where they lost the trail, while the other one scouted out and around. One opening in the trees looked very like another, the light slanting in the same direction, wildflowers blooming in similar clusters beneath the pines and scrub oak.

"No sign of twigs broken or undergrowth disturbed and no sign of the trail on this side," Willa called far off to the left.

The noise from the brook had grown loud or soft as the trail approached and drifted away. Now its sound had almost disappeared with the trail. Willa and Edith were heading inland toward the road, the brook on their right. They had crossed it twice. Edith sat down on the log. Her left shoestring was untied. She glanced back in the direction they had just come. The trail was fairly evident there, so perhaps someone coming in from the road would not have missed it. Edith knew from experience that this was the best of numerous trails leading inland from the waterfall. They had taken it before, several times, stopping for picnics along the way. The brook afforded countless picnic spots and swimming holes. Dipping pools, Edith corrected herself. Even though Cobus built new dams every spring, none of them were large enough for an actual swim, and the water in the brook was generally too cool for anyone to linger.

Eel Brook

Refreshing, Cobus called it. Edith chuckled. Willa's niece was shocked the first summer she visited.

"Those ladies just took off all their clothes in broad daylight and jumped in the water," Mary Virginia's voice rose almost to a squeal. "I didn't know what to do. So I did it, too."

Willa laughed and laughed.

"That's just Cobus," Edith finally intervened. "Cobus thinks it's healthful to bathe where the water is bracing."

"Yes," Mary Virginia said slowly, then glanced at Willa, whose efforts to contain her laughter were beginning to appear painful, "I expect it is."

"You did exactly the right thing," Willa finally managed to say, "though heaven only knows how you came by such good sense."

Willa put an arm around her niece's shoulders and hugged her close to make sure Mary Virginia understood just how good she had been. Thirteen was a difficult age. "You should have seen your mother the time we took her with us to the Wind Mountains. Horrified, all the time, horrified."

Edith smiled at the way Willa pantomimed Jessica's horror and at her own first response to the Wind Mountains. Edith and Willa discovered Wyoming and the Wind Mountains at different times, but all Nebraskans eventually went west for camping and east for culture. Edith fell in love with the mountains the moment she arrived, but Willa's sister Jessica, who was the same age as Edith, paid more attention to her own appearance than she did to the world around her. Jessica despised the mountains and hated tents.

"Animals, she called us. Animals. And she called your uncle Douglass a he-goat." Willa threw back her head to bray like a donkey, "He-goat. He-goat."

At that Mary Virginia, Edith, and Willa caught the giggles and Willa was unable to continue until tears streamed from her eyes.

"That's when your uncle Douglass called your mother Jessicass," another wave of laughter bubbled over, "and the name stuck," Willa wiped her eyes.

Mary Virginia's lips formed a large O.

"Oh, she hated the name. And she hated us," Willa threw her hand to her forehead to assume the pose of Patience Betrayed.

"From then on Jessica was Jessicass, and Douglass was Billy Goat Gruff. And I tried out for the role of the Troll," Willa's grin deepened and she contorted her face and swung her arms and gallumphed several steps backward.

When their laughter subsided and Willa straightened up and shed her silly Troll grin, Mary Virginia was sitting on the ground where the giggles had dropped her, her arms draped across her body, still holding her sides.

"Momma can be a cross to bear," Mary Virginia's face expressed a certain surprise. She had never before said a word of criticism about her mother.

"Mothers are, sometimes," Willa nodded and reached down to help her niece up. "Like a thorn that never lets loose."

EDITH glanced over to see what progress Willa was making in her search for the trail. Amidst all that laughter, she realized, had been a hint of Willa's early turmoil with her own mother and a glimpse of the gargoyle-like character Willa was just then creating in her new manuscript about daughters. She called the character Blinker.

Family, Edith smiled to herself. Mary Virginia still had so much growing to do. Edith remembered her own coming to consciousness and the difficult struggle to define her own footing. Willa's passage had been similar. But independence, they finally realized together, did not have to mean eternal defiance or standing alone or stepping out of one's place in the human family. Memory held, if nothing else did. And all that youthful stomping and strutting about to assert one's place in the world, Edith snorted out loud. That was the chimera.

Ties that bind, and ties that set free. Edith finished tying her shoestrings and resettled herself on the fallen log, then glanced again at Willa, now on her knees checking something in the grass Edith could not see.

The focus of Willa's manuscript had a great deal to do with their current circumstances. Edith's mother and Willa's father died within three months of each other just the previous year. Now Willa's mother lay paralyzed by a stroke in Pasadena, where she had gone to visit Douglass. Edith's father was also in California, under the care of Edith's younger sister.

Life seemed suddenly fragile. Neither Willa nor Edith needed Mr. Brown's final dive to remind them of that. But family ties held fast even past death. The more one strained against them, Edith guessed, the tighter they held. Tentacles, they felt at times, tendrils at others, as capable of choking life out as of bringing it in. The trick, Edith guessed, smiling at Willa, who continued to pat the ground around her knees, lay in staying easy in their grip. And, Edith supposed, in remembering that blood lines were not the only things fastening one to life and to each other.

"EYES like those," Rob Feeney pushed away from his desk for the second time that afternoon, "don't belong on Grand Manan."

"What?" Jason Dobbs, the young man the shipping company had placed under Rob for training, looked up from his desk.

Rob realized he had spoken aloud. "That man Brown," he said now, "he didn't really belong on Grand Manan."

"Brown?"

"Yes," Rob rose to pull a paper cup from the dispenser on the wall behind his desk and fill it with water from the cooler. "He had the look of a man who knew death," Rob swung back to his desk, the cup in his hand, "knew it and didn't mind it."

Jason put down his pen and frowned.

"Oh, never mind me," Rob settled in his chair, grinning at the confusion on the young man's face. "I'm just thinking out loud. I saw him, you know, on the passage over."

"Oh, right," Jason turned back to his work. He had learned some time ago that Rob Feeney occasionally talked to himself and that when he did, he didn't really want to engage in conversation. He was just turning things over. Personal things. Memories of his father. A tough guy, Jason had heard, who died at sea. Memories of the war. Jason didn't much know what to do about those and didn't want to know. His own life took all his energy.

"LOOK what I found," Willa rose and came back through a cut in the trees, one hand extended, palm up and cupped. Edith slid off the log and trotted over to see.

It was a button. The right size for a shirt and a crimson so rich, it was almost burnt carmine.

"It would go well on a red shirt," Edith held the button for a moment in her fingers. "Where did you find it?"

The button had been lying by itself just a few feet beyond where the trail once again became obvious, then split immediately to encircle a thicket. The two paths seemed equally well traveled. The button had been on the path to the right, lying just off to the side, cushioned by decaying leaves. Willa prodded the area with a stick while Edith slipped the button into her pocket. She stood for a moment working it like a worry bead, letting her fingers sense what they could from its shape, size, solidity, and smoothness, before letting it drop into the safe confines of her pocket.

Tell me about your owner, Edith's fingers pressed the question. The button grew warm but remained silent.

"AFTER Willa discovered the button, we searched hard all the way back to Whistle Road," Edith assured Winifred Bromhall later that evening, "but the button was all we found."

"And what do you think of Miss Briggs? Is she a likely suspect, as everyone seems to think?"

Winifred was picking the scallions out of her salad and placing them on the edge of her plate. Winifred can do anything she wants and be beautiful doing it, the thought flitted across Edith's mind.

"Certainly not," Willa's answer was unusually brusque.

"But what if Miss Briggs had known this Mr. Brown from the city? What if he threatened her somehow . . . her livelihood, you know . . . with blackmail or something."

"Rubbish. Nonsense," Willa refused to speculate.

Edith watched the knife and fork separate a scallion from the red fluted edge of a lettuce leaf. They worked like miniature pinchers in Winifred's relaxed grip. What must it be like to live on the inside of such elegance, Willa said just the other day. Willa was right, Edith smiled at Winifred. But then, Willa was usually right. And she didn't like to gossip.

"Where exactly did you come out?" Margaret Byington's soft alto interrupted Edith's reflection.

"Come out?" Edith turned to look at Margaret, who was in the process of settling into the fourth chair at their table. A sturdy, direct woman with dry wit and wonderfully deep laughter, Margaret always made Edith feel somehow warm and pleasureful.

"Just this side of the old logging road into Ashburton Head. You know the place," Willa at least had been paying attention.

"On Whistle Road," Edith smiled. "You're late," she observed, passing the mashed potatoes.

Margaret nodded, "We got lost on the way to Indian Beach. Too many trees downed by storms blocking the trail. Confused us. It took forever to get there and another forever to get back."

Ethelwyn Manning, Margaret's partner in the misadventure, glanced over from a neighboring table where she also had filled a fourth chair. "You should have heard Margaret trying to bargain a fisherman into rowing us home. She tried everything to avoid climbing the steep grade to Eel Lake."

"I had no money with me," Margaret laughed, reaching for the haddock, "and he had never heard of credit. Said it must be an American thing."

"Too bad so many Americans have heard of it," Willa pronounced. "Just last week *The New York Times* ran an enormous list of bankruptcies. And they are constantly publishing advertisements for liquidation auctions. Why, there was even one recently for exclusive lots around a golf course in Rye," she shook her head. "No money for farms, no money for land, no money for homes. But for stocks," she shrugged, "that's another story."

"From what I hear, too many people play the stock market on borrowed dollars," Margaret's eyes grew momentarily serious.

"Gambling, you mean," Winifred's British midlands accent was engagingly droll.

"That's one way of looking at it," Margaret agreed, helping herself to the haddock, "trying to win what there's no way to earn."

"It takes money to make money, they say," Edith cleared a space in the center of the table for the haddock.

"Middle-class greed, I say," Margaret pressed on. "That's what happens when robber barons become heroes, and everyone tries to become part of America's new royalty. Let's join the Mellons, the Morgans, the Vanderbilts, the Rockefellers, the Roosevelts," Margaret beat time with her fork as if she were the drum major at the head of a marching band. "And now there's H. T. Parson," her fork went even higher, "a man from whom we've not heard before. *The Times* says Mr. H. T. began life as bookkeeper, rose to take over the crown at Woolworths, and is now planning to build himself a million-dollar mansion in Paris," her fork plunged for a new note, then rose again in crescendo, "as soon as he finishes erecting his first million-dollar mansion in Long Branch, New Jersey." Her fork rose again with "All-American boy makes good, builds many mansions," and made its final flourish with, "Castles in the Air, compliments of Horatio Alger."

Edith and Winifred laughed. Willa shook her head.

"You are right, though," Margaret lowered her fork to fill it with potatoes, "it does take money to make money." Having conceded Edith's point, she went on to make her own, "It would just be a whole lot better for everyone if investment dollars weren't robbed in the first place from the working class. Hardly anyone makes a living wage anymore."

"It would also be better if they were not borrowed by the middle class," Edith frowned, "especially to be put into the stock market."

"Now there's a silent thief for you. And you do it to yourself," Willa nodded. "I'm in favor of old-fashioned robbers myself. Let's hear it for Robin Hood the Good, a man who robbed only the rich," she grinned.

"Here, here," Margaret seconded her motion.

WILLA enjoyed Margaret as much as she did, Edith guessed. A forceful woman with a new perspective and a first-rate mind. Until this year, Margaret had been too busy working for the Red Cross to take summers off, but now she had taken a job teaching at Columbia, and her summers were free. Ethelwyn Manning and her great friend, Katherine Schwartz, were old friends of Margaret's, going back to 1908 when Manning and Margaret both spent a year in Pittsburgh. Manning, just graduated from Smith, was in training at the Carnegie Institute to be a librarian. Margaret, several years beyond Wellesley with a masters in sociology, was in Pittsburgh doing research on the devastating effects of factory policies in the neighboring mill town of Homestead. Margaret's study turned out to be a milestone, the first of its kind to focus on working-class women and to count their unsalaried labor—taking in washing and putting up boarders—as part of the general economy.

Willa, who had been ambivalent about Pittsburgh the ten years she lived there, was as fascinated by Margaret's findings as Margaret was by Willa's experience. Willa had lived on both sides of Pittsburgh's economic divide, putting up in boarding houses during her early years as a newspaper reporter and then, while she tried her hand at teaching English and Latin at Allegheny High School, luxuriating in the comfortable surroundings of the wealthy McClungs. As a permanent guest in the McClungs' solid home on Squirrel Hill, Willa had found a second family and a place to write. Long after Willa left Pittsburgh, until 1916, in fact, when the Judge died and Isabelle decided after all to marry Jan Hambourg and sell the family home, Willa returned annually for long visits, partly at first to write and then, once she and Edith had settled into their Bank Street apartment, to keep up with old friends.

But no one in Pittsburgh, least of all Willa Cather, was ever far from the steel mills, even on Squirrel Hill. Especially on Squirrel Hill, Willa once declared, and proceeded to point out that Isabelle's brother may have married the girl next door, but her name was Mellon, and Isabelle's father had acquired his reputation as a result of the strike at Homestead. When Judge McClung sentenced Alexander Berkman for attempting to assassinate Henry Clay Frick, their neighbors began calling the Judge the man who saved Pittsburgh—and the world—from anarchism. But how safe was a world, Willa would add, where power and poverty colored men's minds the way the flames from mill furnaces burnished their nights and ashes darkened their days. Willa probably never would write about class wars and western Pennsylvania, not directly, not in a novel, Edith guessed, but they both loved listening to Margaret talk about the households of Homestead. Lately, Edith had noticed a renewed attention to domestic detail and occasional touches from Margaret's stories slipping into the background of Willa's new novel.

Willa always depicted the power of the feminine principle at work in the universe, though Edith realized most of Willa's readers would be shocked to find that out. And these days, feminine had to do with women's appearance. Period. People did not realize what Willa was up to. Men certainly didn't. Men read Willa's books because she wrote about interesting men. And Willa encouraged them, Edith almost chuckled out loud. Recently, in fact, Willa seemed to be ignoring women altogether, but that was deceptive, just like the emphasis on religion in *Death Comes for the Archbishop*. People thought Willa was Roman Catholic after that. Fiction. Pure fiction.

Anyone who really knew literature or myth or history or art would recognize that the Virgin Mary was the main force in that novel, and behind the Virgin, the feminine principle. But these days, it seemed, the only people who knew literature and art were the artists themselves. And a few scholars, Edith granted, all of whom were men. With a few exceptions—Edith glanced at Margaret, deep in the midst of explaining economic theory to Winifred Bromhall—but the exceptions were mostly in professional schools. Social work, librarianship, education. Women's professions. Those women couldn't be expected to analyze fiction, but Willa's novels spoke to them, whether or not they ever heard of the feminine principle. Men posed a different problem. Men only read about men, and Willa wanted them to read her novels, to take seriously what she had to say. Ever since the War, when men had destroyed so much—all in the name of making the world safe—Willa had increasingly focused on men and their moods. She wanted their attention.

We've got it all wrong, Edith knew Willa wanted to shout but couldn't. No one wanted to listen to a woman rant, Edith reminded her. But they would listen to reason. They would listen if Willa spoke in ways that made it seem as if truth did the talking. Then Willa could declare that the world was not safe or simple, that good was not always good and bad not entirely evil, that humans and life were complex. Let the men in her novels say that, and men would listen. Women, too. Women listened when the women in Willa's novels declared romantic love a mistake. Now women and men needed to hear the rest of Willa's message, that maybe we have been hasty with our dreams. Power, progress, competition, conquest, wealth . . . the values we've held, the way we've defined success, the men and women we've learned to admire. Maybe we have been hasty, we Americans.

War's aftermath had given Willa new urgency. Edith felt it, too. More than ever, it seemed, men wanted to forget, to abandon the past, and that is exactly what Willa counseled against. Men especially, Willa would insist, needed to connect with what they had lost—with other men, with women, with children, with the human family, with animals, with the earth around them, with the universe, and with God. Reconnect, interconnect, hold together, all ways, always.

That no one saw or talked about the feminine principle in Willa's work was not surprising. Men talked about men. It's a man's world, everyone said. Men were always at the most important place, the center, the head. Women stood behind or at the side, out of sight and out of mind.

Unless, Edith smiled to herself, they were not all the time stuck in a man's world. One never got out altogether, of course, but there were respites. Smith College had been Edith's first respite. Now she had her life with Willa and the women's editorial division at J. Walter Thompson. And Whale Cove, of course. Winifred, Margaret, Cobus, Felix, Katherine, Manning, Eloise, the Jordan sisters, Helen Master, Lucy Crissy. Librarians, social workers, teachers, writers. All of them well educated, well traveled, highly articulate, and thoroughly accustomed to living in the world and thinking for themselves. And they were interested in absolutely everything. Literature, art, music, history, philosophy, spirituality, religion, sports, sociology, psychology, politics, business, work, finance, philanthropy, humanitarianism, and world affairs. Dinner at Whale Cove was better than a college seminar, Margaret often said. Busman's holiday, Winifred would chuckle.

Still it was a man's world, Edith couldn't deny that. But sometimes in a place like this, Edith picked up her dessert fork to try the apple pie, one forgot to notice. Women held the important place here, the center, the head. Men were off to the side, out of sight. And the women at Whale Cove meant to keep it that way. Only female rusticators allowed, Jacobus had drawn the line. Their bathing facilities, she explained when necessary, were limited to the small pool they dammed up in the brook and to an outdoor shower they called the Bower.

Rustic, private quarters. A woman's world. Their world for the moment. For as long as chivalry could keep men at bay. Edith's fork slid down through inches of apples, slicing off a large chunk of the pie. No one at Whale Cove ever expressed a desire for electricity or modern plumbing. Outhouses, wood stoves, kerosene lamps. Small discomforts.

The pie crust was warm and crisp. Could it be, as Winifred suggested, that Mr. Brown had threatened to interfere with the same sort of tranquility at the other end of the island and that was why he died? Certainly not. Edith savored the hint of nutmeg blended into the tart sweetness of the apples.

CONSTABLE DAGGETT would have to wait until morning to have any kind of extended conversation about yesterday's passengers on the S. S. Grand Manan. The young agent was clearly annoyed. He had just pulled the office door shut and inserted the key when Daggett strode up.

It was late, Daggett realized, and his own dinner long overdue. The young man's too, he surmised.

"Agent Feeney's the man you want to see. He'll be here first thing in the morning. Always opens early."

Feeney. Daggett hadn't heard that name in a while, though he guessed he knew Feeney had come back after the war and trained as an agent. Daggett just hadn't run into him, despite their proximity. Feeney. Robert Feeney. The fellows called him Rob. When they were being kind, Daggett remembered. Otherwise it was Feeney. Freaky Feeney, Wienie Feeney. Daggett had seen little of him since they finished school together. Feeney's father had coached most of the men on the island in soccer. They had all at one time or another had Jagger Feeney for a coach. He was the only one who ever called his son Robert. Always in that odd, authoritarian voice of his that placed heavy emphasis on the ends of everything. *Ert*, Daggett remembered someone starting to call Robert, until he had flattened the fellow's nose. Rob had had to fight often and hard to save his name. Daggett supposed he still did but hopefully without fists, almost middle aged, as he was, and unmarried.

Daggett thanked the young agent, Dobbs he said his name was, and headed for his own office. It would help his state of mind if he took a moment to sort through and file his notes. Then he could take another moment to slip by the house for his evening meal. Elizabeth would be waiting for him.

"Excuse me."

Daggett started, "Yes?"

The young agent stood above Daggett on the steps, his brow furrowed. "The man who died. What do you think he was doing on a hiking trail in a pin-striped suit?"

SALLIE JACOBUS sometimes arranged special activities after dinner, but the women of Whale Cove enjoyed nothing more than an evening's conversation over a crackling fire in the sitting room of the main house. White with dark beams overhead, its walls lined with bookcases that rose to the mullioned windows and covered the whole of the wall leading into the dining room, the sitting room held several tables with straight-backed chairs so that small groups might pair off for playing bridge or quiet reading. But six or more of the women usually settled into the Queen Anne chairs and overstuffed couch surrounding the low coffee table in front of the fireplace. The hearth was large, with a pair of cranes on the left that had been used, when the house was built almost a century before, to suspend pots for cooking. Jacobus kept a fire throughout the season. Paired with the books, the chairs, and the bay window, with its small, leaded, diamond-shaped panes, the hearth created a luxuriant sense of warmth and well-being.

Their evening discussions often carried over several days. Recently, except for the disruptions brought by Mr. Brown's death, they had been concentrating on the economy, which seemed to be thundering out of control. Money, money, money, headlines in *The New York Times* continued to roar. People everywhere gossiped about flappers and speakeasies and talked about grabbing the brass ring, jazzing it up, and living high on the hog. Loose women, loose liquor, and too much loose change, Willa observed during dinner, proposing a toast to loose women. Never in favor of temperance, Willa and Edith maintained a well-stocked wine cellar in New York, for which their summers in Canada proved useful. Pesky Prohibition, Willa called it. But Margaret insisted that the Twenties' roar had grown dangerous, deadening everyone's ears to sharp cries from the working class.

Willa and Edith were hopeful about Hoover. His handling of the food crisis after the war had been brilliant, Willa pointed out. But they all knew Hoover would never tackle the most pressing social issues, or end the suppression of labor unions, or reverse the trend to devalue women and their work. Even his Law Enforcement Commission sidestepped central issues surrounding poverty and crime and the free-wheeling use of federal firearms once bootlegging became a felony.

Margaret was more interested in the cooperative efforts of the Women's Trade Union League. Co-ops were both practical and highly effective, places where individuals could help themselves and each other at the same time. And Governor Roosevelt, she said, was doing interesting things in New York. His wife Eleanor, Willa pointed out, was doing even more interesting things, going into partnership with Marion Dickerman and Nancy Cook to run a school and start a furniture factory at Val-Kill. Now *there* was innovation.

VIII

"BUTTON, BUTTON, WHO'S got the button," Jacobus sang out, leading Constable Daggett into the sitting room to interrupt the evening's conversation.

"I do," Edith pulled the tiny crimson object from its hiding place in her jacket pocket and placed it exactly in the center of Daggett's calloused palm.

Daggett studied the button carefully, then slipped it into the inner pocket of his wallet.

"Well," he pulled out his tobacco pouch and settled into the chair closest to the fireplace, "tell me where you found this."

The circle of expectant faces turned toward Willa, who recounted her discovery and recited the reasons she and Edith settled on the site they had determined as the scene of the crime.

Daggett himself was the next focus of inquisitive stares. He returned their looks. Jacobus, Coney, and Felix he already knew, and now Miss Cather and Miss Lewis, but he still needed introductions to several of them, Winifred Bromhall, Margaret Byington, Ethelwyn Manning, and Alice and Mary Jordan. They had been absent during his earlier visit. He recognized the Jordan name, "The two of you have a cottage near the road to The Whistle, I believe?"

"We have one of the cottages on the hill above Miss Cather and Miss Lewis, yes," Alice Jordan volunteered.

"Did you happen to see Mr. Brown or anyone else pass by yesterday afternoon?"

"Not a soul, except Mr. Sharkey and young James. They were

heading toward North Head sometime before noon, I believe. And later Miss Briggs, but you know about her."

Winifred Bromhall looked up expectantly, but no one said anything further about Miss Briggs or the rumors in the village. Daggett crossed one knee over the other.

Alice Jordan's brown eyes, slightly magnified behind glasses, matched the warm tones of her hair, parted in the middle and swept back into a bun. People might think her stern, but he guessed she was shy. Too much humor and warmth came through those glasses, despite her reserve. Quite right for a woman who headed up the Children's Room at the Boston Public Library.

Daggett glanced around. So many of these women were librarians or school teachers like the other Miss Jordan, and all of them seemed competent and somehow comfortable, shy or not. No wonder Jennifer had been so taken with the Cottage Girls and *Jane Eyre*. He smiled vaguely and turned back to Alice Jordan.

"Well, there was that young man from Swallowtail," Mary Jordan interrupted looking at her sister.

"Oh, that's right. He knocked at the door and asked Mary for directions to Whale Cove."

"And young Herbert Gordon," Mary Jordan brightened. "I don't believe Alice saw him. Mr. Gordon passed by sometime after four. He was riding his bicycle."

"And later Mr. Winslow went by in his wagon," Mary added after a moment and, having finished, cleared her throat and refolded her hands in her lap.

Mary Jordan conveyed even more Yankee taciturnity than her sister, Daggett thought. She sat entirely upright and took up very little room on the couch. Rather severe. A classic New England spinster school teacher. That may be her profession, Daggett understood, but he expected that this had been a fairly long speech for

Mary Jordan. He had no doubt, however, that she had also learned the name of the young man from Swallowtail.

"Matthew Johnson," she responded promptly, "yes, Johnson with an *h*."

Daggett jotted his notes, then glanced up. Alice Jordan was squinting a bit in his direction. He waited for her to speak.

"I remember him, too," Alice finally said. "Natty dresser, in tennis togs, but not the others Mary saw. I was inside most of the afternoon reading." She looked Daggett squarely in the eyes.

Daggett watched as Alice Jordan refolded her hands in her lap also.

"You've been very helpful, both of you. Quite observant," Daggett turned again to his notebook. "Roy Sharkey, James Daniels, Sabra Jane Briggs, Herbert Gordon, Jr., Little John Winslow, Matthew Johnson." He rubbed his forehead as he read the names aloud.

"With an *h*, yes."

Daggett glanced at Mary Jordan, "I had understood Mr. Johnson was bird watching at Castalia with the rest of his party." Daggett looked around the circle and then back at Mary Jordan again, "Did he happen to say what he was doing up this way?"

As Daggett expected, that was beyond the scope of the Jordan sisters' conversation with Matthew Johnson.

Daggett took time to tamp and relight his pipe. He returned the tin of matches to his jacket pocket. They sat silent for a moment while he puffed.

"Can you tell me," Daggett finally lifted his notebook from his knee and turned back to the Jordans, "what they were wearing?"

"Roy Sharkey and his partner wore jackets and work pants." Typical gear, Daggett entered next to their names in his notebook.

"Miss Briggs was in her red shirt and jodhpurs. Somewhat deeper than the hue in your jacket," Daggett felt Mary Jordan's eyes inspecting his uniform, coming to rest at the rumples about his waist. The back of his neck stiffened, and he seemed somehow to be sitting both deeper and taller in his chair. Daggett loosened his grip on the pen. Herb Gordon had on his usual slicker and fishing gear. Little John also wore a jacket, the same one he was wearing when he arrived at Whale Cove after Mr. Brown's death. Buttoned all the way to the neck, Daggett remembered, though the afternoon had turned warm.

Daggett paused to run his eye back down the list. He had already talked to Roy Sharkey and Miss Briggs. Young James was out on Sam Jackson's boat. Herb, Jr. had probably been on his way to The Whistle to check his father's nets. The Gordons kept a boat there for that purpose. Daggett would talk to young Herb in the morning and ask what he was doing and whether he saw anyone at The Whistle. It occurred to Daggett that he had never asked Little John what he was doing at Whale Cove that afternoon. He put a check mark next to Little John's name. And Mr. Johnson, Daggett made the final entry, who wore tennis togs and carried a backpack. Daggett underscored *backpack* and placed a question mark next to it, then he reached over and tapped his pipe out in the fireplace.

Jacobus rose to add a few logs.

"What about you and the others here," Daggett directed the question to Jacobus. "Do you remember seeing Mr. Johnson on the trail to Whale Cove? Or anyone else," he added when Jacobus shook her head.

"Edith and I didn't see him," Willa reminded him.

Margaret Byington shook her head. "Claude Gilmore drove the three of us over to Dark Harbour early that afternoon," she explained, indicating Manning as well as herself, "and we didn't return until well after the excitement was over."

"Miss Bromhall and Peter and Cobus and I were in the garden most of the afternoon," Felix reflected. "I don't recall seeing anyone, do you?" she turned to Winifred.

"Two men," Winifred frowned, "but I didn't really see them. Only their legs. And heard them talking. I was bent over picking beans and not really looking at the trail, you know."

Daggett waited for Miss Bromhall to recall more details. When she didn't, he asked what the men were wearing. She had only a vague impression, she said. They could have been wearing any kind of pants, except, perhaps, jodhpurs. The legs were loose, not snug. And dark, but she couldn't say about colors. They were in the shade. She frowned again. She hadn't seen their feet, only the bottoms of their legs. One of them walked in front of the other. Could she be certain they were men, Daggett asked to be sure. Oh, yes, she heard their voices but only a murmur.

Whale Cove Inn Living Room

Daggett raised his pencil off the page.

"I'm sorry. I can't tell you what they were saying," she looked around at the group, "but there were two voices," she turned to Daggett, "I am certain of that."

Daggett leaned forward, "Could you tell what sort of accent they had?"

"American, I believe, but I'm not at all certain. I'm afraid I can't always tell the difference from Canadian, and I couldn't really hear their words," Winifred watched Daggett's pencil move on the page.

"Did they speak in regular tones or might they have been arguing?"

"Oh, I can't say," Winifred shook her head.

"Would you recognize their voices if you heard them again?" Jacobus interjected, moving to take her seat on the couch next to Winifred again.

"No, no, I can't say," Winifred shook her head at Jacobus and, frowning again in concentration, slumped deeper into the couch. "Oh, let me think," she finally declared, staring vaguely in Daggett's direction, her eyes not quite focused.

Lovely woman, Daggett sat quietly, waiting. Illustrated children's books, he understood. British, professional, independent, and really quite lovely, he cocked his head on one side. Perhaps she was the reason Elizabeth and the others were occasionally so diffident about the Cottage Girls. Surely Elizabeth could see there was nothing to worry about here where Jennifer was concerned. These women might very well prove to be a good influence.

It was true Jennifer would acquire notions from them that were grander than Grand Manan, but Daggett himself had gone off island as a youngster. It hadn't hurt him, and it wouldn't hurt Jennifer. And it should be quite all right if Jennifer were to go to somewhere like the States or decide to get an education. Women did that these days. Then she could come back and start an island library as well as a family. The Cottage Girls would like that, Daggett glanced again at the books lining the shelves around room. It wasn't like his wife to be so difficult. Besides, he returned to his internal argument with Elizabeth, look at all the fellows who went off island. They came back when they could. Young James, now, he was just back after two years in the States. Mary Daniels said he was glad

85

to be back and wanted to stay. Most sons did who could figure out how to make a living on Grand Manan. Jennifer wouldn't have to worry about that.

"It's no use," Winifred finally halted her retrospection. "I can't remember anything more. I just didn't pay that much attention," her eyes conveyed genuine sorrow.

No one else recalled anything further. Jacobus and Felix had returned to the kitchen before the men passed by. They saw and heard nothing at all. And the others had told him all they could remember.

"What now?" Jacobus rose to poke the logs into a better position. The fire leapt up.

"Find out where the red button belongs, I guess, first thing in the morning," Daggett closed his notebook and stretched his legs. Then he tucked the little notebook into the inner pocket of his jacket and let his open hand rest for a moment on his chest. He was reluctant to rise. It was warm and peaceful here.

Rob Feeney's late evening constitutional took him past Newton's Bakery, where he remembered the encounter. The man with the vacant eyes meeting the woman with the blazing hair. And red shirt, Rob reminded himself. And now the whole island was gossiping about Sabra Jane Briggs. The Amazon killed the misogynist, everyone was saying, and did so because she hated men.

Rob had to laugh. He was certain that when he saw them in front of the bakery, they were meeting for the first time. Those eyes had widened before they narrowed, Rob remembered, and widened not from meeting the familiar but from discovering the unexpected . . . a woman dressed like a man.

"I suppose I should have asked, but I didn't want Constable Daggett to think we, like everyone else, suspected Sabra Jane Briggs," Alice

Jordan was clearly rueful over the missed opportunity to hear about village gossip. And to hear it from the constable's point of view, Mary reminded her.

When Daggett departed, the group around the fireplace broke up and the Jordans were just about to turn onto the path that ran along the orchard and up the hill to their cottage near the road. Willa and Edith would go straight on through the pines.

"Sabra Jane is planning to work on our wall again tomorrow afternoon," Edith was happy to point out.

"Yes," Willa finished Edith's thought. "Perhaps we can ask her what she did when she left here yesterday," Willa's voice softened, "and about the button."

"The missing button," Alice's voice dropped to a whisper.

"I believe she would tell us," Edith began to speculate. "She does seem to be a direct sort of person. Straightforward, I mean."

"Like me is what you mean," Willa laughed. "Edith tries to be diplomatic about my lack of polish, but we both know it's a matter of country and class. Edith at least had Smith College to smooth out her western edges, but despite the years I spent in Pittsburgh, there's not a drop of small talk in me and I have no patience for etiquette," Willa tilted her head. "Of course, those are nothing compared to Yankee roundaboutness."

Both Jordans smiled.

"But, seriously," Willa added as an afterthought, "do you think Sabra Jane would be offended by our asking?"

"I wish I knew her better," Alice turned to her sister, whose shoulders were in the midst of a shrug. "Cobus knows her fairly well. Why not ask her advice at breakfast?"

"Excellent idea," Willa agreed and said good night, taking Edith by the elbow for their trek through the woods.

Moonlight slipped through the pines ahead, picking out in pencil points the path that led from the main house to their cottage.

Behind them the orchard stood motionless in a light so stark it seemed almost to etch the young apples on their boughs.

"I'm not ready for sleep," Edith turned her back to the woods and paced in reverse to keep the orchard in view, "are you?"

"I could sleep for days," Willa yawned, "but I'll settle for one good night." She paused to look back. Edith had stopped.

"It is so beautiful," Edith spoke each word separately, looking first at the orchard and then at the moon-full sky, too bright for stars.

Willa responded softly, "'That tender light which heaven to gaudy day denies.'"

Edith smiled at Willa's Byron and countered with Ben Jonson.

"Queen and huntress, chaste and fair, / ...Now the sun is laid to sleep, / Thou that mak'st a day of night, / Goddess excellently bright."

Willa yawned deeply.

"My favorite," Edith confessed.

"Mmmm, but you omitted the poem in between."

"I know. Somehow the poem doesn't matter right now."

"The moon matters. Fair Diana, 'tis a-hunting she will go."

"We must, too," Edith caught Willa's hand to pull her along, "but not a-hunting. 'Tis too late this night for us."

"Ummm, well beyond our bedtime."

Edith responded with a yawn.

"This sleuthing is a tiring business," Willa complained, "all that hiking in the afternoon and so much puzzling in the evening."

"It does require a different kind of concentration," Edith agreed. She saw again the intensity in Winifred's eyes, and their conversation with Daggett began to replay itself in her mind.

"I wonder if Mr. Brown was one of the men Winifred saw. What do you think?"

"I am too sleepy to think and wondering about Mr. Brown will just keep us awake."

"That and the moon," Edith agreed. She often had a touch of insomnia.

When the path broke out of the woods just above their cottage, Edith halted again, her hand on Willa's arm. The splash of moon-glow flooding the area struck her like a physical force. So moved she could not contain herself, Edith stretched as high over her head as her hands could reach, then drew her arms down and out, as if to encompass the whole of the scene before them, their cottage, the cliffs, the sea beyond.

"Listen to the crickets," Willa said after a moment and touched Edith's arm.

IX

DAGGETT LEFT THE house early the next morning to walk the trail from Whistle Road to the waterfalls and inspect more carefully the sites Miss Cather and Miss Lewis described. He had removed the button from his wallet and placed it in his jacket pocket, where every now and then he touched it like a talisman. It was, he knew, exactly like the button missing from the left sleeve of Miss Briggs' red shirt.

Daggett was in no hurry to arrest Miss Briggs. As far as he had been able to tell, even with opportunity and means, she had no motive. And there were several things he needed to check on first, not the least of which were the two men Miss Bromhall had noticed and the question marks he had placed in his notebook.

He had also to locate the third passenger to arrive with Mr. Brown and Miss Driscoll on the S. S. Grand Manan. The man had to be somewhere on the island. Daggett just didn't know how to look for him. He should have insisted that Feeney's young assistant open up the office the night before and retrieve the list of passengers. At least then he would have had a name. But it had been so late in the evening. And now it was so early, Daggett could only plan to swing by to see Feeney as soon as he finished checking out the trail. Or if something else intervened, perhaps when the steamer returned to North Head later that morning, Daggett could at least get a physical description. Possibly one of the crew had overheard a name.

Miss Driscoll had been of little help. She told Daggett she had not really looked at the man and had spoken only a word or two with Mr. Brown, nothing worth jotting into the notebook. Daggett could only hope the crew would prove more useful. He also intended to stop by Jackson's Drygoods and ask about their supply of red shirts, Daggett touched the button again, but first he wanted to see for himself where the button had been lodged and look once more at the cliff. Miss Briggs could wait. It wasn't likely she would leave the island.

"COME on, man. What are you waiting for?" Little John Winslow's voice was insistent, his manner abrasive.

Little John had arranged his stocky body, legs spread, elbows crooked, to occupy most of the room on the sidewalk in front of the North Head Bank. His small audience blocked Daggett's progress toward the boat landing, where the S. S. Grand Manan was preparing to dock.

Little John's entourage was already excited. Eva McDaniels, his eager disciple, had hitched her thin shoulders as high as she could and posted herself firmly beside Little John to glare at Daggett. The Winslow's black-and-white puppy pranced and yapped and jumped against Daggett's legs. Daggett reached down and patted the puppy's head, then picked him up and handed him to Little John's son Jocko.

"Just the man I've been looking for," Daggett worked hard to make his voice sound hearty, but Little John was not to be distracted.

"I always said it would come to no good having so many women on the island."

"My words exactly," Eva McDaniels joined in, her voice threatening to turn shrill. "Women should be at home with their families."

"It's against nature's laws, that's what it is. Women need husbands to take care of them and babies to keep them out of trouble," Little John's mustache twitched violently. He clapped one hand down hard against Jocko's shoulder. Jocko tightened his grip on the puppy.

"A woman's home is her domain," Eva's lips drew tight.

Daggett had heard that before, usually from Eva. She ran it as a kind of subtitle in the *Recipe Exchange*. Elizabeth repeated it at times. Odd how women's mouths shaped themselves around those words. Rather like sucking lemons. Daggett felt his own lips purse with the thought.

"What do these women think they're doing, earning money and, and, and taking vacations," Little John fairly sputtered. Spittle that formed little puddles at the edges of his lips became flexible strings when he opened his mouth and blew into bubbles that never quite popped. Daggett found himself almost amused.

"You'd think they were ladies of leisure, the way they come here," Eva interjected, her lips pursing tighter still.

"Well, they're not. There's no lady in them. And I'll tell you what they're doing," Little John slapped one hand against the other, "they're taking jobs away from men, that's what they're doing."

"Women shouldn't have money of their own," Eva's head bobbed up and down. "Just look at what they do with it. Throw it away on their own pleasure, that's what they do. I tell you it's not right. Women should not have jobs or money of their own."

"I beg your pardon," Emma Parker came bustling out of the bank, gray curls swinging, her purse clasped tight against her stomach.

Daggett grinned. Eva McDaniels had gone too far this time.

"I work for my living," Emma's eyes snapped.

"You're a widow," Eva responded sharply. "That's different."

"I make my own way. Always have."

"Yes, yes, yes," Little John tried to wrest control of the argument again, "but we're talking about women that have never been married. They're bad luck around the sea. Everyone knows that. A bad lot altogether, that's what they are. And they're invading the island."

Eva's head began to bob again.

Little John continued his diatribe, "Worse and worse it gets. So many new ones coming to The Anchorage to stay with that, that, that scarlet woman."

"There's nothing wrong with Miss Briggs," Emma Parker held her voice steady.

"High-falutin' ways," Little John growled.

"Floosies," Eva could no longer stay quiet, "all of them, floosies."

"Flappers," Emma corrected, turning her gaze to the rest of the assemblage. "It is true," she addressed them, "that the women at The Anchorage are younger and perhaps more lively than the Cottage Girls at Whale Cove, but . . . "

"The Cottage Girls," Little John mimicked in falsetto, "the Poor Soiled Doves, Disappointed in Love."

Daggett feared Little John could go on for some time chanting the names islanders had devised for the two summer colonies. Winters were long on Grand Manan and islanders could be creative in their amusements. Little John, in particular, was known for his doggerel.

"You must excuse me," James Enderby's formidable height appeared in the doorway directly behind Emma Parker, his hands spread against his waistcoat, thumbs hooked in his watch chain.

Daggett gave up any notion of interrupting. Enderby would take care of it, his polite baritone shutting Little John off like a faucet.

But Eva McDaniels didn't miss a beat, "You've heard, haven't you, James, about the red button?"

Daggett felt his jaw drop. He had told no one. If Eva McDaniels knew about the button, all of Grand Manan must be fully apprised or would be before long.

Enderby did not answer but turned to Little John, "I'm afraid I could not help but overhear your remarks just now." He paused to clear his throat and lift his hand from his vest.

"What's the matter now, James? Cat got your tongue?"

Little John's surliness surprised even Daggett. This could hardly be the beginning of a conversation. What was happening here?

"No cat has ever gotten my tongue, Little John, though I am not at all certain I can say the same for the two of you," Enderby's gray eyes narrowed.

Enderby hooked his right thumb over his watch chain and placed his left hand, fist folded, against the small of his back. It was characteristic of Enderby to stand so when he had something serious to say. Daggett was delighted by the prospects.

"As I told you earlier," Enderby's mild tone belied the anger that flashed behind his glasses, "I believe you are being quite unreasonable. Miss Lewis, Miss Cather, Miss Cobus, Miss Felix and all the rest of the Cottage Girls are each of them the soul of propriety," Enderby's gray-suited form seemed to grow taller as he spoke. "You should not carry on with your spurious jokes."

"Call me unreasonable! Call me unreasonable!" Little John sputtered. "What do you call murder then?" And without waiting for an answer, he declared, "Murderess. That's what Sabra Jane Briggs is. She did it. You all know it."

"And the red button proves it," Eva spun around toward Daggett.

"Well, not exactly," Daggett cleared his throat.

"You," Little John swung the whole of his body to face Daggett, "You've not done a thing to stop her."

"Now, Little John," Daggett tried soothing.

"A man's not safe in his bed with the likes of them on the island."

"Don't be silly," Daggett raised his voice and took a step toward Little John. He got no closer. Jocko's puppy crooned, and just as suddenly Daggett felt his pant leg pull stiff one way then another, as if it had been caught by a fierce wind. Sharp teeth grazed his ankle.

"You," Daggett exploded, pointing his finger at Jocko, "you take care of your dog. And you," he jabbed the finger at Little John, "you come with me. There are questions here that need answers," Daggett turned on his heel. "Now."

Jason Tinsley, suspended in midstride at the door of his pharmacy, raised his hand and opened his mouth as if he were about to make a speech of his own.

"I mean *now*," Daggett flung over his shoulder again from the middle of the street, without looking to see whether Little John followed. The hair on the back of Daggett's neck stood stiff against his collar. He realized he would need every minute it took to reach his office to regain his composure.

"THAT'S what Emma Parker told me not more than ten minutes ago," Rebecca Jackson almost danced on her tiptoes. "Constable Daggett stormed off so fast, Little John was out of breath trying to catch up."

Edith laughed, "I met Little John the day of Mr. Brown's death. He does seem a blustery sort of fellow."

"The town clown, my husband calls him," Rebecca Jackson's hand fluttered near her mouth, "when no one's listening except me, of course."

"I'll keep it to myself," Edith smiled and moved toward the rear of the store where the Jacksons kept their men's wear. "Now, let's have a look at your shirts."

Rebecca followed on her side of the counter, its dark walnut polished by more than thirty years of service. Shelves lining the walls behind her rose all the way to the ceiling, their cubicles filled with bolts of material and ready-made clothing. On a middle shelf at the very back were three red shirts, neatly folded and stacked.

"We had eight to begin with when the order first came in," Rebecca placed the stack on the counter.

Edith looked from the shirts to Rebecca.

"I already told the constable we sold five. Sabra Jane's was the second. The first went to Sam Jackson. It's nice and warm for being out on his boat, he says." Sam was Rebecca's brother-in-law.

Rebecca ran her hand over the shirt on top, then handed it to Edith.

"See how soft it is."

It was soft, Edith glanced back at the shelf. Too bad it did not come in other colors. Willa would love the light wool but the red was all wrong. Willa liked rich, primary colors, but she did much better in green. Edith preferred mauve and pastels for herself or black when they were in the city.

"Mary Daniels bought one of these shirts two weeks ago. For a present, I believe she said. And yesterday one of the young fellows in that party at Swallowtail got one. The fellow that wears the tennis outfits all the time. You know the one I mean?"

Edith nodded. His pinkened forehead hovered before her with the Lucky Strikes he had extended to his wife.

"Matthew Johnson, yes," Edith glanced up, "Johnson with an *h*."

His shirt made a total of four, but Rebecca had halted there, a faint smile playing across her lips.

"And Monday, four days ago I guess," when Rebecca spoke again, her voice had become almost languorous, "Little John Winslow bought one for himself. Said if he liked it, he would order another for Jocko."

"Are you quite certain?"

"Sold it to him myself," Rebecca smiled with her eyes.

"All that talk about Sabra Jane's shirt," Edith scoffed. "He said nothing about having one himself."

Rebecca's eyes smiled, "Rather like the pot calling the kettle black, isn't it?"

The light wool seemed to move by itself under Edith's hand. She continued to stroke the material without quite realizing. Now she occupied herself by taking the pins out of its folds and shaking it loose.

The buttons on the sleeves were colored exactly like the one Willa found on the trail. And they were the same size. Edith rubbed the buttons on both sleeves. They felt exactly the same as the button she had carried around in her pocket for safe keeping. But, she rubbed again, the left one felt different from the right. The thread was loose. She raised both sleeves for close examination.

Rebecca watched, eyes quizzical at first, then she undid the pins on both of the remaining shirts, shook them out and rubbed the buttons on their sleeves. "The thread on the left sleeve is unknotted," Rebecca finally announced, nodding. "On both of them. I'm sure of it."

She turned the cuffs and pointed. Tiny knots were barely discernible on the two right sleeves, but no knots appeared on the left.

The thread on the shirt in Edith's hand revealed the same problem.

"My heavens," Rebecca was the first to speak. "All five of the shirts we sold might well have lost the very same button."

"We must tell Mr. Daggett," Edith agreed.

"Immediately."

AT that moment, Daggett stood in the center of Little John's parlor staring at the red shirt in Anna Winslow's hands. Jamie, the youngest of the Winslows, lay sprawled on the carpet near her feet. Hues in the border of its floral design matched the red in her hands. Little John stood near the front door. Daggett had to turn around to speak to him.

"That's the shirt you bought at Jackson's Drygoods a few days ago?"

Little John crossed the room to take the shirt from his wife's hands. He inspected it as though he had never seen the shirt before.

"I guess so," Little John finally mumbled, glancing at Daggett. "How did you . . . I suppose you want to look at it," he changed course.

"I do, yes," Daggett took hold of the shirt by its collar, then ran his fingers down the front and reached for the sleeves. All buttons were in place, but the left cuff felt odd. Daggett raised the sleeve for closer examination. This button was a slightly different shade from the others. Daggett glanced at Little John, then rested his eyes on Anna.

"I mended it this morning," Anna gestured vaguely in the direction of the shirt. Her eyes were busy tracing her youngest son's tentative crawl across the floor toward the door. When Jamie reversed direction, Anna brushed the hair from her face. She had worn it loose this morning.

Daggett offered the shirt to Little John for further inspection. Little John made a slight shake of the head. His moustache twitched and he took a step backward and sat down without looking. The armchair held. Little John stared at the sleeve.

"Little John probably didn't even realize that button had come off," Anna's voice broke the silence. "He doesn't notice things like that. Never has."

Anna moved closer to Little John. Jamie followed.

"You should see the pile of mending I do every week," Anna's voice picked up speed. "Between Little John and Jocko and Jamie, I swear I can hardly keep up. And now with that puppy chewing," she paused for breath, "well, there's just so much I can do."

"I'm sure," Daggett nodded and raised the sleeve, intending the gesture to pose a new question. But Little John's face remained blank. Daggett turned back to Anna and waited for her to tell him about the additional mending his thumb discovered just below the elbow.

"I had to fix a few rips," Anna nodded and rubbed her fingers against her thumb as if she too were feeling the stitches. "Can you believe it? A brand-new shirt like that?"

Daggett waited for Little John to speak. He didn't. Finally, Anna snatched the shirt from Daggett's hands and shook it in Little John's face.

"How many times must I beg you to be careful? You and your sons?"

Little John made no response. He stared at his feet.

"Careless, just careless," Anna's hands trembled, and when she faced Daggett again, her eyes had turned deeply angry. "It doesn't matter that a shirt's new. He'll wear it to do the dirtiest of jobs, then drop it wherever he takes it off. And Jocko's just like him," her lips drew firm.

Daggett watched Little John, who was looking up now, staring first at one of them then the other. But Little John might as well have been on a boat in the middle of the Atlantic. His eyes were glazed and his face held no expression. Daggett frowned.

"Have you nothing to say about this?"

Little John focused for the first time on the shirt.

"Where did you find that?"

"Where do you suppose? Right where you dropped it. On the floor of your bedroom," Anna's voice was still harsh. "Where do you suppose it was? Where do I find any of the clothes you wear?"

Jamie reached up to give the shirt a sharp tug. Anna lifted its sleeve out of his reach, barely breaking the stride of her words.

"Everything Little John wears winds up on the floor," she glared at her husband then at Daggett. "He has a closet, but he makes no," her "no" continued, growing louder, "no use of it, no use at all," she gave the shirt another shake.

Little John looked again at Daggett.

"I don't remember it ripping. The button. Well, I don't know about that either," Little John shook his head. "The pup," he began. "The shirt was all right when I wore it."

"And when was that?" Daggett reached for his notebook.

Little John took a moment to consider.

"Day before yesterday," Anna remembered.

"That's right, it was," Little John agreed.

"Were you wearing it when you arrived at Whale Cove just after Eric Dawson brought the body in?"

"I don't remember."

"He never knows what he has on."

"What do you remember?"

"Putting it on in the morning. It was new," Little John's hands ran down the front of his chest, "I liked the way it felt."

Daggett jotted in the notebook, relieved that Little John was cooperating. The brief session in Daggett's office, where Daggett had managed to curb his own temper long enough to ask Little John about buying the red shirt after Rebecca Jackson informed him about all the purchases, had taken some of the puff out of Little John's sails. Now, Anna's scolding and Little John's apparent surprise had further subdued him. Daggett didn't know how much of Anna's tirade could be an effort to cover for Little John's sins. He would think about that later. For now it was enough that Little John's bluster had blown itself out, even if the lull was only temporary.

"I hauled nets and poles for Herb Gordon all day that day. Back and forth, back and forth, from The Whistle to Whale Cove. I suppose I got wet a couple of times. I don't remember whether I changed clothes. Sometimes I do when I come home for a hot meal at noon."

Little John's eyes had grown serious. Daggett turned a page in his notebook.

"I don't remember either," Anna watched Daggett write.

A high yelp intervened. Everyone jumped. The yelp was followed immediately by the sounds of furious feet and several loud shouts. Then Jocko's puppy burst into the room and careened full tilt around the outside pattern in the carpet, a blue-and-white shirt locked between his jaws, its sleeves streaming, buttons clattering. Then Jocko arrived with a roar, and together the boy and his pup raced out, leaving Jamie shrieking with delight.

TEN minutes later Daggett stuffed the two telegrams Captain Whitson handed him into his pocket and strode aboard the S. S. Grand Manan. The business with Little John had taken much too long. The telegrams would have to wait until he finished interviewing the crew and returned to his office where he could read them without interference.

"It's a pity you didn't arrive an hour sooner, Constable," Captain Whitson admonished Daggett as they crossed the deck. "We've been here that long and more, and we're due to cast off in fifteen minutes, you know."

Daggett explained that the delay was both unexpected and unavoidable. He repeated the words several times and threw in "murder case, you know" before adding gratitude for the trouble the captain had taken to assemble his crew in the mess.

"Well," Captain Whitson sat down at the head of the table, "ask away, but I don't think you will find any of us much help."

Except for three pieces of information, the captain was correct. The first was that the unknown man turned out to be Burt Isaacs on his way home from a lumbering job near Eastport. The second was that Rob Feeney, who had the complete lists of passengers and crew, had also been on board. And the third was that Mr. Brown was "a gen-u-wine odd duck," as the first mate put it. Brown had stood off by himself on the other side of the wharf from where passengers usually waited, and he had let no one touch his luggage, not on the wharf and not on the ship.

"He managed it all himself, he did," the first mate shifted a toothpick from one side of his mouth to the other, "when most gentlemen don't like to do that, you know."

X

"Buttons loose on all the left sleeves," read the note on Daggett's desk. It was signed, "Respectfully, Edith Lewis and Rebecca Jackson."

Daggett sighed and sat down heavily. For a moment he remained motionless, then he pulled the two telegrams Captain Whitson had given him from his pocket, slit open their yellow envelopes, and spread them both on the blotter before him. Marvin Gates, Boston's Finest Tailor, had died January third. No shop records remained. Five John T. Browns lived in Boston, eight in New York. None with a record. All present and accounted for. All in Boston. All in New York. Now, just how helpful was that, Daggett inquired of the large face staring back at him from the clock on his wall. Had he any more particulars, New York wanted to know. How would you like a red shirt, he said to the clock. Its black hands clicked forward.

Worst of all, Burt Isaacs, the unknown third passenger, probably wouldn't be of any help either. Difficult as he could be at times, Rob Feeney was a better bet. Observant, intelligent, and generally friendly. How much he could help would depend on how busy he had been during the passage over. Isaacs, on the other hand, was a son of a gun. Surly, self-absorbed. A loner just right for the Maine woods. If lumbering was what he was doing there.

So many fellows ran liquor to the States these days, it was sometimes hard to tell who was doing what, both in the woods and on the water. But Canadians didn't usually get involved below the border. Didn't have to take that chance. Depending on the province, of course. Daggett eased his back deeper into the chair and reached for his pipe. He hadn't thought much about it because New Brunswick was open to liquor again after a brief flirtation with prohibition.

Once his pipe was lit, Daggett placed his feet on the desk and crossed his ankles. The toe of his right boot was showing some wear. He would have to take time to polish them one of these days. Here it was mid afternoon and he had not even had his noon meal. Well, he would finish his pipe first. Elizabeth fussed about bits of tobacco and the smell on his clothes, but a pipe came in handy at times like this.

Daggett had no desire to give up tobacco, any more than Canadians in general were prepared to give up alcohol. Or the brewing of it, despite demands from the United States government. The war had been more effective with prohibition in Canada than threats or moral suasion. Daggett watched a smoke ring rise until it became too relaxed to hold its shape and rocked back and forth, its oval becoming increasingly lazy. Finally, it dissipated altogether. Canada had used its valuable grains during the war to produce bread, not liquor. But the war was over, well over now, and Canadians had given up their emergency measures. The United States, too, but at the same time Americans had also tightened their grip on prohibition. To no avail. People still drank, Daggett blew another smoke ring. But now they got arrested. And some of them got shot. The smoke ring took its lazy course upward. Shot by law enforcement agents. Daggett blew a stream through the puff's widening hole. Law enforcement agents who were too often overly zealous.

But Americans these days were making angry noises about law and law enforcement, so much so that no one was doing any real police work. No one had time. Daggett had been aware of the fierce growling and snarling when prohibition first began in the United States almost ten years earlier with the passage of the Volstead Act. He had never been happier to be posted in this quiet, out-of-the-way island. Just as he expected, things got noisier and messier on both sides of the border, until finally the United States Treasury boys joined the fray. Now it was an all-out fight, with the big Treasury tom cats strutting and yowling right in broad daylight, their volume turned high. Daggett wouldn't be surprised to learn that no one in Boston or New York had made an honest effort to find out about Mr. John T. Brown. Those fellows were too busy doing their own pissing and preening.

All anyone on both sides of the border had heard about for the last month or more was how United States federal agents had taken to shooting innocent victims. They were out of control, cried reporters, as violent as the criminals they sought. Canadian newspapers were full of the stories and, Daggett was willing to bet, newspapers in Boston and New York were too. One man out for a Sunday drive with his family in Minnesota took twenty-six slugs from a border patrolman's shotgun. What a customs officer was doing with a riot gun in the countryside defied Daggett's understanding. And then federal agents had opened fire on a motorboat full of people near Detroit. Guilty or not, armed or not, that seemed like a lot of cowboy gunslinging to Daggett.

He had never been able to grasp the American penchant for violence or how Americans chose their heroes. It apparently mattered not at all on what side of the law a man stood as long as his aim was quick and deadly. He could even be on both sides of the law. Wyatt Earp, Wild Bill Hickock, Daggett had heard plenty about both of them. And now gangsters like Capone, free to come and go as they pleased. And famous. They got writeups in American newspapers as if they were aviators or kings.

Daggett shook his head. Odd set of values those Americans had. But that's what sold newspapers, he supposed, and paid the salaries of Treasury agents. Well, Daggett would like to know what those agents would do with Mr. Brown, a man from nowhere and a murder that, except for a single witness, looked like an accident. A murder where the one lead he had, the red shirt with its lost button, was unraveling in his hands.

"BASIL, borage, calendula, chives, fennel, marjoram, parsley."

"Parsley, yes, lots of parsley."

"Sage, savory, tarragon, thyme," Edith checked off herbs on the sheet Sabra Jane had given her.

"And coriander," Willa prompted again from behind Edith's shoulder. "Be sure to add coriander. And rosemary. And what about rue?"

"Do you think all of these herbs will grow here behind the cottage? This spot may not get enough sun," Edith turned to Sabra Jane, brilliant today in various shades of green and blue.

"We'll just have to see. It's a little late in the season for some things, but I can bring sets or cuttings of just about everything on the list. Those needing sun, we'll plant toward the top."

"And horehound? We could grow horehound? What about peppermint? You forgot peppermint," Willa, still reading over Edith's shoulder, reached for the list.

"I'll bring something of everything," Sabra Jane laughed, "How about that for a plan?"

"Exactly right," Willa handed the list to Sabra Jane and pulled on her gloves.

Sabra Jane had arrived bearing vinca and several varieties of sedum, along with a small American flag to celebrate the Fourth of July. There were enough rocks to occupy the three of them for the rest of the afternoon with the promise of more the next day. Young James was due back on Sam Jackson's boat sometime that evening, and Sabra Jane had extracted Roy Sharkey's word that once James was back, they would deliver another wagon load as soon as possible.

"You seem none the worse for village gossip," Edith opened the conversation she had been waiting to have.

"Old biddies. Little John and Eva. The both of them," Sabra Jane plunged her trowel in the earth. "I don't like gossip," the trowel scraped against rock, "and I don't like gossipers."

Rock Wall with Herbs

"Invasion of privacy," Willa pulled at a root.

"I'll bet you have trouble with that," Sabra Jane rocked back on her heels. "Not just autograph seekers, but people who feel free to make you into whomever they please."

"We guard against that as well as we can," Edith handed her several sprigs of sedum with well-developed rootstock.

"Next thing you know you'll be pilloried and they'll be piling firewood around a stake erected just for you," Willa reached for more vinca.

"I hate it most when women spread rumors," Sabra Jane's hands held still. "The violation seems deeper somehow."

"It's certainly not a sisterly thing to do," Edith agreed.

"Not all women are sisters," Willa reminded them. "And maybe I should add, not all sisters are women, if by women we mean grown up, sentient, thinking, compassionate human beings."

Sabra Jane grinned. "*Rumor* and *gossip*," she paused. "Have you ever noticed how those words are used to refer only to women?"

"*Information gathering* and *mob violence.* Those are words we reserve for men," Edith nodded.

"I feel better already," Sabra Jane's grin lengthened. "It's good to be understood."

LESS than a hour later, long before they depleted their pile of rocks, Sabra Jane, Willa, and Edith sped off in the Reo, aimed toward Daggett's office, a red button clutched securely in Edith's left hand. She had discovered it among the rocks only minutes before they leapt into the Reo.

Edith planted her right hand on the seat of the rumble to hold herself upright during the rush around corners. Willa's auburn hair streamed back, while Sabra Jane's strawberry red was encased in a bright plaid cap. The sharp breeze on Edith's face felt delicious, like the wind off the Plains on a hot August day. Edith missed those days and the creak of a saddle and swing of a horse loping beneath her. She knew Willa did too. But this was exciting, a red button turning up in the pile of rocks and a dash to tell Daggett.

Sabra Jane would be cleared of suspicion. Edith felt sure of it. But if Sabra Jane were innocent, Edith surprised herself with the thought, who was guilty? Until this moment, Edith realized, she had focused so thoroughly on disassociating Sabra Jane from the person on the cliff, she had forgotten to consider who did belong to the outflung arm and red-shirted back.

While the car lurched and gathered speed, Edith went over in her mind the list of people she knew to be suspects. The Jordans had seen Roy Sharkey, young James, Sabra Jane, Herb Gordon, Little John Winslow, and Matthew Johnson. And Rebecca Jackson had sold red shirts to Sam Jackson, Sabra Jane, Mary Daniels, Little John Winslow, and Matthew Johnson. Edith's mind began to make automatic matches, but she caught herself in the midst of another lurch and skid as the car came to a stop at Tattons Corner before turning left into North Head. Those five were surely not the only red shirts on Grand Manan. Every fisherman probably owned at least one, and the men who went over to the mainland to work in the woods more than likely had several.

About all the red shirt did, Edith braced herself for the sudden stop in front of Daggett's office, was to eliminate most of the wives on Grand Manan. Every one of their husbands remained fair game. But why would an islander, Edith brushed road dust from her knees, want to kill a man who had never before set foot on the island?

"YES, indeed," Daggett agreed, "motive is the key," once Sabra Jane, Willa, and Edith crowded their chairs around the large desk in the middle of his office. Daggett had no secretary or secondary officer, so he was free to arrange furniture anyway he liked. He chose openness with a sense of balance. Edith liked that about him.

"Motive and opportunity, watch words for detectives," Daggett halted. He obviously was not paying attention even to his own little speech. His eyes were fixed on the pair of red buttons staring up from his blotter. They were identical.

"You had opportunity," Daggett finally lifted his eyes to meet Sabra Jane's. "Others did too. But even without this button to suggest your innocence, Miss Briggs, I've not been able to guess what possible reason you might have for killing that man," Daggett shrugged and took a moment to tamp down his pipe.

"Trouble is," Daggett continued, striking a match and leaning back in his chair, "I come up with a similar blank for every person I can think of who might have had opportunity."

"Who does that include?" Sabra Jane's brows were knit, the freckles on her forehead muted by tan.

"Well, there's still a small list I haven't yet dealt with," Daggett shook his head.

"Mr. Johnson is among them, I suppose," Edith prompted.

Daggett raised an eyebrow.

"I know nothing about the fellow, actually," Edith shifted in her chair, "I just remember Mary Jordan mentioned seeing him. And I saw him the next day with his wife and friends at Rose Cottage when I stopped in for tea. He seemed regular enough. City man, of course. Tennis is a city sport."

Daggett drew on his pipe.

"What happens if we start from the other direction?" Willa leaned forward, her voice meditative. "I mean, what exactly do we know about Mr. Brown?"

"Unfortunately little," Daggett pushed the telegrams from Boston and New York across his desk. "I've had no help from outside, and you know as much as I do about his activities here," Daggett rose to retrieve a file lying on top of the cabinets at the back of his office.

"Captain Whitson said he signed the passenger list and had a passport," Daggett flipped through the notes in the file, "but no one remembered checking the passport and there were no signs of either passport or wallet on his body. Nothing among his things at Swallowtail, either. Hardly anything personal, for that matter."

Daggett returned to his desk, the file still in his hands. He flipped through several more sheets.

"St. John sends word they have no record of any Yanks by that name. So I'm down to the one place that hasn't responded to my request for information. New Bedford, Massachusetts." Daggett glanced up, "Any of you know the place?"

No one did.

"His shirts were done by a laundry there."

"Mr. Brown's suit was badly ripped," Willa's words were measured, her brow furrowed. "His passport and wallet might have been lost on the rocks."

"Yes, and with the tide on its way out, they could be anywhere by now," Sabra Jane completed Willa's thought.

Daggett placed the open file on his desk.

"What about New York and Boston," Edith lifted the telegrams still in her hands, "what was Mr. Brown's connection there?"

Daggett closed the file and turned to his notes.

"Tailor tags. Marvin Gates, Boston's Finest Tailor. And in New York, Abercrombie and Fitch."

"My favorite wishing place," Sabra Jane's grin included her eyes.

"Beg your pardon?"

"They carry all the finest equipment for the outdoors, right down to safari jackets and elephant guns," Willa chuckled. "Teddy Roosevelt alone has kept them busy for years."

"But what did Mr. Brown buy there," Edith wondered aloud.

"Binoculars?" Willa guessed.

"A gun," Sabra Jane pronounced.

"No, no, no," Daggett halted speculation. "There was a bird book but no gun. No binoculars, either. At least, none that I know of. Just a navy blue sweater."

"That's odd," Willa sounded speculative.

"Odd?"

"In a place like this, birders carry binoculars."

"Well, this birder carried an Abercrombie and Fitch sweater," Daggett glanced back at his notes, "a navy blue pullover."

"Mr. Brown would not have had to be in New York to get that,"

Willa suggested. "Someone might have given it to him."

Again, they sat in silence.

"I've never been to New Bedford," Sabra Jane tried a new tack. "What's in New Bedford that would interest Mr. Brown?"

"I don't know," Edith shook her head.

"Mills, water, docks," Willa offered a guess. "It's close to Martha's Vineyard and Nantucket."

"If only we knew more about Mr. Brown and his interests," Edith returned the telegrams to their place on Daggett's desk.

ROB Feeney heard the Chevrolet's sputter and glanced up from his desk. The Chevrolet paused and Rob half expected the constable to pull up in front of his office, but Daggett turned toward the docks. There's a man with too much on his mind, Rob almost said the words aloud and glanced at the lists of passengers and crew waiting for Daggett on the corner of his desk. Rob wondered whether he should take them over to Daggett's office, but he had his own work to do and Daggett was clearly off on an errand.

Rob didn't envy Daggett. All that running around must produce very little certain progress and when it did it brought a great many surprises. The definition of mystery. The bumpy business of making the unknown known. Rob much preferred the steady beat of his own routine.

"LISTEN here, Isaacs, you may not want to talk to me, but I want a word with you," Daggett placed a hand on Burt Isaacs' arm. "We can talk here, now, or you can come to my office."

Isaacs pulled loose and turned away, leaving Daggett with his profile, the set of his jaw broken only by a wad of chewing tobacco wedged between his back teeth. Isaacs stared intently ahead, apparently focused on a sailboat about a hundred yards out. Not far to its left, two whales leapt out of the sea.

112

Daggett watched them also, alerted by the sound. Humpbacks, both of them, the first of this season.

"Aren't they something now," Isaacs' belligerence had vanished, like wind from the boat's sails. He rested his elbows on the railing that ran along this section of the wharf.

The whales disappeared. The sailboat picked up speed.

"I'm asking what you were doing on the mainland," Daggett refused to be distracted. "And I'm asking whether you ever met this fellow before and what you noticed about him."

"Like I told the Captain, I was logging for Jack Watson," Isaacs kept his eyes on the sea. "I never saw that man before in my life. Wouldn't know him if he walked up to us right now," Isaacs spat and wiped his mouth. "And I don't know a damn about his passport or his wallet or his luggage. Why would I," Isaacs flicked his eyes toward Daggett. It was a statement, not a question.

"From what I've heard, Jack Watson runs bourbon over the border."

"What's it to you?" The wad of tobacco shifted from one side of Isaacs' jaw to the other.

"I understand you talked to Mr. Brown coming over on the ferry."

"Who says?"

"Doesn't matter, it's what I heard," Daggett studied the side of Isaacs' tanned face. The lips were taut, jaw firm. A muscle twitched next to his eye.

"There they go again," Isaacs nodded.

First one whale, then the other leapt high into a dive, arching until their fluted tails ended their long, sleek glide, like flags hailing the powerful grace of their rise and return.

"Next time they'll beat the boat," Isaacs looked directly at Daggett, his brown eyes glinting, then back out to sea. "See if they don't."

"You think it's a contest?"

The sailboat shot forward.

"Everything's a contest," a stream of brown saliva shot out from between Isaacs' lips. It arched out and down, then disappeared into the blue-green swirl at the base of the pier. "Winning's what counts," Isaacs shifted the wad to the other side of his mouth.

Daggett heard first one, then the other whale spout. Towers of water rose high into the air, then the bend of their backs and their tails signaled the start of another long descent.

Ten yards behind, the sailboat sped on.

"THERE'S nothing that adds up about this Mr. Brown, is there?" Willa leaned back against the Adirondack chair and swirled her glass until ice clinked against its sides.

"Whatever adds up is certainly not apparent," Edith agreed, settling into her own Adirondack, placing her glass on its wide arm.

Edith and Willa enjoyed an evening cocktail to whet their appetites before dinner. They were starting a bit early this evening, but they agreed that they needed to take a break and the gin tasted especially good. Not only had they gone to the extravagance of chipping ice for their drinks, they were ready for some serious relaxation after moving rocks with Sabra Jane and then racing off to see Daggett, red button in hand.

"You would think by now with Daggett's inquiries and all these telegrams coming in, Mr. Brown's personal story would be taking shape," Edith complained, "but it's only pointing to loose ends."

"And loose buttons," Willa chuckled.

"Yes," Edith smiled, "but at least this last one made it much harder to point a finger at Sabra Jane."

XI

COMPARED TO BURT ISAACS, Herb Gordon, Jr. had proved a font of information. Words tumbled from his mouth before Daggett could finish a question. Trouble was, Herb Jr. had nothing to tell Daggett about Mr. Brown or his demise.

But Herb Jr. did have first-hand experience with every rumor racing through North Head, and he had plenty to say on the subject of Sabra Jane Briggs—her clothes, her pottery, her Reo, her lodgers, the sort of food she chose to put on her table, the way she loped through the woods, how she came from New York with a woman named Marjorie, what she had done to the old Ingersoll place, what she was doing to the farm she now called The Anchorage. But all Herb Jr. could say about Mr. Brown or the afternoon of his death was that he had ridden his bicycle to The Whistle and back between the hours of one and three. During that time, he had seen a flock of sheep but not one person, no one at all, either coming or going.

Mary Daniels proved equally forthcoming and uninformative. Mary was delighted Daggett stopped by. She fed him a piece of gooseberry pie and made him walk every step of the way around the outside of her cottage to admire the new roof her son had installed when he returned from the mainland, where he had been making more money working on commercial fishing boats than he could for Sam Jackson on Grand Manan. Mary had been widowed when James was a toddler, and it was hard for her with no man around while James was off making his way in the world. Now James was home and wanted to start his own family with Eric

Dawson's sister, a fair-haired beauty if Mary did say so herself. The problem was still money. James managed to find work with Sam Jackson and Roy Sharkey, though Mr. Sharkey just wanted help delivering rocks to those famous ladies at Whale Cove, such nice women they are, Mary added, nodding. She thought they could make do, the three of them together, under this new roof.

But when it came to answering Daggett's questions about the red shirt, all Mary could tell Daggett was that she bought it for James, who was still out on Sam Jackson's boat. The shirt was not in James' room, and Mary could not say when or even whether James had worn it. James was due back that evening, but everything depended on their catch. The season had been slow and dragging for scallops could be a difficult business, as Daggett well knew.

Tourist Brochure 1927

MATTHEW JOHNSON was another matter altogether. Daggett found him with his wife Maggie, sitting on opposite ends of the arbor swing behind Swallowtail. Wisteria entwined with grape vines covered the lattice, providing shade from the late afternoon sun.

Among a semicircle of lawn chairs facing the arbor, two carried wet spots on their arms, apparently left by tumblers like the one Maggie Johnson still cradled in her right hand. Daggett could see two cubes of ice and some sort of pale liquid. He raised an eyebrow. Ice cubes were rare on the island.

A third wet spot glistened on the arm of the swing near Matthew Johnson's elbow. He seemed perfectly comfortable, lounging next to his wife in spotless tennis whites. His wife wore something drapey and loose with a bold blue design. Beach pajamas, Daggett thought they were called, though he never expected to see anyone in an outfit like that on Grand Manan. A wide-brimmed straw hat took up the center of the swing. Its baby blue sash fluttered with each back and forth roll.

"I doubt that I can be of much help, Constable," Johnson bent his head over a match, then leaned back to blow cigarette smoke with measured force. His blue eyes watched intently as the white puff dispersed the air. His face was framed by light chestnut hair, slicked back and spare, with deep vees on each side, the top of his forehead pink from the sun.

"The man who died, well, we have no idea who that man was," Maggie Johnson spoke with a certain listlessness, her voice low, the words throaty, "but we are eminently curious about the details of your investigation."

"The details, yes."

Maggie Johnson surprised Daggett. By now he had heard a great deal about this young couple and expected Johnson to be, as he seemed, distant, relaxed, fit. But Johnson's wife Daggett expected to be edgy, brittle, almost high-strung, yet her words came slow and listless, tinged with arrogance and boredom. Daggett had heard she smoked cigarettes, and now it seemed she drank liquor as well. The women he knew did neither.

Fast living, Daggett watched Maggie Johnson sip from her glass. Her lips matched the enameled blaze on her nails. Johnson blew another precise stream of smoke, this time directed toward Daggett, then flicked at an ash poised on the crease of his trousered left leg. Fast living and a great deal of money, Daggett concluded.

"Ah, Constable, won't you join us in a gin fizz?" The voice came from behind, then attached itself, as Daggett turned, to the male half of the other couple in Johnson's party, a lanky fellow named Jameson according to The Swallowtail registry, Samuel Jameson.

"Name's Sam."

With drinks in both hands, Jameson nodded instead of offering to shake.

"We're celebrating Independence eve, Constable," the willowy blond in Jameson's wake bore a dish of crackers along with her drink. "We've already celebrated your Canada Day."

"My wife Jean," Jameson nodded toward the blond. "You've met Matt and Maggie, I guess," Jameson's glance took in the swing.

"Independence eve?"

"American independence from the Brits. You know," Jean Jameson's lips rose lazily at the corners.

"Oh, Fourth of July. Of course."

Daggett waited while Jameson handed Johnson his drink and his wife resumed her seat and balanced the plate of crackers on her knees. Jean Jameson was also adorned in beach pajamas, though hers were all lemony and pale orange. Daggett preferred them to the blue.

"Come on now, Mags, give us a smile, why don't you," Jameson cajoled, nudging the swing with his knee. "The girls are tired of life on the island," he turned to Daggett. "Can't seem to think of anything to do with their time."

"There is nothing to do," Jean Jameson corrected her husband,

118

smiling vaguely in Daggett's direction. "I don't like to hike, and I'm not the least bit interested in boats or birds."

"What did I tell you," Jameson shrugged toward Daggett. "Now, how about that drink," he took a step toward the inn.

"None for me, thank you. Not while I'm on duty."

"On duty? How formal that sounds."

No mistaking it this time, Maggie Johnson was trying to be droll. Daggett offered a smile.

"Well, have a biscuit then," Jameson sank into his chair. "That is what you call crackers, isn't it?" He put a hand on the empty chair next to him, "At the very least, you can sit and chat for a moment."

"Yes, thank you," Daggett pulled out his notebook before he sat down.

"An inquisition?"

Rays from the late sun slanted through the wisteria, striking Maggie Johnson on the crown. Her brown hair fitted snug, like an aviator's cap, and her eyes, turned fully on Daggett for the first time, overpowered the rest of her features. They were large and a very deep brown. She was, Daggett guessed, considered handsome. Possibly even beautiful, like a model in one of those magazines displaying women's clothes.

"You like to play tennis, do you?" Daggett returned Maggie Johnson's gaze but decided to ignore her question, aiming his own directly at her husband.

"Best game in the world," Johnson's tan exaggerated the whiteness of his teeth. "Even Maggie likes it, don't you, Mags?"

"I play, if that's what you mean," Maggie Johnson continued to rest her eyes on Daggett's.

"You have courts near where you live?"

"We have courts where we live," Maggie Johnson underscored the *where*.

"I don't believe I caught the location?"

"Massachusetts," Jameson held the plate of crackers in one hand and gestured with the other, "near Boston."

"With a summer place on Martha's Vineyard," Maggie glanced at her husband. "That's why this trip is so absurd," she paused to raise an eyebrow.

Jean Jameson giggled.

"I don't mean to be rude," Maggie continued, "this is a marvelous little island. For a while." Her hand draped itself over the left arm of the swing and made a languid sweep in an apparent effort to indicate the whole of Grand Manan. "I'm sure you enjoy living here immensely," she crooned. "It's just that we needn't be here with you."

"Matt lured us all into coming," Jameson said heartily, "with marvelous tales about puffins."

"I'm an avid birder," Matthew Johnson acknowledged over the rim of his glass.

"I have yet to see a single puffin," Jean Jameson complained, her voice flat.

"Machias is the place for that," Daggett began to explain. "The next island over. Any fisherman will take you and there's an excursion motor launch," he stopped. It was not his job to make Grand Manan palatable to these people. "But, tell me what you do in Boston," he veered back onto course, aiming again at Matthew Johnson.

"Do? In Boston? Oh, what business, you mean. Investments. Banking. Desk work. Nothing so vigorous as here."

"Matt hardly does anything anywhere, really," Jameson put in. "Midas touch," he nodded toward the couple on the swing, "and a rich wife."

"Don't be jealous, Sammy," Maggie Johnson chided. Jean Jameson laughed.

"It's Jean who has more money than God," Matthew Johnson

allowed, tipping his glass in her direction and bowing his head with great solemnity.

DINNER that evening at Whale Cove began even livelier than usual, with everyone puzzling aloud over all the red shirts and all the loose buttons.

"How did you ever think to go to Jackson's Drygoods to look at the buttons on those shirts?" Winifred Bromhall had placed her hand on Edith's arm, her eyes wide.

"I didn't, actually," Edith confessed. "I just wanted to look at the shirts and perhaps find out how many people had bought them. They were wonderfully soft and I let my hands run over the fabric. That's when I felt the loose thread."

"What a detective," Margaret Byington exclaimed from across the table.

"Here, here," Willa laughed in agreement.

"No, no, no. Not at all," Edith felt herself blush. "It was purely by accident. The truth of the matter is Rebecca and I were engaged in gossip about Little John Winslow, and I wasn't really thinking about what I was doing."

"Little John Winslow," Margaret exploded, "what a silly little man."

"Yes," Winifred agreed. "We stopped by the bakery this afternoon and heard all about his nasty allegations. And not just about Sabra Jane. But about all of us."

"I'll never understand such men," the corners of Margaret's mouth turned down and she shook her head. "What a trial he must be for his wife."

"Yes," Edith agreed and reached for the salad.

"Yes," Willa nodded.

Willa, Edith knew, encountered enough such men to make the horrifying effects of ignorance and misogyny clear in her fiction.

Wick Cutter, Buck Scales, two of the worst of her misogynists, were evil. But Little John was really not a bad man. Just very ignorant. Yet it was the nonsense men like Little John spouted that made the evils of misogyny possible, Edith thought. Also, it seemed, the evils of a misogynist like Mr. Brown. And again she saw the body, angled slightly toward her, plummet from the cliff wearing what she now knew to be a pin-striped suit and wing-tipped shoes.

LATER, much later, Daggett stared at the notebook outstretched before him on the desk. One line said *Boston, Martha's Vineyard, investments, new rich.* Another said *hiked alone, tiff, others Castalia, check Gilmore.* Farther down, Daggett studied again the third line in his handwriting. *Red shirt, backpack, button missing left sleeve.*

Yes, Matthew Johnson had walked from Tattons Corner to The Whistle early in the afternoon of the day Mr. Brown died. He was alone on the road and saw no one. On the way back, he took the Red Trail around Ashburton Head and got as far as the waterfall at Seven Days Work. At that point, Johnson said, he cut inland along the brook. About half way to the road, near where a fallen log crossed the trail, he stopped to rest and eat some pemmican. It was well beyond noon, he had had no lunch, and the others in his party had taken the picnic hamper with them. When he finished the pemmican, he removed the light wool shirt he had been wearing in lieu of a jacket and tied it loosely around his neck. Once the sun burned off that morning's fog, the day turned warm, even in the woods. He grew so warm by the time he reached the road that he put the shirt in his backpack. Yes, the shirt was red. He had purchased it at Jackson's Drygoods earlier that day. And yes, when he untied the sleeves from around his neck, he noticed the button on the left sleeve was missing.

Johnson stayed on the road until he came to a cottage and stopped to ask how to get to Whale Cove. Once there, he made his way back to the Red Trail and walked on into North Head. An older woman, Boston accent, gave him the necessary directions. He couldn't remember who told him about the hiking trails in the first place. Someone he spoke to in the village, perhaps the banker, perhaps Andrews or his wife. Johnson saw no one on the trail at Seven Days Work or on the road, certainly not Mr. Brown. And no one else in a red shirt. Johnson did not believe anyone saw him either. With further prompting, he recalled hearing the sound of a bicycle on gravel as he neared the road. That was all he remembered.

Yes, Johnson nodded again in answer to Daggett's question, the button was in place shortly before noon when he began his walk. He remembered distinctly fastening the buttons on both sleeves. He first put the shirt on when Claude Gilmore stopped at Tattons Corner to let him out. The four of them were on the way to Castalia, to watch birds on the marsh. Johnson planned the excursion and was to have gone with them, but his wife's irritability was more than he could bear that afternoon. He had gone off by himself to maintain the equilibrium of their marriage. That's exactly what he said, the equilibrium of their marriage. The Jamesons affirmed his statement, as did Maggie Johnson. According to her they often chose not to be together.

Matthew Johnson was absolutely certain about when he noticed the button missing. That happened when he untied the sleeves and rolled the shirt up to put it in his backpack. By that time, he had achieved a pleasant mood again. The missing button threatened to destroy it. Johnson was not in the habit of purchasing ready-made clothes, but having forgotten his sweater when they set out, he asked Claude Gilmore to stop long enough for him to run in to get something warm. The fog had taken its time burning off and the air felt raw well into the afternoon. The tiff with his wife began when Johnson asked Gilmore to make the stop at Jackson's Drygoods and picked up steam when Maggie caught sight of what he bought. She did not like the color red. Johnson did. She thought the workmanship shoddy and had a great deal to say about the garment workers who produced it. Johnson found himself in the ridiculous position of defending his purchase by upholding the general standard of quality in the garment industry over the last twenty years. The missing button not only brought back the whole quarrel, it served to affirm Maggie's opinion of the garment industry.

The hands on the clock on Daggett's office wall said eight forty-five. So much to do, Daggett glanced again through his notebook. He hadn't yet managed to talk to Rob Feeney. Well, nothing there that couldn't wait another day, Daggett reached for his pipe. The sun would go down soon.

XII

"HUH, HUH, HUH, huh," Edith could barely distinguish the sound of her own from Willa's breathing, Willa was that close, running near Edith through the quiet night air. Silent except for regular explosions of breath and an occasional crunch of rock underfoot, they ran with measured pace in the moonlight.

Thank God for moonlight, Edith glanced ahead to where the trail etched its way through a meadow, then cut into the darkened woods beyond. Sharp as the part in a person's hair, Edith described the scene to herself, then found her mind roaming and pulled it up short. She did not want to think about what lay ahead. She would force herself to concentrate on the moment. The throb of her lungs, the huh, huh of their breath, the rushed fall of each foot, the scene around, the surround. Edith caught herself. She was slipping into an old habit of repeating words and sounds in her head, nonsensical words, serious words, words for the sake of their sounds. Sibilants, consonants, vowels. From here she would slide into scenes and imaginings.

Edith shook herself back to the moment, to wonder how moonlight could so blur the familiar yet sharpen detail. The wildflowers off to her left Edith knew by day to be a mass of blazing purple, but to her night eye they registered as individual and distinct, shadowy spikes with particular twists and solitary heads. Not a mass at all, but hundreds, even thousands, of individuals. It took moonlight to show them that way, moonlight to see, Edith chuckled to herself, lunar lucidity. Thank God for moonlight and for their knowledge of the trail, Edith glanced up to investigate a bank of encroaching clouds, then jumped a tiny rivulet emanating from the spring she knew to be near but could not discern.

Willa set the pace when they came to the woods. Edith picked it up again at Seven Days Work, and they snaked their way in and out along the cliffs, almost without thought daring the edge, racing always toward a pinpoint of light. A pinpoint that moved. A pinpoint they had noticed and wanted to reach because it moved, because it bobbed and bounced and flashed and yet stayed put.

The bobbing light had been stationary for a long while now. They had first seen it from the edge of their cliff. Home alone for the evening, Edith and Willa had been out on their lawn chairs watching the sun set and the moon rise. Everyone else had gone into North Head to see the latest film showing at the Happy Hour Theatre. After Edith spotted the light, they watched it for a moment together, then Edith stood sentinel while Willa ran to the main house to phone Daggett. He was on his way now in the Chevrolet. He planned to meet them where the trail headed inland near the waterfall, but he would have to come in from the road and use a torch because he didn't know the trails the way they did. Willa had told him they would try to reach the waterfall without using a flashlight, for the surprise factor. You shouldn't go at all, he had said. But he supposed he couldn't stop them. Be careful, was all he said at the end, you know the danger.

Care-ful, dan-ger. The words ran through Edith's mind like a mantra, pairing the fall of her feet. Care-ful, dan-ger.

A plosive for landing with a hold on the *n*, soft *g* for rocking to take off again. Care-ful, dan-ger. The words entered her consciousness in quite the same way, Edith remembered with a start, as they had years before when, as a child, she had touched a match to a firecracker for the very first time. Her father had called out the warning at a large garden party. Everyone had come, even William

Jennings Bryan, who was about to run for president of the United States. He was just one of their neighbors as far as Edith was concerned, but she remembered that Fourth of July because of the way he roared his approval, louder than anyone, when Edith succeeded. A display of fireworks had followed. Boom. Boom. Boom. Huge, sparkling displays and the shooting flares of Roman candles. Edith saw them all again and heard the long ahhhhs that came after.

A forest fire began to roar through Edith's lungs. Repeated, searing pain, flame after flame after flame. Her head ached. She had only her mind to hold on to her stride, willing her legs to keep pumping, arms to keep moving through air. Care-ful, dan-ger, her feet continued to fly down the trail.

There it was again. Close now, that light. Very close. Two more bends in the trail, an eighth of a mile, no more. Edith reached back to signal Willa to an abrupt stop, then dropped to her knees and at the same time clamped a hand over the lower portion of her face. She was dimly aware that Willa had halted beside her.

Edith's chest heaved fire. Fierce pains shot through her shoulders, legs, the soles of her feet. Her ears pounded. She hoped the hand gripping her mouth would quiet the sound of her breathing. She could no longer hear and had no time for her body. Not now, not with the light right there.

It was more than a pinpoint now. It was a beam, a large beam. It stroked the trees inland from the cliff. Back and forth, back and forth, back and forth. Then it halted and turned, as they had seen it do earlier from the cliffs by their cottage, to shoot down the rocks and rake across the shore to the sea.

Edith felt rather than heard Willa crouch beside her, but they both heard the stone Willa's shoe dislodged. It made three sharp pings in a vertical drop to the rocks below. No cascade, no great rush. Just three sharp pings.

Edith caught her breath and felt her abdomen pressed hard against her spine. The beam suspended its progress, hovered momentarily, and then swung violently upward to hit Edith directly in the eyes.

Edith felt herself lurch and Willa's hand clutch her shoulder. Then she reeled backward and down, falling out of the light. She felt the sudden warmth of Willa's hand on her arm and heard a muttered damnation. Her elbow scraped rock. Her feet slipped toward the edge of the cliff. They slid off.

Involuntary, that was the word that presented itself. Edith's hands clutched the earth. A sharp pain shot through her left palm. Then she felt Willa's arm cross her waist and hold firm. Safe. Saved.

Had that been what happened to Mr. Brown, an involuntary slip? But there had been no arm to catch him, only the red-shirted arm that flung itself out before he went off the cliff.

Edith blinked at the halo of brightness just ahead. But the beam had vanished, she knew that. And with it, the person who held the light.

"Identify yourself."

Willa's words boomed across the void. They exploded and reverberated but drew no other sound.

"Which way did he go?" Willa tightened her grip.

Edith shook her head.

"Did you hear anything?"

"Nothing."

"See anything?"

"No."

"Damnation."

"WHOEVER it was saw Edith, that's for certain," Willa glanced around the dining room until her eyes came to rest again on Daggett's face.

"And parts of you as well," Edith laughed.

"The two of us were all stirred together like scrambled eggs," Willa's laugh was deep and rich. "Edith was just about to go over the cliff."

"You must have been frightened half to death," Margaret Byington's eyes showed her concern.

"Only about a quarter to death," Willa chuckled and turned her attention back to the steaming cup of Sanka Jacobus shoved toward her across the blue-checkered oilcloth.

"The truth is it didn't occur to either of us to be really frightened until it was all over," Edith reached across the table to take Willa's hand, "and then we were terrified."

Edith's left hand, the jagged cut on her palm swathed with gauze, lay still in her lap.

"Neither of us moved for at least five minutes after he'd gone."

"The light had been so bright," Edith nodded, "I couldn't see to move."

"Yes," Daggett leaned back in his chair and contemplated Edith's face, "let's go back to that point."

Daggett's notebook lay open next to the empty cobbler dish on the checkered cloth. He flipped back through the top few pages, coming to rest on the third, his finger tracing a line midway down.

"Just how big was that light?"

"I have no idea," Edith shrugged.

"Big," Willa set down her cup and retrieved her hand, then spread her fingers and drew her hands back and forth in the air until they settled on creating a circle about eight inches in diameter.

"What made it so bright do you think?"

"Number of batteries? Size of bulb?" it was Willa's turn to shrug.

"How high off the ground was it?"

"How high did the person hold it? Good question," Willa frowned. "Three feet, maybe three and a half," she turned to Edith, "What would you say?"

Edith closed her eyes to return to the cliff. Before its glare hit, she had been able to see the light. When they rounded the curve, it was trained on the twisted trunks of cedars near the edge. It spent several moments caressing the base of each tree, flooding the large outcropping of rocks nearby. From there it had inched back into the pines that formed the woods beyond the trail. It would pick out one pine, then another, and starting about midway up, move slowly down and around, until it had embraced each pine the way it had the cedars. Then suddenly, abruptly, in the seconds before Willa's foot disturbed the stone, the beam had swung away from the trees and shot down the rocks toward the waves below.

But that's not what Daggett asked. Height, that's what he wanted, height. Edith refocused her mind and saw again the backlighted legs, loosely trousered, with laced boots, pants tucked in at mid-calf, legs spread, one planted slightly ahead of the other. A strong stance, but relaxed. No plan to run there. The light had moved but not the legs until . . . Edith caught her mind wandering again and looked up.

"Three and a half feet at least," Edith paused to watch Daggett write the figures, their lines straight, curves firm, then she glanced at Willa.

"Yes," Willa drew the word out, "I believe Edith has it right."

"The person had to be a good six feet," Edith moved on to the real point of Daggett's question, still looking at Willa, "wouldn't you say?"

"Six feet and comfortable in his socks," Willa nodded.

Daggett's pen moved quickly.

"All we could see were his legs, of course. The outline of his legs," Edith corrected herself, "and a faint hint of his torso."

"But he was easy in his body," Willa was thinking aloud again. "Almost nonchalant in the way he held the flashlight," she extended her left hand and held it, wrist relaxed.

"Until he heard the stone fall," Edith interjected, "then he moved fast."

Willa's hand jerked up and swung dramatically to the left, "Extraordinarily fast," she agreed, "and quiet."

"Amazingly quiet," Edith's voice had dropped almost to a whisper.

Jacobus pulled out a chair and sat down.

"Left handed, was he?" Daggett's pen hovered above the page awaiting their answer.

"He?" Jacobus wanted to know.

XIII

By LATE MORNING, the gale winds and sheets of rain that startled the island shortly before midnight tapered to a drizzle. The front was already blowing out to sea. No time to waste, Edith decided. By afternoon everything would change. The sky would be blue, the air crisp, the grass freshly green. Beautiful in aftermath, but what Edith wanted was happening now. The storm's colors intensified to their fiercest hues. Dazzling purples and cobalt blues, dashing grays and thundering greens.

The deep tinge stretching across the rounded bottom of the enormous cloud hanging now over the weir. Plum. Positively plum, Edith dipped her brush into the jar of water she kept for that purpose and tried again to get just the right mix before the cloud scudded off. Looking through a rain-drenched window, one could never be sure of shape. But accuracy didn't matter here, she tried a stroke, impression did.

Had their impressions the night before been accurate, Edith shifted her position on the stool and winced.

The word *involuntary* flitted again through her mind. Her body ached, every bone bruised, every muscle strained. The run last night had been long, long enough to stiffen them both for several days, without all that scrambling around on the side of the cliff. Edith set her brush near the paint box and reached down with her right hand to rub the backs of her legs. They were tighter than she had realized.

Willa had given Edith's shoulders and back a thorough massage before heading up to the attic room for her morning's work. But with her left hand bandaged, its cut still fresh, Edith was able to reciprocate only by applying liniment to Willa's shoulders and lower back. It's a wonder Willa managed to do such a thorough job, Edith marveled. For too long now, the thumb on Willa's writing hand had given her so much trouble she often wore a splint, but the splint got in her way and relieved only part of the pain. That turned her growly and depressed. But Willa's thumb finally improved and now she wouldn't notice how cramped her legs were, Edith guessed, until she got up from her desk. When her hand worked and her writing was going well, Willa rarely noticed anything until she was finished for the day.

Edith tried stretching in her sitting position, one leg at a time. Creaky, that's what Willa said the night before. We're getting old and creaky.

"Nonsense," Edith heard herself say aloud. But maybe Willa was right. Maybe she was getting creaky. Cracked, too. Here she was talking to herself just like Crazy Eddie, the neighbor who so frightened her as a child.

Edward Williams had been notorious throughout Lincoln, but nowhere more than on the block where they lived. Everyone knew he talked to himself and made strange, batting motions with his hands. Children imitated him and adults laughed. He's harmless, their elders would say, he's just old. But old held no meaning for Edith then, and Crazy Eddie wandered into their yard many more times than she liked. He was always getting lost, trying, he would say, to find his way home. Often as not he was at home when he said that.

Edith's best friend Jamie had busied himself adding hundreds of stories to the neighborhood lore about Crazy Eddie. Malevolent inventions, close to the truth. Too close to tell the difference. And Jamie had used those stories to taunt Edith, claiming that if she refused to do whatever he told her to do, he would tell Crazy Eddie to come and carry her off. Edith learned immediately to obey. But when she caught on to the lie, she caught on to power and that was the end of Jamie.

Later that year, when Crazy Eddie finally died, Edith acquired her first awareness of death. Such gifts we bring each other, Edith stretched her arms in the air and sighed deeply, then brought them down slowly and suspended them momentarily at shoulder height before letting them drop into her lap.

Ready to concentrate again, she hooked her heels on the bottom rung of the stool, looked back at the clouds, then studied again the shapes on her paper.

Hamstrings, tight hamstrings, the thought flitted through, then dissolved in the swirls of plum and purple before her. Edith reached again for her brush.

In the window the round-bottomed cloud gave way to wisps of dark gray edged with lavender and indigo. There seemed to be a race on, the field so crowded, clouds rushing neck and neck. Individual colors streamed together, then broke free. Edith dipped her brush. Lavender leading, indigo on the outside.

What had that man been doing? What could make him stay in the same place during the whole of their long run, Edith tried a mixture of violet and mauve.

He must have been in that spot for at least twenty minutes. Easily twenty, Edith pulled a stroke across. This one arched high above the others. She let her hand pause in the air.

It must have taken Willa a good ten minutes to make the phone call. And then the long run. She decided on a touch of azure, there, just above the others.

Why didn't he simply look around and leave? Why swing that light back over exactly the same territory time after time? The words slowed in her mind then repeated.

"I AM beginning to think none of this will ever fit together. So many pieces, no apparent design," Willa pushed herself up from the rock wall with a hand on each knee. She stepped back and stretched, then brushed her hands firmly against each other.

"Last night's rain didn't help any, either," Edith glanced up. "What a soggy mess."

"Patience, patience. You'll see," Sabra Jane Briggs shoved her trowel deep in the earth.

Willa took off her hat and swirled several loose hairs away from her eyes, then bent over to pat her forehead with the loose end of her shirt tail and wipe the sweat from her eyes. When she straightened, the tail was still in her hand.

"Why on earth did you let me choose a white blouse to do this sort of work?" Willa turned to Edith to demand. With the chuckle that followed, Willa's dimples deepened. She tucked in her shirt tail, ran her fingers through her hair and shook her head vigorously. Then she replaced her hat. It was her favorite hat, a close-woven straw with flat brim and wide ribbon, the blue of her eyes.

"Why don't we take a break and have some of the lemonade Jacobus brought over," Edith rocked back on her heels. "I, for one, could use a respite," she removed her work gloves, taking special care with the left. The wound on her palm would be tender for days.

"This business with the flashlight," Sabra Jane stood up and brushed damp earth from her knees, "tell me more about it."

"Talk about too many pieces with no apparent design," Edith said over her shoulder, letting the screen door slam behind her. Willa filled in the story while she retrieved the oatmeal cookies and lemonade.

So thoughtful, Jacobus, Edith smiled to herself. She knew they would choose to work on their rock wall while everyone else from the main house, Jacobus included, took off for an afternoon's hike to Money Cove.

Actually, Edith corrected herself, Matt, the tricolored dog of no particular breed, brought the cookies. Matt was short for Mattie, which was short for Mathilda, but Edith thought of Matt as a descriptor for Matt's favorite position and place, a full-length sprawl in front of the door to the main house.

Just before lunch, when Edith caught sight of Matt and Jacobus swinging along the path from the main house, she had laughed out loud. Jacobus carried a huge jug of lemonade, and Matt, head high, ears alert, body taut, bore a wicker hamper full of sandwiches and cookies, its handle firmly clamped between her teeth. Matt was wonderfully serious and well mannered and devoted to Jacobus, but she was also young and good humored and crazy about Willa. When Jacobus had put the lemonade on the counter and reached for the basket, Matt leapt past her and thundered through the cottage to the attic stairs. Taking their tight, old-fashioned turns in two strides, Matt did not stop until she had deposited the basket in Willa's lap and planted both front paws directly on the center keys of Willa's typewriter. The old Oliver gave a tremendous clack.

Edith chuckled and finished arranging her tray. She paused at the screen door. Willa and Sabra Jane were engaged in waving simultaneous but opposite directions to Roy Sharkey, whose wagon Edith could not see. She could hear it, however, on the lawn by the side of the cottage. She guessed young James must be turning the horses to back the wagon closer in toward their burgeoning wall.

"Fine job you're doing there," Roy Sharkey stood with his hands deep in his pockets, studying their handiwork. The folds of his belly rolled over his belt and pulled his back into an exaggerated curve. Just like a broken-backed mule, Edith decided about Roy Sharkey's spine. But this is a swayback, Willa would say, that has nothing to do with hard work. Minus his jacket, Roy Sharkey looked even less accustomed to physical labor than he had when he delivered the first load of rocks. But then, Edith remembered, young James had done most of the actual work.

"You can put this load in the same place you put the last one," Sabra Jane stood near the dwindling pile of flat, charcoal-gray stones. Dull streaks of red zigzagged along their edges and cut through their centers.

"Why not put the load over here, instead? This would be closer to the wall," Willa's hand aimed in a general direction to the north of the previous pile.

"Whatever you say, ladies," Roy Sharkey's face maintained its stillness, except for his mouth. His grin was blessed by straight teeth.

Roy Sharkey's smile was his best feature, Edith decided, though it was difficult to tell what his face might look like without the grizzled stubble and jutting cigar that, along with his belly, served as his trademark.

Sabra Jane held her silence. Willa looked at Sabra Jane, then at Roy Sharkey, and then at the wall. No one moved. "I guess over there would be better, after all. More out of the way when we're not handling rocks."

"Right you are," the cigar bobbed.

Edith advanced with the tray, "Will you join us, Mr. Sharkey?"

"Thank you, Miss. Later, perhaps," the cigar bobbed. "Right now James and me best be unloading these stones," he gestured at his wagon, making its slow, heavy progress backward around the edge of the house.

"We'll see if we can save you some lemonade, then," Willa nodded and led the way around the cottage to their lawn chairs, still sitting near the edge of the cliff. When they arrived at the chairs, she placed a hand on each hip and stood for a moment with her back arched, arms akimbo. "Lord, I'm stiff," she sighed.

"I'm not surprised after a jaunt like that," Sabra Jane shaded her eyes to survey the cliffs where they had run the night before. "How ever did you manage that in the dark?"

"Actually, it wasn't so dark," Edith shaded her eyes to look as well. Sunlight glinted off the waterfalls and brightened the cliffs all along Seven Days Work. Sharp details from the night before had long ago disappeared, washed away by the sun. Different features drew Edith's attention now. The dark cedars and rugged cliffs, masses of yellow tinged with red and brown, and below gray-green boulders strewn like pebbles to the edge of the sea. Daylight rendered the trail at the top of the cliff altogether invisible. But it had never been visible from here, Edith reminded herself, unless someone like Mr. Brown stepped too near the edge.

"Moonlight," Willa settled into the Adirondack chair next to Edith, "you'd be surprised how well you can see by moonlight."

"That's true," Sabra Jane turned away from the cliff. "It was bright last night before the clouds moved in, I remember."

"It was a lovely evening," Edith nodded. "We sat here for the longest while just watching the moon and listening."

"Yes," Sabra Jane glanced out toward the weir, "I love that sort of evening. The waves, the night sounds," she looked at Willa. "Actually," her voice turned suddenly brisk, "how stupid of me. We often take midnight hikes to Southern Head. Moonlight hikes. Of course you can see. It's a whole other experience to be guided by moonlight, isn't it?"

Willa laughed, "I thoroughly enjoyed last night. I expect I would have enjoyed the running, too, had we a different reason for doing it."

Sabra Jane accepted a lemonade and sat down.

"Actually, I did enjoy it," Willa corrected herself, "up to the moment my foot found that stone."

"From beauty and fear to sheer terror," Edith handed the cookies to Willa with a melodramatic flourish, "all in the flick of an instant."

"That's one dramatic catharsis I choose to live for a long while without repeating," Willa chuckled.

"For a moment there," Edith raised her glass, "I was afraid we had lost the opportunity to make such choices."

"You were awfully lucky not to fall," Sabra Jane's words carried separate emphases.

"Yes," Edith and Willa agreed simultaneously.

They sat for a moment in silence. Edith glanced again at Seven Days Work. The height was stupefying. And no one except the fellow with the flashlight would have seen or heard them during their long fall. No one at all.

"What if he'd had a gun," Sabra Jane's eyes had widened. "What if he had tried to shoot you. What if he had tried to force you off the cliff."

"Daggett thought he might have had a gun," Willa's response was almost contemplative, "and for some reason chose not to use it. Maybe with the dark, the noise, he didn't want to risk a shot."

"He may have realized we weren't close enough to see him," Edith tried to make a different sense of it, "not to identify him, anyway."

"And don't forget, he had been there all that time inspecting the place," Willa continued to think out loud. "He must have realized there was nothing there to incriminate him, so why shoot. He took off running instead."

"Yes," the word came quickly with Sabra Jane's nod, red waves following the toss of her hair, "but what was he looking for? And who was he?"

THE sound of the Chevrolet's motor gave way to the sharp bang of a car door.

"Hey, what's all this now? You best watch where you step,"

Roy Sharkey's hoarse protest barely preceded Little John Winslow and Constable Daggett. They rounded the corner of the cottage, Daggett carrying a large pillowcase with something heavy inside. Loosely draped, it swung with his stride.

"Good day, ladies," Daggett called out. Little John, a few paces behind, nodded at them.

"Hello," Willa rose. Sabra Jane was already on her feet.

"Don't disturb yourselves, ladies, please," Daggett waved with his free hand.

Edith sank back. Willa and Sabra Jane, already up, started across the lawn to retrieve more chairs. At a stern glance from Daggett, Little John joined them but managed to maintain his distance from Sabra Jane.

"I've brought something to show you," Daggett raised the pillowcase toward Edith. When the chairs were in place, Daggett still stood. He held the bag forward.

"Show us," Willa commanded.

Daggett took his time with the unveiling, scrunching the pillowcase to bring the object to the surface yet keeping cloth between his fingers and the object inside.

It turned out to be the largest flashlight Willa and Edith had ever seen. The light itself was at least eight inches in diameter, possibly ten, Edith guessed. And its handle must hold a dozen batteries, easily a dozen. It must weigh a great deal, she reached out to touch it.

"Sorry," Daggett swung the bag away, "I can't let you do that. Possible prints. But I simply couldn't wait to show you," he confessed.

"Wonderful," Willa leaned forward. "It looks like it must be the flashlight, all right. But where on earth did you find it?"

"That's the wonderful part," Daggett's laugh was self-conscious, "I can't say that I did." He placed the pillowcase on the ground at his feet and sat down. "It simply appeared on the seat of my car."

"I beg your pardon?" Willa asked.

"There it was when I came out after dinner. Could have been there all day," Daggett opened his hand and pointed toward the light again. "There it was, large as life, sitting by itself on the passenger's side."

"But who? Why?" Willa puzzled.

"I have no idea."

"No idea?" It was Sabra Jane's turn to express surprise.

"That's right, none," Daggett eyes met Sabra Jane's.

Willa interrupted, "Where were you when it happened?"

"At home, eating dinner. First real meal Elizabeth and I have had in some time," Daggett mused. "Sat down at noon and probably didn't finish until shortly before two." He glanced at Edith, "I'm sure the person who put the torch there wiped off any finger prints, but you just can't be too careful about things like that. I have to check it out."

"Of course," Edith smiled, "it was thoughtless of me to try to touch it. I've read Agatha Christie, after all."

Daggett laughed, and Little John, whose silence had become notable, finally asked, "Who's Christie?"

Daggett laughed again. "I was on my way after dinner to pay visits to Rob Feeney and young James, but when I opened my car door, there was this torch. It took me a minute to realize what it was."

They sat in silence, everyone looking at the bag with the torch. Daggett accepted a cookie from the dish but shook his head at lemonade. Little John helped himself to both, ignoring for the moment that it was Sabra Jane who passed the cookies.

"I checked for footprints, of course," Daggett chewed for a moment then shrugged. "Nothing there. Gravel driveway must have obscured them," he swung his foot across the grass as though covering his tracks. "Elizabeth saw no one, and Jennifer was gone. So I retrieved an old pillowcase and got ready to take the torch into the office. But I wanted you to see it first. Then I remembered that young James might actually be here. And then Little John flagged me. And then, well, here we are."

"Yes, well," Little John moved his body toward the front of his chair.

All three women turned to look at him.

"You do think this might be the torch you saw last night?" Daggett's question recaptured their attention.

"It certainly looks like it could be," Edith responded.

"I agree," Willa nodded.

"Perhaps if we saw it lit at night," Edith glanced over at Seven Days Work, "we would be certain."

"Yes. Good idea," Willa shifted toward the front of her chair.

"Only a few fellows use a torch like this," Daggett advised, "almost all of them on their boats."

"Wonderful," Sabra Jane cried out, "you'll get him now."

Daggett gave his full attention to Sabra Jane for the first time that afternoon.

"I didn't expect to find you here," Daggett's smile remained pleasant. "When did you arrive?"

XIV

"THANKS AGAIN FOR the vote of confidence," Sabra Jane hugged them both and slid behind the wheel of her Reo, "and for the lemonade, as well."

"Think nothing of it. It's we who owe you," Willa swept her hand toward the partial wall where sprigs of sedum and herbs already rode jauntily among the rocks, their roots taking hold.

Willa and Edith watched as the Reo followed Roy Sharkey's wagon, then swung around it and disappeared into the trees. Sharkey had promised that he and young James would deliver the final loads the next afternoon. Daggett's Chevrolet, bearing the flashlight and Little John Winslow, had already driven off.

From the Red Trail

"That putrid, puffed-up pouch of foul air," Willa growled on the way back to their chairs.

Edith picked up the lemonade jug and several glasses. Willa retrieved the tray.

"Why Constable Daggett ever allows Little John Winslow to tag along, I'll never understand."

Edith held her peace. Willa had been in and out of sorts all afternoon. She was out again, Edith surmised. And sympathized. Little John Winslow was an impossible man.

"Detective Winslow, reporting for duty," Willa tut-tutted and pulled herself to attention, adding a mock salute. Then she glared at the chair in which Sabra Jane Briggs had been sitting, "You. You with the red hair. You're the guilty party. Must be. No one else here with red hair, is there."

Edith laughed.

"Logic, deduction. That's the ticket," Willa harrumphed and grabbed Edith's arm. "I demand you arrest this red-haired heathen, Constable," Willa pointed to the empty chair and shook Edith's arm. "Well, sir, what are you waiting for?"

"Exactly like," Edith applauded Willa's performance.

"It's nice to know such intellect is on the loose," Willa began to chuckle, "don't you think?"

"We should always be so safe," Edith felt almost like giggling.

DAGGETT found it mildly amusing that Little John's mustache made several violent leaps, almost as if his lips had gone into spasm.

"Why ask me where I was?" Little John's mustache made another leap. He placed great emphasis on the *I*.

Daggett pressed his foot on the accelerator.

"Why don't you ask the witch where she was?" Little John squared his shoulders against the seat. "Or James where he was? Young James has one of those shirts, I heard you say so."

Daggett looked forward to the moment he could drop Little John off at Tinsley's Pharmacy.

"Well?"

"I will ask James, you needn't worry," Daggett spoke with just enough volume to carry over the noise of the Chevrolet's engine. "But I'm asking you now. Routine, remember? Means we ask everyone everything."

Daggett momentarily considered going into Tinsley's himself to purchase some aspirin. He should never have given Little John a ride in the first place. Daggett patted his pocket for the reassuring pipe. Little John seemed so contrite, almost remorseful when Daggett stopped the car. He said he wanted to go along, he didn't care where, he wanted someone to talk to.

Then Little John got in and said nothing. Daggett shook his head. Nothing at all. Except that nonsense he spouted before the ladies. Daggett's hand reached again for his pipe. Perhaps the aspirin could wait. He should waste no time checking out Jackson's Drygoods and the Boat Supply at Seal Cove. One of them must sell oversized torches. And he still had to drop by Rob Feeney's office and swing over to visit with young James. It would be another long day.

Daggett glanced again at Little John, "I'm waiting for your answer."

"I wasn't anywhere special."

Little John actually squirmed. Daggett was amazed.

"I was home and in bed by ten," Little John turned to face Daggett fully. "Ask Anna if you don't believe me."

"And this afternoon?"

"When you saw me," Little John returned his eyes to the road, "I was heading toward Tinsley's from McDaniels'. Eva had asked me to stop by after noon. Had something she wanted me to look at," he turned his head away.

"What time did you get there?"

"Must have been half-past one."

"When did you leave?"

"Soon after. You saw me."

"When did you leave home to go to McDaniels'?"

"I didn't leave home," Little John glanced out the window on his side of the car again, "I wasn't there. Had some biscuits at the bakery."

"You had a large breakfast?"

"If you must know," Little John swung around to face Daggett again, his cheeks bearing odd purple splotches, "Anna isn't speaking to me."

"Sorry to hear that."

"This morning she refused to cook my breakfast," the words flew out of Little John's mouth. "I don't know what's gotten into that woman."

Daggett kept his eyes on the road.

"Can't anybody understand women anyway," Little John shrugged, "ever since Eve. Adam sure never understood her. If he had, we wouldn't be in this mess," he gestured broadly.

Daggett felt a smile rise. He suppressed it.

"I don't know why I try," Little John sighed.

By the time Daggett returned to his office from Seal Cove, it was ten minutes past six. He had already missed Feeney, and he had promised young James he wouldn't stop by until well after six. He could afford half an hour or so for his pipe. Time enough, he hoped, to go through the day's mail and check back through his notes. Too many places sold oversized torches, Daggett placed the notebook on his desk. And too many people bought them.

A quick glance at the pile on his desk suggested that his mail contained the usual assortment of government correspondence. Daggett's occasional secretary, Jane Hobson, had apparently come in to straighten up the office and open his mail. She left it stacked to the right of his blotter.

Daggett let himself sink deep into his chair. He undid the buttons on his jacket and placed his notebook on the blotter. Then he took out his tobacco pouch and pipe. No sense rushing, no matter how short the time.

Daggett raised his feet to the desktop and tamped tobacco firmly into the bowl, but when he reached for the tin of matches, which he had taken out of his pocket and placed next to the ashtray, he noticed the sheet on the bottom of the mail. It was a telegram. New Bedford, Massachusetts. He began there.

Not one John T. Brown in all of New Bedford. No such customer at Chin's Chinese Laundry on West 13th Street.

Chin's did, however, do shirts on a regular basis for a John Thomas Bush. White shirts with French cuffs, Daggett drew deep on his pipe. Chin's was concerned about this Mr. Bush. He had dropped off his last order Saturday, June twenty-ninth and never returned. The order he picked up on the twenty-ninth contained six starched shirts and a navy blue suit. Daggett opened his notebook and reached for a pen.

John Thomas Bush's clothes were expensive. His suits carried a Boston tailor's label, Daggett began to place check marks next to parallel items in his notebook. The physical description of John Thomas Bush matched precisely what Daggett knew of John T. Brown, Daggett expelled the smoke from his lungs in a concentrated stream.

Mr. Bush had no criminal record in New Bedford, but he was well known to the police. A girlfriend had disappeared. The police investigated but had never been able to pin anything on him. Bush might be an alias. He divided his time between New Bedford and Detroit, Daggett found himself breaking into a grin.

The New Bedford police thought Bush a gambler and probable bootlegger. Rum customer, the telegram concluded. Wry sense of humor, the lieutenant from New Bedford. With a wide grin,

147

Daggett placed the yellow sheet exactly in the center of his blotter and ran his hand over it several times, as though ironing out wrinkles.

Whatever else he did this evening, he would take time to fire a telegram back to New Bedford asking for everything they had on John Thomas Bush. He would send new telegrams to New York and Boston to see what they had on a Mr. John Thomas Bush. Maybe if he made their jobs easier, they would come up with something after all. And he would ask Doc McCauley to get what prints he could from the corpse. The Federal Bureau of Investigation in Washington, DC might be able to find a match. If Bush was an alias like Brown, the FBI could tell him. Daggett had never had occasion to use them before, but he understood the FBI now had the best records in the world.

"JAMES isn't usually so careless, you know," Mary Daniels placed one hand on her son's shoulder and lowered the coffee pot in the other to pour steaming black coffee into Constable Daggett's cup, "especially not with a brand-new shirt."

"No, I'm sure James is not careless," Daggett reached for the sugar.

"Well, I was this time, that's for certain," for one second James Daniels looked directly at Daggett. "Before I could catch it, it went overboard. So I'm sorry, Mr. Daggett, I just don't have that shirt anymore."

Mary Daniels gestured with the coffee pot toward James. He nodded and raised his cup. She poured his coffee and moved around the table to pour herself another cup. Then she returned the pot to the stove and filled a large plate with freshly baked gingerbread. She placed it on the flower-patterned oilcloth next to Daggett's notebook. Daggett sat with his pencil poised.

"When did you wear the shirt?"

"I wore it that morning, first day out," James blew on his coffee, "because of the chill."

"It was a nice warm shirt," Mary Daniels sipped from her cup and nudged the gingerbread closer to Daggett.

Daggett lowered his pencil.

"Then, I don't know," James glanced at the clock above the stove, "by ten or eleven it warmed up and I took the shirt off. I don't remember what I was doing, but I put it down on the side of the boat. Guess I wasn't thinking," he tried a sip, then blew again on his cup. "Next I knew, it was gone."

"Notice anything unusual about the shirt?" Daggett helped himself to a piece of gingerbread and pushed the plate toward James, "any loose seams or tears or rips that you remember?"

"Don't recall any," James traced the pattern on the oilcloth with his cup. "Why?"

"Buttons missing, anything like that?"

"Don't think so," James reached for the gingerbread.

"Sam carry a torch on his boat?"

James paused and cocked his head, "Of course."

"What size?"

"The usual."

"Any oversized?"

"The long one, you mean?"

Daggett nodded.

"S'pose so," James took a large bite of gingerbread.

"Know where he got it?"

"No, why do you want to know?"

"Sam ever run liquor on his boat?"

"Of course not," James swallowed and swung his head away to cough. Something was caught in his throat.

"James wouldn't go out with Sam if he did anything like that," Mary watched until her son stopped coughing.

Daggett pressed on, "You and Sam got back when, did you say?"

"Not until eleven or so," James cleared his throat and sat straighter in his chair, then glanced again at the clock, "just ahead of the storm."

"Not enough ahead. James came in dripping wet, he did," Mary began to laugh.

"That's true," James confessed.

"Very soon now he's going to drip water all over somebody else's clean floor," Mary winked at Daggett, "at least he will if Jenny Dawson has anything to say about it."

Daggett watched the flush rise from the base of James' neck. It had been a long time since anyone had teased him that way about Elizabeth.

"Got water all over my floor last night, he did," Mary continued. "Always does," she raised her hands in a shrug. "That's a man for you."

Daggett chuckled, enjoying Mary's warmth.

"What I don't understand," Edith trimmed the wick in their oil lamp, "is why anyone would put that flashlight right in the Constable's lap." Light leapt again into the corners of their sitting room.

"That is a puzzle," Willa rested the open pages of Francis Parkman against her stomach. "Perhaps the idea was that if the man turned it in, so to speak, he wouldn't have to hide it."

"As long as Daggett has the flashlight, he doesn't have to find it, is that what you mean?" Edith rose to stir the ashes in the fireplace and put another log on to burn.

"That's right."

"Clever," Edith poked the log into place.

"Yes," Willa tapped an open pack of cigarettes against her palm.

"And plausible," Edith settled into her rocker and put her feet on the hassock. Willa moved her slippered feet to make room.

"That would mean our man has a certain assurance and a cool sort of intelligence, wouldn't it?"

"I suppose," Willa struck a safety match, "at least he would have to be wise to the ways of the police," she said between puffs.

The Lucky Strikes were damp from the previous night. They had forgotten to put the open pack in the sun to dry.

"That would mean an experienced criminal," Edith picked up her book, "or a very smart prankster."

"Exactly," Willa exhaled.

"SOMEONE either knew very well what he was doing and had good reason for doing it," Daggett nodded to his wife, "or he was confused beyond measure."

"Well, finish buttoning your pajamas and come to bed," Elizabeth plumped up his pillow.

"What I can't figure out is why. Why he was there in the first place," Daggett sat on the edge of the bed and removed his shoes and socks.

"No need to figure anything more tonight."

"Had to be an islander," Daggett swung his legs under the covers and shoved his shoulders deep into the pillow.

"Why an islander?"

"Who else would carry an oversized torch?"

"But an islander," Elizabeth turned to Daggett, her voice hushed, "why would an islander kill someone from the States?"

"That's a good question," Daggett smiled at his wife. "Of course," he paused to yawn deeply, "it is still possible that Mr. Bush's death was accidental."

Daggett closed his eyes and felt the tension ease out of his body. This was his lull before the storm, his chance to think through what he had to do next. He stretched until he felt his toes reach the bottom of the bed.

"Accidental?"

The pillow next to Daggett's ear crinkled. Elizabeth was leaning toward him.

"We know that the person in the red shirt was with Mr. Bush, but we don't know that his actions caused Mr. Bush's death."

"Oh. But then how . . . "

"The person in the red shirt stood close to the cliff, closer than Mr. Bush. And Mr. Bush went off head first. That could suggest a plunge or a leap," Daggett opened his eyes to glance at his wife, "not a shove. So the correct question is why," he closed his eyes again.

"And where," Elizabeth touched his shoulder, "where is that person in the red shirt and why did he hide."

"Yes," Daggett felt a second yawn begin somewhere near the base of his diaphragm. "It is also possible," he struggled to continue around the edges of the yawn, "that the person in the red shirt and the person with the torch are not one and the same."

"But then why . . . "

"The person with the torch may simply have been curious about what happened to Mr. Bush," Daggett forced his eyes open and reached for the clock on the nightstand. "Maybe he was afraid to go during the day. Didn't want to raise suspicion. Or maybe he couldn't go then. Tied up at work," Daggett finished winding the clock and set the alarm for five-thirty, "or maybe he was out at sea."

"And the red shirt?" Elizabeth propped herself on one elbow.

"The red shirt was free enough to be on the trail at Seven Days Work during at least one afternoon," Daggett lay back and stared at the pattern on the bedroom's tin ceiling. Elizabeth had painted it an off-white.

"Wouldn't that suggest that the man in the red shirt was not an islander?"

Daggett turned his head to face Elizabeth, "That's another question altogether."

152

"Are there others?"

"Well," Daggett wiggled his toes, "just who was John Thomas Bush? Why did he use an alias? Is Bush a second alias? And what was he doing on Grand Manan?"

"Four good questions."

"And here's a fifth," Daggett reached over to push a stray hair off Elizabeth's forehead and slip it behind her ear, "who on Grand Manan knew John Thomas Bush?"

"Yes, that is a good one," Elizabeth nestled her head on her husband's shoulder.

Daggett reached to extinguish the light.

ERIC DAWSON heard the rustle a moment before Jocko's puppy burst through the hedge. The Dawsons' porch light caught the puppy in full flight. The moment it landed, it leapt again.

"A little late to be walking your dog, isn't it?"

The sight of Little John Winslow struggling with his son's puppy over a heavy string grocery sack filled with pink papers was as good as any slapstick in the moving pictures. Little John pulled, the puppy skidded. Then the puppy pulled, and Little John braced his legs. Then Little John began to tip forward.

"Need help?"

"Blasted dog," Little John planted himself more firmly.

The puppy tugged and swayed. Finally Little John succeeded in raising the sack and brought it to rest on his chest.

"Jocko out this late?"

"In bed with the rest."

The puppy yapped. Little John stuck a foot out to hold him at bay. The dog grabbed the toe of his boot began to wag Little John's foot back and forth. Little John ignored him.

"Here," he handed a sheaf of papers to Eric, "might as well lighten my load."

Eric raised the top page up to the light.

"Got to distribute these. All of them. Special edition I helped put together," Little John's mustache twitched once above his grin.

Emblazoned just below the *Recipe Exchange* was The Dragon Lady, followed by a recipe consisting chiefly of ladyfingers topped with red frosting. Directly across from The Dragon Lady, in equally large letters, appeared Daggett's Delight, A Rocky Beach Fudge.

"Can't you and Eva McDaniels find something else to make jokes about?"

"Murder is no joke." Little John shook his foot, but the puppy's sharp teeth held tight.

XV

"NOTHING LIKE THIS has ever happened before," Geneva Andrews exclaimed at the door of the room John Thomas Bush had occupied. The door stood open.

Daggett studied the room's disheveled contents. Drawers from both bureau and wash stand littered the bed. Blankets and sheets and the bed's yellow chenille spread trailed off its edge and onto the floor. Pillows lay rumpled, one still on its side, its case half torn. Only the rocker remained as it was.

"I just came up to clean Mr. Brown's room, the next guest comes today," Geneva rushed through her explanation, "and this is what I found."

"His name turns out not to be Brown, Geneva," the cadence of Daggett's speech was thoughtful. "It was apparently Bush, John Thomas Bush."

"He lied about his name?"

Daggett watched Geneva's eyes grow large.

"Seems so."

"Frightening business this, Constable," Harvey Andrews' heavy tread came up the stairs behind them. Harvey nodded toward the open door of the room, "No idea anything might be wrong in here. Never heard a thing."

Both the stairs and the hallway were carpeted. A thin carpet also covered most of the floor in the room.

"It could have happened any time between Wednesday and today."

Harvey put his arm around his wife.

155

Geneva seemed about to cry.

"No one needed the room, so we just left it the way it was after you took his things away."

"Makes you wonder, doesn't it," Daggett moved forward.

Harvey nodded, "Why would anyone search a room when it was clear that all of Mr. Brown's . . . or Mr. Bush's," Harvey caught himself, "that all of Mr. Bush's personal belongings had been removed?"

"That's a mystery, all right," Geneva perked up.

Of the two windows occupying the outer wall, one stood open. Not unusual for July, Daggett glanced at the door. No marks near the latch.

"We don't lock our doors," Harvey followed the course of Daggett's gaze. "Never felt the need. May have to now, I suppose."

"I doubt it. This doesn't change much on a permanent basis," Daggett bent down to check under the bed. "Whoever did this probably won't do anything like it again. Not here anyway," he finished his inspection. "For now, though, I would like for everyone to stay out of this room," Daggett pulled the door shut, wrapping his hand first in his handkerchief. "Just until I come back to dust for prints, you understand," he smiled his reassurance.

"I'm sure Constable Daggett will take care of everything," Geneva's responding smile was meant to be brave.

"Back stairs?" Daggett glanced again at Harvey.

"Around the corner there," Harvey nodded toward the hallway that ran from the main staircase to the rear of the building, "goes down to the kitchen."

"I'll have a look," Daggett led the way, "then I'd like to see your guest list again."

CONSTABLE DAGGETT would simply have to wait until later that evening for the S. S. Grand Manan to return from St. Andrews, Rob Feeney repeated. No way to tell who the passengers would be before the steamer docked in North Head. Yes, Agent Feeney would be happy to give Daggett the lists of passengers and crew from the day John Thomas Bush died. Yes, Feeney had been on the crossing with John Thomas Bush, though he remembered little beyond his suit and his eyes. Especially his eyes. And yes, the fellow named Matthew Johnson had arrived at the dock this morning in time for the crossing. Feeney had noticed he was a little out of breath. Feeney knew him by sight. One of that foursome at Swallowtail. Modern, wealthy, played a lot of tennis. Or so it would seem from his clothes.

Daggett nodded hello to Feeney's assistant, the pleasant young man named Dobbs, and settled into the chair next to Feeney's desk. His body felt heavy. He glanced over the list Feeney handed him of Tuesday's passengers and crew. No surprises there. Feeney kept a neat desk. Daggett tucked the list into his pocket and retrieved his notebook. He opened it against his knee and directed Feeney's attention to this morning.

The steamer had left at seven, with stops at Campobello, Eastport, and Cumming's Grove. It arrived in St. Andrews at eleven and would turn around again to make all the same stops, leaving St. Andrews at one-thirty that afternoon and arriving in North Head sometime around seven, depending on the tides. Rob Feeney had no way of knowing who would be on it. Passengers often bought their tickets on board.

Between Tuesday afternoon, when John Thomas Bush had died, and Friday evening, most of those who had come and gone were islanders, Rob Feeney was sure of that. On Wednesday, a party of three arrived, headed for The Anchorage. Young women, all regulars from New York. Feeney remembered them from the previous year. They laughed a lot and told funny stories. On Thursday, three older women for Rose Cottage and on Friday, a family of four for The Marathon. The women came from Massachusetts. The family were Canadians, Rob believed, from Montreal. Business was unusually slow this year.

As for those leaving the island, two sets of two from Rose Cottage left on Wednesday, along with a threesome from The Marathon and a couple from Swallowtail. Wednesday's passengers had disembarked, as usual, at the various ports between Grand Manan and St. Stephen. Thursdays, the steamer was unavailable for outward bound travel, the constable knew that. On Friday, only a single non-islander was outward bound, a man from The Swallowtail Inn. Boarding with him was Burt Isaacs.

Wednesday's twosome from The Swallowtail were the Reimers, the Friday solitaire was Jackson Knoll. The Reimers were older, white haired, probably retired. Knoll was thirtyish and muscular with dark curly hair. He stood well over six feet tall and wore a dark green windbreaker with light pants and a tie. He seemed extremely athletic and fit. Rob Feeney was certain Isaacs was traveling with him.

Daggett remembered Knoll from his handwriting on The Swallowtail register. The pen had spread to accommodate him. Jackson Knoll from Toronto. When questioned, Knoll had said he did not know Mr. Brown or anyone else on the island. Daggett had thought it unnecessary to question him further. An oversight, perhaps serious. Daggett would wire Toronto.

According to Feeney, Isaacs had said little to Knoll and nothing at all to Rob Feeney. But Isaacs and Knoll were definitely traveling together, the agent declared. And they knew each other, he was sure of that. They shared a certain level of comfort in each other's proximity.

"You can always tell when people know each other," Rob Feeney explained, "you just know. You don't always know how you know, but you do. Friends, relatives, lovers, married couples. Maybe you don't know what they are to each other, but you can feel the connection. There's a certain ease between them. It's like overhearing a conversation without words. You know?"

Daggett said he did.

There may have been a flicker of familiarity between Isaacs and that fellow Bush, too. Rob Feeney paused to remember but he couldn't be certain.

Daggett cleared his throat and turned a page in his notebook.

This morning, at any rate, had been a different matter, according to Feeney. No one seemed to know anyone else. Crossing with Matthew Johnson were the Ridleys, a middle-aged couple from Rose Cottage, and Richard Miller, a young man from The Marathon. Feeney exchanged pleasantries with each of the men before they boarded, but none of them had talked to anyone else. The Rose Cottage couple kept entirely to themselves.

Feeney had no idea why Johnson was traveling alone or where he was going. Daggett thought again about Johnson's claim that he used separations to maintain his marriage.

"IT is a scandal," James Enderby's hand found its way to his vest, "an absolute scandal." Enderby hooked his right thumb in his watch pocket. His other hand grasped a bag of fresh sugar donuts, "The notion of Sabra Jane Briggs as some sort of scarlet woman is preposterous."

"Surely people will see how silly this is," Jesse Martin agreed.

Edith spread the large pink sheet of paper on the counter next to the bakery's cash register and read it through carefully. "Ludicrous," she agreed when she finished reading. "And they call her a murderer," her voice raised in rare emphasis, "such nonsense."

"Some folks are talking about asking the constable to interfere," Emma Parker brought a tray of lemon cupcakes from the back room to the display case.

"Well, censorship is never . . ."

"Confiscate all those papers, I say," Emma's gray curls bounced in Edith's direction.

"If you ask me," Jesse Martin interrupted, her blue eyes flashing, "Constable Daggett should arrest the pair of them. Recipes are one thing, jokes or no. But this," Jesse stabbed her finger at the article entitled VIXEN SKIRTS CONSTABLE, "this has got to break some kind of law." The byline announced the author as J. Winslow, Sr.

"Perhaps Miss Briggs or Constable Daggett will consider bringing suit," James Enderby raised his hand from his watch fob and cleared his throat.

"Wouldn't bother me to see the constable throw Mr. J. Winslow, Sr. into jail," Emma Parker unloaded her tray three donuts at a time. "Teach him a lesson."

"Make life easier for his wife too," Jesse Martin giggled.

"ALL of North Head is incensed," Edith reported to the women of Whale Cove, who were gathering in the dining room for their noon meal.

"It's too bad. It's just too bad," Jacobus shook her head and set the coffee pot down long enough to order Matt out of the dining room.

Matt's tail drooped but she began her lone journey through the sitting room and out the front door.

"It's not libel they should be arrested for so much as bad writing," Ethelwyn Manning raised her eyes from the pink sheet in her hands.

Jacobus chuckled.

"And even worse jokes," Katherine Schwartz nudged Manning, who turned the sheet over. They continued to read.

"I had not planned to go with you to The Anchorage this evening," Eloise Derby took a moment to smooth the material of her blue skirt before drawing her legs under the table and draping a napkin across her lap, "but I believe now I shall. Miss Briggs needs our support."

"Voorhees the Viking and Brunnhilde Briggs," Peter Coney called from the kitchen door as though advertising a burlesque show. A serving girl with a large tray squeezed past her.

"It's going to be a delightful evening," Winifred Bromhall breezed into the dining room.

"Valkyries to the rescue," Margaret Byington called from across the room.

Willa flourished a fist.

Everyone laughed.

Edith joined in. She loved to hear them laugh.

"I can hardly wait until evening," Margaret's voice carried more energy than usual. "You'll join us, won't you?" She pulled out her chair between Willa and Edith.

"I'm afraid not, and I'm actually sorry we won't be going with you this time," Willa looked rueful.

"Sabra Jane will be in rare form, you know."

"Brunnhilde Briggs, indeed," Winifred Bromhall sat down opposite Margaret. She put a hand on Willa's arm, "You and Edith really should come with us."

"I'm sure there'll be room," Margaret was hearty. "Claude Gilmore is driving."

Edith looked at Willa, who smiled back, her expression shifting from sad to mirthfull. "I'm afraid not. But this way," she turned to Margaret, "we'll have your breakfast stories to look forward to."

"Stories are better when the audience doesn't know the plot, you know," Willa reached into the basket of fresh biscuits the serving girl placed before her.

"Yes," Edith laughed, "but we'll let you in on something not exactly in their script at the moment. Watch for the horns on their helmets. They're in grave danger of sudden removal."

161

"Those sort of Valkyrie cattle horn affairs?" Margaret raised her hands and drew them away as though she were shaping a pair of horns on her head.

"That's right," Willa approved of the demonstration, "they're made of papier mache."

"Yesterday while we were working on the wall," Edith explained, "Sabra Jane described their costumes to us."

"And confided that they had a desperate problem. They ran out of glue and could find none on the island," Willa finished Edith's thought.

"Perhaps we have some glue," Mary Jordan interrupted from the next table. Her eyes reflected concern.

"I'm sure we must have some here somewhere," Jacobus finished filling Mary's cup and moved over to their table, "I'll have a look."

"Are you quite certain you won't join us tonight?" Alice Jordan leaned across to address Edith.

"I'm afraid running around in the night has taken its toll on us," Willa pointed to Edith's bandages.

"This whole incident," Edith confided, "has been, well, frankly unsettling."

"You both must be exhilarated and exhausted at the same time," Jacobus switched pots to pour Sanka in Willa's cup.

"Exactly," Willa took a sip.

"The truth is," Edith added, "Willa is falling behind in her writing, and we simply cannot let that happen. She's had too many interruptions already with her poor, painful thumb and trips to California to be with her mother. So tonight we turn in early."

"Hmmm," Margaret nodded with understanding, "and disruptive business this, death and detection."

"Too disruptive," Willa agreed, "makes morning schedules unworkable."

"Morning schedules are always unworkable," Margaret growled.

"No, no," Winifred concurred with Willa, "it's late nights that make mornings impossible. Whenever I'm working on a publisher's deadline, I cannot allow myself even an evening for the theater. It's not the time away or the sleepy morning after," she helped herself to a biscuit, "it's the distraction. I cannot get my mind back into an illustration no matter how interesting the work."

"Precisely," Willa nodded.

"We do understand, but should you change your mind anyway," Alice Jordan left her thought unfinished.

"Thank you," Edith ladled herself a portion of savory mutton stew.

"But you forget," Willa passed the butter, "I also have a reputation to maintain as an irascible recluse." Her eyes crinkled again.

"Let's hear it for the irascibles," Margaret's laughter rolled out.

"That's American slang for the Valkyries, isn't it?" Winifred liked to be sly.

WE generally put the singles in the rear wing. That is what Harvey Andrews had said, nodding toward the hallway that led eventually to Swallowtail's back stairs. Daggett rested his hand midway down the page of his notebook and with his other hand loosened the buttons on his jacket. They're usually not as particular as married folks, that was Harvey's explanation.

But John Thomas Bush had been particular, according to Harvey. He had arranged to have himself placed exactly in the middle of the front section, in a bedroom next to the suite of rooms occupied by the Johnsons and diagonally across from the Jamesons.

Why had he done that, Daggett contemplated the clock on his office wall. Its minute hand clicked forward.

The Reimers had occupied the end room, just beyond the Johnsons and across from the Blackalls of New York. After the Reimers left, their room remained empty. The Jamesons were opposite the

Johnsons, on the back side of the building. No view of the sea there, Daggett narrowed his eyes, though the garden was pleasant enough, he supposed.

The Ainsworths, Harts, and McKinneys were in the other end of the front section. The Ainsworths' two children and their nanny, a Miss Jacobs, had rooms in the rear. So did Jackson Knoll, a big, swaggery fellow Harvey had called him, whose room was opposite Miss Anna Driscoll's. The back stairs were wooden, circular, and narrow. They opened into the kitchen below.

There was usually someone in the kitchen during the day, Geneva had pointed out, and often well into the evening. Except for about two hours Thursday afternoon, someone was usually at the front desk as well, Harvey insisted. The desk was next to the staircase and if Harvey were not there, he was usually in the sitting room or parlor, somewhere close to the stairs. Thursday Geneva kept an eye on the desk while Harvey went to get supplies and have his hair cut. No one should have been able to slip up to rifle through Mr. Bush's room without their knowledge.

But someone did rifle through Mr. Bush's room, Daggett's hand paused again near the bottom of the page. Mr. Bush's empty room.

Daggett had made no effort to curtail anyone's movements. Perhaps he should have.

According to Harvey, Jackson Knoll's leave-taking had been unexpected. Knoll's original booking was to have extended another week, through the following Friday. Knoll told Andrews he was leaving because there was nothing to do on Grand Manan.

So where had Jackson Knoll gone? Did he really know Burt Isaacs? What about the possibility that Isaacs knew Bush? And where was Matthew Johnson? Too many questions, too many unanswered questions.

The Jamesons and Johnsons were booked through the following Saturday. As originally Mr. Bush had been, Daggett's hand paused again.

Did Mr. Bush know the Johnsons? The Jamesons? Anyone on Grand Manan? Daggett reached for his pipe, glad for a quiet moment. The hands on the clock continued to tick forward.

Once Little John got hold of these complications—a rummaged room and disappearing guests—Sabra Jane Briggs might be loosed from the pillory, but Daggett's competence would certainly be challenged. Daggett questioned it himself.

XVI

"Well, Miss, I'm sure I don't know what's happened exactly, but I cannot deliver your rocks today," Roy Sharkey's cigar bobbed, "not without young James to help me."

"No, of course not," Edith lowered her paint brush and glanced back toward the cottage. They hadn't expected Roy Sharkey this early in the afternoon. Willa had gone back to the attic to write letters.

"You've still got quite a pile of rocks back there," Sharkey nodded toward the cottage. "Should keep you busy enough."

"Absolutely. And Miss Briggs is putting on a program at The Anchorage tonight so she is not joining us this afternoon. We're in no rush."

"Yes, ma'am," Sharkey's nod was vigorous. "The Missus was talking about going tonight, but I say it's too far. A lot of North Headers are going, though. Eva McDaniels, now, she's our neighbor, she's riding with the Winslows. Leastways with Little John and his boy," Sharkey's smile grew wide.

"Yes," Edith wetted her brush.

"You read the *Recipe Exchange*?"

"I did the last issue."

"Then you know who Eva McDaniels is," Sharkey looked hopeful. Edith nodded gravely.

Sharkey put his hands in his pockets and took them out again. "Can't account for young James," he lifted his cap to scratch the top of his head. "He wasn't home like he said he would be, and his mother had no idea where he might be. His fiancée neither," Sharkey rested most of his weight on one leg. The folds of his stomach followed the tilt of his body. "Mary was all in a fluster. Said James hasn't been himself lately, worrying as he does about money and wanting to get married."

"He seems a nice enough young man," Edith cocked her heels on her stool. "Polite, industrious." This could take a while, she flicked her brush and wetted it again.

"William Dawson's Jenny," Sharkey pulled a blue bandana out of his pocket. "That's who James plans to marry," he wiped grit off his forehead just below the line of his cap. The afternoon had turned warm. "It's her brother found the body."

"Yes. Well," Edith smiled and rested her hand on her knee, "if Eric Dawson's sister is anything like her brother, young James will have a fine wife."

"That's how I came to get him to haul these rocks," Sharkey stuffed the bandana into his pocket and placed his cap on his head. His fingernails were crusted with dirt.

Edith shifted the brush to her bandaged hand and used her good hand to scratch her ear.

"James has always done odd jobs because his mother needed the money. Jim Daniels died when James was a baby, you see, and Mary never would have anyone else. Proud woman that one," Sharkey's frown seemed to still his cigar.

Edith waited.

"Yes," Sharkey cleared his throat. "Well," he did it again. "But now that James wants a wife, he's taking on even more work."

"Perhaps that is what happened today. Something more lucrative came up," Edith shifted the brush back to her good hand.

Two gulls swung through the air. Edith turned to watch them fly over the weir.

"Yes, ma'am, could be," Sharkey glanced at the gulls. "All the same, it's an odd bit of business."

DAGGETT felt enormously foolish standing by himself on the cliff at Seven Days Work. This would be the third time he had been over this territory. But he also felt reasonably certain that whoever had gone to the trouble of searching the cliff in the middle of the night and turning John Thomas Bush's Swallowtail room inside out had not found what they were looking for.

Daggett checked the room thoroughly himself before removing Mr. Bush's belongings. He felt under pillows and blankets, raised the mattress, looked behind pictures, ran his hand along the edges of shelves in the wardrobe. Routine, by-the-book how-to-find when you don't know what you're looking for, when you don't even know whether you should be looking for something.

Daggett was looking for identification, the missing wallet and passport and keys, anything to say more about the man. He found nothing. Not at Swallowtail and not on Seven Days Work. He hiked the trail several times, searched under and around rocks, and gazed down the cliff toward the sea. Nothing turned up.

What made today different was that someone else was also looking. For what, he couldn't say, but it was obvious they were searching all the same places.

Another difference was that Daggett brought a pair of binoculars with him to study more carefully the sides of the cliff and the beach below. A rain storm and several tides had intervened since his last visit, but a gun, a wallet, a set of keys, or a passport might still be lodged somewhere among the rocks.

Daggett focused his binoculars on the jagged cuts below his feet and began a determined sweep, taking in hundred-yard swathes every ten feet or so. He forced his hands to be slow and his mind to register detail. He prolonged his investigations of crevices and inched his eyes through deepening shadows. The cliff's two-hundred-foot drop took well over an hour to search thoroughly. Finally, Daggett rested his back against a rock and slid down to sit. He rubbed his eyes, stretched his legs, and reached for his pipe. There was plenty of time, he told himself, for a methodical scan of the boulders and rocks on the beach below. It was just four o'clock.

Earlier that afternoon, Daggett had added to his list of telegrams, sending them this time to St. Andrews, St. Stephen, and Montreal. He wanted to follow up on the activities of Jackson Knoll, Burt Isaacs, and Matthew Johnson. Another set of telegrams went to Machias, Calais, and Bangor, three places in Maine Daggett guessed might be able to supply him with information about Jack Watson. Bootlegging was no crime in Canada, but murder was. A last set of telegrams went to Boston and New Bedford. In all of them Daggett requested information about current bootleggers and their runs, added the name of John Thomas Bush, and suggested that Bush might be an alias. The earliest answers, he figured, would not come in before late that evening.

Just off Seven Days Work three seals leapt in unison out of the sea. Two more followed, all five heading north, swimming away from Whale Cove along the north end of the island toward Ashburton Head. Were they to continue on their journey, Daggett shook a match out of his tin box, they would swim past Campobello and the tip of Maine, and head right up the bay past Eastport to St. Andrews. From there they could, if they chose, Daggett struck the match and held it to his pipe, go on in narrowing waters until they reached St. Stephen where the St. Croix River emptied fresh water into the bay. Those were the choices the steamer also made, Daggett blew out a long stream of smoke, the S. S. Grand Manan, which would return this evening from St. Andrews with or without Matthew Johnson on board.

EDITH lowered her binoculars and rested them on the back of Willa's Adirondack.

"That is Constable Daggett, isn't it?"

Edith nodded.

For some moments, Willa had been leaning forward, her hand raised to shade her eyes, squinting toward the two waterfalls on Seven Days Work.

"I wonder what he's looking for," her voice trailed off.

Edith raised the binoculars again and scanned down Seven Days Work. She paused to adjust the focus.

Willa and Edith were watching three seals play their way up the coast when Willa noticed movement on the trail at Seven Days Work. Edith retrieved their binoculars from the cottage, and together they had spent several minutes watching Daggett use his binoculars to scan the cliff.

"Whatever it is he's looking for, he's stopped now. He just propped up his legs and lit his pipe."

"Well, sit and finish your tea then," Willa leaned back in her chair. She placed her feet, still in the loose slippers she preferred for the attic, on the edge of their low wicker table. A saucy red tea pot with two cups perched in the middle.

"Yes," Edith sat down and reached for her cup. Daggett was engrossed in his pipe, his binoculars idle in his lap. He apparently was waiting for the seals to make their next leap. Edith waited too.

"Wait a minute," Willa half rose, pointing up the beach toward Ashburton Head. "What's that?"

Edith set her cup down and focused the glasses for the greater distance. A lone man made his way along the shore, his head covered, eyes lowered to the rocks at his feet. The brim of his hat prohibited Edith from seeing the whole of his face. He paused frequently and changed directions often to skirt the rocks and pockets of salt water left by the tide.

"Do you think he's helping Daggett?"

"I think Daggett would have signaled to him if he were," Edith kept her eyes on the man. He must have been out there for some time without their noticing. His pace was slow, but he had already come a long way down the shore.

"Umm," Willa leaned forward, "it's hard to believe Daggett would send anyone out there with the tide coming in."

The boulders and rocks on the beach below Seven Days Work were so random and large it was rare for anyone to walk there. And the distance between Eel Brook and Whale Cove, the only two places one could get inland and away from the sea, would be intimidating even had there been no danger from the tides. High tide along that coast reached all the way to the cliffs, leaving virtually no beach at all for several hours.

Low Tide Seven Days Work

"You know," Willa ventured, "I don't believe Daggett has noticed him yet."

"He hasn't looked up," Edith observed. "Maybe he hasn't seen Daggett either."

Without binoculars, Willa had the larger view. Edith lifted her eyes a moment to glance at Daggett, then went back to the man.

"Can you see his face?"

"No," Edith scanned the glasses down, "but he's wearing canvas shoes," she stared at a foot taking off from a rock, "and white cotton pants," she caught up with his legs.

"Tennis whites," Willa's voice was excited. "Not an islander, surely."

Edith moved to study the man's head. She could tell that his jaw was clean shaven, but the brim of his hat obscured most his face. The hat was canvas, like his shoes. Its brim flopped.

"Has Daggett seen him yet?"

Edith panned her glasses up. Daggett was enjoying his pipe.

"I don't think so."

"What's that on his back?"

Edith lowered the glasses again to the beach. The man was almost directly below Daggett now and stood bent over at the waist. He seemed to be studying a pool of water at his feet. A brown pack covered his back. Its flap was buckled, but the pack itself looked empty, deflated and slack.

"A hiker's pack, I believe," Edith handed the glasses to Willa, "but he can't be carrying much."

"Ahhh," Willa agreed.

"Do you suppose he doesn't know how dangerous it is with the tide coming in?"

The man had less than an hour if Edith's calculations were correct.

"An off-islander, he might not."

"Daggett could warn him off."

Willa ran the binoculars up the side of the cliff, "I don't think he has seen him yet."

A flash of color caught Edith's eye. "There," Edith grabbed Willa's arm, "over there. Look at Eel Brook." Edith saw the flash again. Blue, a brilliant blue. "Look for something blue."

Willa swung the glasses up and scanned the valley between Seven Days Work and Ashburton Head where Eel Brook worked its way to the sea.

"I don't see anything."

"No." The blue had not returned. "Perhaps I was wrong," Edith dropped her eyes to the bent figure on shore.

"What could it have been?"

"I don't know."

The man uncovered his head.

"Look," Edith reached for Willa's arm again, "he's taking off his hat."

Willa swung the glasses, and Edith shaded her eyes, willing herself to see. The man turned toward them and then away.

"I don't recognize him," Willa tilted her head, then handed the binoculars to Edith, "could be one of those tennis players at Swallowtail."

Edith aimed the glasses at the man and worked up the length of his body. He was certainly fit. The hat had returned to his head. He was leaning over again, reaching down, his left side toward Edith. She couldn't see what attracted him.

"Could be," Edith exhaled slowly. Tennis had never been Edith's game. Louise Pound had so dominated the sport in Lincoln that Edith's younger set had never quite taken an interest. Edith much preferred horseback riding, as had her whole family, but there wasn't much of that on Grand Manan.

The man straightened and put his hand in his pocket. Then he put his hands on his hips and leaned against them so that his back arched. His face rose. Suddenly his body froze, as if he were playing the child's game of Statue. Edith followed his gaze, swinging the glasses upward in time to catch Daggett, binoculars trained down, rising to his feet.

"Look," Willa grabbed Edith's arm and pointed.

Edith shot the glasses down. The man had turned toward them. He began to run.

"Daggett's seen him."

"Yes."

"He's coming this way."

"Yes."

"Do you know him?"

"It may be the man you thought. Johnson, I think his name is."

"With an *h*?"

"Yes."

"Are you certain?"

"No," Edith watched the man leap across rocks. At this rate he would reach Whale Cove in thirty or forty minutes.

The man's hat blew back. The top of his forehead was pink from the sun.

"Daggett will know."

"Yes," Edith raised her glasses.

Daggett had disappeared.

THE glint of light recurred. Eric Dawson dipped his oars, tentatively this time, and stared at the cliff. The dory rolled smoothly beneath him, no longer shooting toward the weir.

"What's this now?"

The sound of his own voice steadied the thumping in Eric's ears. His pulse slowed with the boat. He wasn't sure whether the pounding in his ears was due to exertion or to the sudden start he experienced at the sight of someone on Seven Days Work. Someone in the very place the man had gone off the cliff. Someone wearing red.

Whoever it was was gone now. The glint was the last of him. Sunlight hitting glass or metal, Eric couldn't tell.

Someone else, someone in white, was running along the beach. That's all right, Eric grinned, I'd run too this time of day with the tide coming in. Odd place to be, though, Eric watched the man zigzag.

Eric pulled on the oars. The dory shot forward and Eric's mind with it. He had to get on with his work. How he had let Lizzie talk him into going to The Anchorage tonight when there was so much to do, Eric shook his head. He didn't understand himself sometimes. And that idiot Little John was certain to cause a row.

A gull lifted to Eric's right, and far up the coast, three seals leapt in unison.

The oars creaked. Eric pulled for the weir.

"THEN your understanding," Daggett's eyes narrowed, he made his words deliberate, his voice uninflected, "is that your husband boarded the S. S. Grand Manan this morning for Eastport?"

"That is what I said, Constable Daggett," Maggie Johnson arched an eyebrow and tipped her head in Daggett's direction. She was again ensconced in the arbor swing behind Swallowtail, this time with Jean Jameson beside her. Both women held drinks.

"Never fear, Constable Daggett," Sam Jameson sat opposite, crossing his legs at the knee, "Matt will be back this evening. I'm sure whatever it is can wait."

"Yes," Jameson's wife drained her glass, "what possible hurry could there be? It's not as though any of us are actually leaving this island. Matt has simply gone to a great deal of trouble to find good telephone connections with the States."

"Telephone service on this island is a joke," Maggie Johnson pushed at the ground with her foot.

"Can't do business without good phones, you know."

Daggett thought Jameson's heartiness hollow. Maggie Johnson rattled ice against the sides of her glass.

"Here, let me fix you another," Jameson leapt to his feet, "there's plenty of time before dinner."

Jameson retrieved the women's glasses and turned toward Daggett, an invitation in the lift of his brow.

"None for me."

Jameson disappeared into the Inn.

Daggett's breathing had returned to normal during the drive

from Seven Days Work. He headed straight for Swallowtail in order to arrive before Johnson could reach his wife and friends. What would Johnson's story be, Daggett pushed the accelerator as far down as he dared on the loose gravel of the road to The Whistle. At Tattons Corner, he actually spun the Chevrolet's tires, and when he arrived at the Inn, he leapt from the car without shutting his door.

Johnson couldn't possibly continue to pretend that he had gone to Eastport. But what did his wife or Jameson know of his plans? If Johnson intended to go to Eastport, why hadn't he gone? If he never intended to go, then the whole thing was a dodge. But who was he dodging. And why.

Daggett thought his best chance for getting answers involved alerting no one to the urgency of his visit. Jameson's trek for more drinks could prove troublesome if he happened to notice the driver's door standing ajar on the Chevrolet. But Daggett couldn't be bothered about that now. It was the whereabouts of Matthew Johnson Daggett cared about most. Jameson and the others either didn't know or were pretending not to know about anything Johnson had done since he left them this morning.

It was all Daggett could do not to leap into the Chevrolet and spin away after Johnson. But where to look. And when he found Johnson, as eventually he would, what questions should he ask. What's all this about Eastport? Why did you slip away from the S. S. Grand Manan? How did you spend the day? What were you doing on the beach? What did you put in your pocket? Why did you run? Yes, Daggett reached for his notebook and shifted his weight, when you saw me, why did you run. But Johnson was not there to give answers. Had he been? Could he be hiding now somewhere in the Inn? Daggett had no way of knowing. He turned back to Maggie Johnson.

"Tell me about the business your husband felt he had to conduct."

"Business is business, Constable Daggett. It's all one to me," Maggie Johnson patted a yawn.

"Business is boring, don't you think, Constable?" Jean Jameson pushed the swing away with her foot.

"I pay no attention to any of it," Maggie Johnson leaned into the swing.

Daggett pressed forward, "When did your husband decide to make this trip?"

"During breakfast, I believe. We had nothing else planned for the day," Maggie Johnson inspected her nails. Her hands lay idle in her lap.

"Who did you say your husband planned to call?"

"I have no idea," Maggie Johnson found an imperfection. She rubbed the nail with her thumb.

"Come, Constable," Jean Jameson ran her fingers through her hair, "what has any of this to do with the case you are investigating?"

By the time Willa changed into her shoes and the two of them raced down the trail to Whale Cove, Edith was able to catch only a glimpse of Mr. Johnson. He had almost reached Church Lane on the other side of the cove. He was no longer running but still set a swift pace.

Edith and Willa moved as fast as they dared across the rocky beach. Edith was glad the man had slowed. She had enough running the night before to last a very long while, and they didn't want to catch Mr. Johnson, only keep him in sight.

Neither of them knew why it was important to chase after this fellow, but they were certain they should. Willa said as much lacing her shoes. Edith had simply cried, "Let's go." The expression on Daggett's face had been enough.

The rough footing of Whale Cove demanded most of their

attention, but Edith managed to see that the man did not, as she expected, turn right into North Head. Instead he slipped into the trees and headed up the trail toward Hole in the Wall. For a moment the man's tennis whites flitted through the evergreens that wound in and out, rising above the shoreline with the trail.

"ABSOLUTELY," it was Rob Feeney's turn to frown. "I swear he was on board. I saw him with my own eyes," Feeney shuffled his papers into a pile, then folded his hands and rested them on his desk. He glanced at his calendar and at his clock.

Daggett's eyes followed Feeney's. Ten after six. Feeney should have gone home over an hour ago. But he could keep his own time, he lived by himself.

"Couldn't Johnson have gotten off after you saw him board?"

Feeney returned Daggett's gaze, then let his eyes drift to Daggett's collar and down onto his chest. Daggett knew that Feeney was not really seeing his collar or the buttons on his jacket. Feeney was looking again at the S. S. Grand Manan with Matthew Johnson on board.

"Well, I was busy," Feeney looked Daggett in the eye again, "I suppose he could have slipped off when I wasn't looking."

The rise in Feeney's voice made it almost a question. Daggett chose not to answer.

"No, that doesn't make sense," Feeney shook his head. "Why would he do that," Feeney's voice became insistent, "and why would his wife not know where he was?"

Daggett shrugged. Harvey Andrews had promised to send a boy over the minute Johnson turned up. Daggett glanced out the window. There was no one in sight.

"I'm sure Johnson didn't know Richard Miller, the other fellow on board. Sure of it," Feeney's eyes rose to an area above Daggett's head and began to trace the edges of schedules posted on the wall across from his desk.

Daggett watched Feeney think.

"Or the couple from Rose Cottage."

The clock on Feeney's desk said it would be forty-five minutes until the S. S. Grand Manan returned to its berth. Daggett wished he had help. An assistant, a sergeant. Almost anyone would do. It was not the first time in Daggett's career that he experienced a need to be in three places at once or wanted someone with whom he could discuss the details of a case.

Daggett reached for his pipe, "Tell me again what he wore."

"Tennis whites. Canvas shoes. One of those backpacks the hikers use. A red shirt."

"A red shirt? He was wearing it?"

"Had it slung over his shoulder."

"And what exactly did he say?"

"Nice day for a boat ride, something like that," Feeney shrugged and took a pack of Players out of the center drawer of his desk. He extracted a cigarette, placed it between his lips, and struck a match.

"I don't know what I'm waiting for," Daggett turned in his chair and stretched out his legs. He crossed them at the ankle, "He won't be on board, you know."

Feeney exhaled.

XVII

"DAMN YOU, DAGGETT, let go of me," Little John tried to shake free. "You have no right to do this."

Little John's bluster was no match for Daggett, but Daggett loosened his grip only long enough to push Little John into the Chevrolet and latch onto Jocko.

"You leave that man alone," Eva McDaniels shrilled from behind, "and don't you dare touch that boy."

Daggett shoved Jocko into the back seat of his car and placed his puppy in his lap.

At that moment Daggett felt several sharp tugs at his sleeve. He turned just in time to see Eva McDaniels' paisley clad arm fling itself high in the air and realized with astonishment that the satchel Eva carried for a purse was about to crash into the right side of his head. Daggett deflected the blow.

"What a woman," Little John howled.

"Try something like that again, Eva McDaniels, and I'll consider your purse a weapon and lock you up, too," Daggett roared and brandished the shotgun he had just wrested from Little John.

"You wouldn't dare," Eva took a step back.

"Now see here," Little John tried to push open the car door.

Daggett held it shut.

"Don't worry, folks," Little John puffed himself up to address his remarks to the small audience he had assembled, "not even Daggett would throw a lady into jail."

The McDaniels, the Tinsleys, and Daisy Edwards were arranged in a semicircle before the open car window. Daggett wasn't sure whether they just fell into that formation or meant to separate him from Eva McDaniels, who had lost none of her fierceness.

Finally, Dan McDaniels put a restraining hand on his wife's arm. Eva continued to glare at Daggett, but her anger had lost its edge.

"Take her home now, Dan. Please," Daggett stood braced against the car door. "And the rest of you folks, you leave now, too."

"Dan, Eva," Jason Tinsley offered, backing up to unlock the door to his pharmacy, "why don't you come in and sit down." He turned to the others, "You can all come. Soda's on the house."

Little John pushed against the car door.

"Not you," Daggett blocked Little John. "You sit right there and listen to what I say."

Daggett stepped away from the car, his voice pitched to the small crowd.

"There will be no vigilante justice," Daggett shook Little John's shotgun, "not while I am constable on this island."

"Fine constable you are," Little John growled, "arresting an honest man and letting the guilty go free."

Daggett swung back around, "No posse. No shotguns. No nonsense." He shook the gun again.

Little John turned forward, deliberately ignoring the constable.

Daggett waited until he heard the pharmacy door close behind him, then he popped the shells out of Little John's gun and walked around the car. He tossed the empty gun onto the back seat next to Jocko and put the shells in his pocket.

Jocko took up no room at all. Only his eyes looked large in the back of the car. Daggett slid behind the wheel, opened the choke, and hit the accelerator with his foot. The Chevrolet coughed.

"That woman is a bat out of Hades," Little John hissed between clenched teeth.

"Stop that," Daggett eased in the choke.

"She's guilty as sin," the hiss continued. "Killed him because she hates men."

The engine sputtered and died.

"It's plain as day. But you, you're doing nothing about it," Little John's eyes darted left. His mustache twitched violently.

Daggett pressed the starter. It whirred.

"Why don't you arrest her?"

"Little John," Daggett's voice threatened.

"Everyone knows she wears men's clothes and lopes through the woods. Jodhpurs and shirts," Little John sneered.

Daggett began an audible count. The engine had flooded.

"It's not natural what she does, you know that."

"Eight, nine . . . "

"She's cut off her hair. She makes pots out of mud. Acts like a man herself and wears tall lace-up boots."

"Little John," Daggett warned and tried the starter again.

"Do you arrest her? No, you arrest me," Little John turned in his seat and gestured toward the rear of the car. "Me and my young son here. And even his dog you threw in the car."

"Now," this time Daggett's voice actually reverberated. "Stop that now."

Little John's mustache clamped down, hiding his lips. His jaw twitched.

The engine caught and they jolted forward just as the S. S. Grand Manan sounded its warning.

The steamer always blew twice when it passed by Whale Cove, after which it remained silent until its final swing into Long Island Bay toward the dock at North Head. It would be less than thirty minutes before passengers disembarked.

Daggett gripped the wheel. He already had guessed the ship would reach North Head before he could dispose of Little John. Daggett rarely swore, even to himself, but he damned Little John now. Once again he would have to trust Rob Feeney's eyes.

Daggett realized he would miss the boat's landing the minute James Enderby had burst into Feeney's office to report that Little

182

John Winslow was in the middle of the main street shouting about how the island should turn out to wrestle the Briggs witch down and tie her to the stake. This is one harlot who won't be getting up out of any circle of fire, Little John was reported to vow. He was trying to rouse all of North Head to follow him to The Anchorage to break up what he had labeled Brunnhilde's Blasphemy. A bunch of women, he roared, swaggering around in men's armor and dress.

There was to be an entertainment tonight, Daggett suddenly remembered. Men's dress is right, Feeney had pointed out. That's when warriors wore short skirts that weren't even called kilts. Feeney had started to laugh. Daggett considered joining him until Enderby added that Little John was carrying a shotgun and waving it in the air.

Serious as Daggett considered Little John's offense, he had no intention of putting Little John in jail, only of disarming him and forcing him into silence. A more serious problem for Daggett was finding a way to impress Little John's errors upon Jocko without entirely destroying the father for the boy. The size of Jocko's eyes reflected in the rear view mirror suggested that the lesson might already be working.

One thing Daggett was certain about. When he delivered Little John and Jocko to Anna and insisted they stay home, Anna would see that they did. Anna might be in the midst of giving the silent treatment to Little John, but she was the one person on Grand Manan who could make Little John listen. Anna was a reasonable woman. She would speak to Little John and do whatever she needed to take care of her son. The shotgun would stay with Daggett.

At Hole in the Wall, the man called Johnson paused briefly and leaned against a tree. Then, rather than head for the trail to The Swallowtail Light as most people did, he turned inland on a little-used path that went sharply uphill until it met several old logging roads high in the woods. Any one of them, Willa observed, would allow the man to drop down into North Head without being noticed.

It was, Willa said when Edith pointed out the way he had gone, like taking the back door into town. But, she added, it was a back door he didn't seem to know much about. He was going the long way round.

Because Edith and Willa knew a shortcut, they decided to take advantage of the man's meandering. Edith badly wanted a rest. Shortly after Church Lane she had tripped on a root and stopped herself from falling by grabbing a tree limb with her bandaged hand. The palm still throbbed and she was having trouble concentrating on the trail.

Willa found a comfortable spot on the arch above Hole in the Wall, and Edith stretched out flat, raising her arm in a vertical slant. Once she slowed the flow of blood, the throbbing would cease. Edith closed her eyes and drew her mind inward, then let go of the man and focused on her breathing. Her pulse slowed and muscles relaxed. She sent inner breath to her wound. Finally, she let go of the wound. Her hand dropped to her side.

Two long wails from the S. S. Grand Manan broke the silence. Edith let its measured pace slide across her mind. The steamer was crossing the mouth of Whale Cove. Soon it would dock in North Head.

"Blue. Didn't you say you saw blue?"

Willa's voice seemed to come from a distance. Edith opened her eyes. Willa stood at the far end of Hole in the Wall, her back toward Edith. She was staring not at the steamer but at a point half way along the trail they had just come.

"Look for blue," Willa turned her head, "isn't that what you said?"

Edith saw the blue from Eel Brook again in her mind, "Brilliant blue, a flash, yes."

"Brilliant, yes," Willa repeated.

The blue at Eel Brook had been a transitory flicker near the beach. It never left the woods.

"I just saw it," Willa pointed, "there."

Edith followed the direction of Willa's hand in her mind and registered the image of a blue-shirted figure moving their way. Quickly, she sat up and stared at the trees along the trail.

"Someone else must also be tracking Mr. Johnson."

"Yes," Edith long ago had ceased to be surprised whenever Willa read her mind.

"You're wrong, Feeney. You must be wrong," Daggett lost control of his voice. It was much louder than he intended.

Feeney flinched.

"Johnson did not get off that ship."

Feeney backed to the side of his desk.

Daggett advanced, "I saw him myself not two hours ago. He was on the beach below Seven Days Work."

"I know, I know," Feeney nodded energetically, "that's what you said."

"He couldn't be on the beach and on the boat. That's a physical impossibility."

"I promise you he was on the boat," Feeney's shoulders rose to the height of his ears in an extensive shrug, "he came down the gangplank."

"Tall? Physically fit? Tennis togs? Chestnut hair?" Daggett touched his hair with his hand, "Deep vees on each side?"

"That's the man."

"Can't be."

"Well, we'll just have to wait a little longer," Willa chose a spot on the top step and settled her back against the door to Daggett's office.

Edith took the next step, drawing her knees to her chin. She

185

wrapped her arms around her legs and balanced the bandaged hand loosely on top.

"I hope he comes soon," Willa began to rub Edith's shoulders, "I am famished."

Edith's stomach grumbled in response.

"You, too?"

"Starved," Edith glanced up, "and exhausted."

If they chose the right table, the Rose Cottage dining room would give them a view of Daggett's office. Edith could almost feel the surge of energy a cup of tea would provide, and Mary Robbins would certainly find them some leftover stew or a bowl of chowder.

Mary had done that before. Edith remembered one night the S. S. Grand Manan had been delayed by a storm. They were terribly late arriving in North Head and Edith had been almost delirious with sea sickness, so they stopped at Rose Cottage rather than going directly to Whale Cove. Mary had fed Willa supper and put Edith to bed.

"What do you suppose that fellow was up to?"

"I can't imagine," Edith leaned back into Willa's hands.

"Do you think he knew he was being followed?"

"He didn't seem to," Edith's interest revived, "though he certainly looked over his shoulder enough times."

"Do you think he saw us?"

"No."

"Maybe he thought Daggett was after him."

"I'll bet that was it," Edith tipped her head. Willa began to massage the back of her neck.

"Where do you think he was going?"

"I wish I knew," Edith rolled her head back. Willa began to knead the area between Edith's shoulder blades. Edith raised one shoulder, then the other.

"How could he disappear like that?"

Edith shrugged. Willa squeezed the top of her shoulders and held them for a moment.

"We had him all the way into the woods above town and then he was gone," Willa released her grip, "that's the real mystery."

Edith exhaled.

Willa squeezed the top of her shoulders again.

"And why didn't he notice young James," Willa drew Edith back with her hands, "James' shirt was such a brilliant blue."

"We would never have seen him otherwise."

"WHAT do you mean Johnson never returned?"

At that moment, Daggett would have taken great pleasure in throttling Harvey Andrews. The innkeeper at Swallowtail may not have done anything wrong, but nothing was right.

"He never did. That's why I never sent my Henry to fetch you," Harvey leaned against the wall behind his counter and worked his toothpick between his teeth. "I told you I'd send him the minute Johnson came in," Harvey moved the toothpick to the other side of his mouth. "Well, he never came in."

"And the others?"

"They went to meet him at the boat, Geneva said."

"That's right, they did," Geneva came in from the dining room and stood in front of the counter next to Daggett, her apron clasped in her hands.

"And they never came back after that?" Daggett looked from Geneva to Harvey and back again.

"No. Said they were going to The Anchorage. There's an entertainment there tonight," Harvey took the toothpick out of his mouth and placed it on the edge of the counter near the cash register.

"That's right," Geneva nodded, "they took a box lunch with them."

"Bit late leaving, if you ask me," Harvey leaned forward and put his elbows on the counter.

"THAT'S how I heard it," Mary Robbins set a plate of crackers between the steaming bowls of chowder she unloaded from her tray, "Constable Daggett ran Little John all the way home in the Chevrolet and told him to stay there."

Edith picked up her spoon. There were only the three of them in the Rose Cottage dining room, and the street in front of Daggett's office was empty of cars. Daggett must have gone elsewhere after taking Little John home.

"Disturbing the peace, I suppose," Willa buttered a roll.

"Carrying a firearm, too," Mary brushed crumbs off the nearest table.

"A firearm?"

"Loaded shotgun," Mary stopped brushing to look at them.

"What on earth good did he think that would do?" Edith swallowed a spoonful of chowder. Its heat made her blink.

" 'Save us from witches' is what he said."

"More likely he shouted," Willa stirred her soup with her spoon.

Edith applauded Daggett's handling of Little John. Things could so easily get out of hand. Edith remembered the blaze of torches, the stench of kerosene, and the heat of men's voices on one hot August night in her childhood. Lincoln's widest avenues had been too narrow for the vigilantes that night, as nice a name as anyone could give the throng of drunken, hotheaded men who raced through the streets demanding death for Earl James, a man convicted of rape and child killing, though her father maintained no one really knew who had done what. Justice, they shouted, justice. And they brandished guns and swords and knives and clubs. The leaders carried ropes. Edith had pressed her nose to the parlor window until her father carried her away. For weeks after, Edith heard how they got their man, how his brown body had swung naked and maimed. It was years before the nightmares died. And many of those same voices Edith heard on other summer nights, in celebrations and torchlight parades, calling for speeches from William Jennings Bryan or pledging allegiance on the Fourth of July.

"That Little John," Willa broke into Edith's memory, "that Little John ought to move to Louisiana. He'd fit right in, after all." She began to grin broadly, "Just another Southern demagogue."

Mary Robbins turned and put a hand on her hip to consider Willa.

Edith ate her chowder.

"It's true that people call us backwoods," Mary moved to the next table, "but we do have a little bit of everything here."

"Geography holds no bounds for demagogues," Willa smiled and glanced out of the window. "Even out-of-the-way fishing villages come equipped with their own," she nodded toward the empty street.

"Yes," Mary let the word linger and bent to her task. Then she paused and looked up to add, "but I really don't think Little John should be likened to one of your American political parties."

Willa cocked her head.

"Southern Democrats," Edith guessed with a grin.

XVIII

"WHAT LO, VOORHEES the Viking," Brunnhilde cried, staring wistfully toward the door at the side of the makeshift stage. She raised bound hands and pulled against the stake fastened to the floor to the right of the door. "Pray the fair Viking secures my release."

Brunnhilde's short red hair shone like a cap. Her eyes, grown wide, rolled toward the pair of sheets serving as a temporary backdrop, where her so-called captors had earlier retired.

Several loud thumps preceded the entry of Voorhees, who strode through the door with helmet flashing, eyes ferocious, body leather-clad. A fearsome head, echoing her own, bristled from the painted shield clasped to her left side, a spear threatened from her right.

Voorhees swaggered to center stage and took a moment to glare at individuals in the audience. The brightly painted helmet, bedecked with horns, covered her ears and curled forward toward her chin, adding to the terror of her stare. With great fanfare, she unlocked her word-hoard.

"Your treasure and your fealty belong to me. Loose your prisoners and pile your wealth here," Voorhees thumped the floor with her spear, "or my ships will invade."

Voorhees' hateful words and baleful glare reached to the outer limits of the room. Someone down front drew a sharp breath. Voorhees raised her shield and shook her spear. Enormous muscles bulged beneath her sleeves.

A trembling Brunnhilde pulled against the thongs binding her hands to the stake. She fluttered her eyes.

"Oh," Brunnhilde finally said, "Oh, my savior has come."

Without even so much as a glance in Brunnhilde's direction, Voorhees thundered again, "Defy me and die," her voice ringing like Thor toward the pair of hanging sheets behind which Brunnhilde's captors supposedly lurked.

The Viking's words bounced off the sheets and then died. No one flung themselves through to her challenge.

"Oh," Brunnhilde gasped, "Oh," and sank to the floor.

Someone tittered off to the right.

Voorhees turned to glare at the audience, and after a great threatening with shield and spear, she finally bent toward the fallen Brunnhilde.

"I will free you, fair maiden, never fear," Voorhees lay heavy emphasis on the word *I*. "But first," she stomped her right foot, "I will ensure your good name."

Voorhees glared again at the crowd with baleful eyes then locked her stare on Eva McDaniels.

Eva sat smaller.

"Come forth, any who dare," Voorhees threatened. "No one shall defame this fair Amazon," she curled her lip, "and live."

After a long moment, Voorhees spun back toward Brunnhilde, but this time as she whirled, her helmet stayed still, its horns pointed skyward. Voorhees strode at once purposefully toward Brunnhilde, but her helmet aimed at the audience.

Voorhees whirled. The helmet wobbled. The ferocious face reappeared then disappeared beneath the horns. Voorhees could not use her hands to right the helmet. It slid and pointed off to the side. She poked it with her spear. The helmet tilted. She tossed her head. The helmet slid to the other side. One baleful eye finally glared forth beneath the horns.

"What lo, the Viking befuddled," a voice yelled from the rear.

"Besotted, you mean," another yelled from the front.

"Mead, that's what she needs," someone joined from the side.

"That's what we all need," another one whooped, "if we're to sit through any more of this."

"Glue is more like it," the laugh belonged to Jacobus.

"To hold us in our seats, you mean," the whoop shifted to a howl.

THE ANCHORAGE dining room was packed. Daggett had arrived too late to have any clear idea of what was going on, but at that point the crowd began to clap and someone guffawed. Others stomped their feet. Laughter shifted to uproar. Daggett dodged elbows all along the wall.

Jennifer, snuggled next to her friend Alice in the front row, laughed so hard she threw her head back. On Jennifer's left, Elizabeth sat with her arms wrapped around her belly. Her whole body shook. Daggett grinned. When they first courted, Daggett had discovered Elizabeth's trouble with delight. Whenever something struck her funny, her whole body would laugh. She had no modulation, no giggles or simpers or little-girl grins, just rich, full-bodied, belly-shaking laughs that ranged all the way from fluted falsettos to vibrating basses. Elizabeth once laughed so hard at something Daggett had said, she popped all her buttons. Daggett no longer remembered what it was that struck her funny but ever since, unless Elizabeth were home and wearing comfortable clothes, she rarely ventured beyond a smile. People thought her somehow soured. Daggett wished she would just let her dresses out at the waist.

EDITH finished folding the Rose Cottage vellum and slipped the sheet into the envelope she had already addressed.

"We'll just have to let this play itself out," Willa stood in the road while Edith taped the note to Daggett's office door.

"When the time is right, Daggett will find us," Edith descended the steps and looked up at the sky. The sun had set.

"It's already past nine," Willa looked at her watch. "I certainly hope he doesn't want to find us until tomorrow," she yawned, "and then not until some very convenient time."

"I asked him not to stop by before noon," Edith smiled and took Willa by the elbow, "I'd like you to be part of the conversation."

Pink fingers of afterglow invaded the dusky blue above North Head. The moon had risen. Willa and Edith decided to forgo Church Lane in favor of Swamp Road. It would be dark by the time they reached Whale Cove, too late to navigate the rocks across the beach even with moonlight.

"In the meantime," Willa patted her stomach, "we've had a fine meal."

"With two pieces of carrot cake," Edith cast a sly glance at Willa, "I would say you found it to be quite satisfactory."

"Every bite a sinful joy," Willa made deliberate smacking noises with her lips.

"THIS is by far the most damnable case I've ever been involved with," Daggett let the screen door slam behind him.

Daggett helped Elizabeth with her coat. The evening was cool for July.

"I saw him," Elizabeth patted Daggett's arm, then left to go up stairs to turn down Jennifer's bed.

Daggett took Edith Lewis' note and the unopened telegrams out of his jacket pocket, placed them on the hall table, and went out to collect the sleeping Jennifer from the back of the Chevrolet.

"Coffee or tea," Elizabeth asked when they had finished putting Jennifer to bed.

Elizabeth and Jennifer had eaten dinner before the Brights picked them up for the drive to The Anchorage, but Daggett had not taken time to eat.

"Coffee," Daggett loosened the top button on his jacket.

"Come along then," Elizabeth led the way to the kitchen.

Miss Lewis' note said that they wanted to see him but not until the next afternoon. The telegrams would keep. He would savor them with dessert. There was nothing he could do tonight, anyway.

"Every lead simply evaporates," Daggett followed Elizabeth and picked up where he left off. "It's like someone is pulling strings or making cards disappear. Tricks. Magic."

"And that someone is Matthew Johnson, is that what you think?"

"It's apparently too soon to do that kind of thinking," Daggett shook his head and pulled out a chair.

Elizabeth put silverware on the kitchen table and struck a match to heat water for coffee. She put out two cups, uncovered the butter, and set leftover pot roast and a fresh loaf of bread before her husband.

"Black magic, that's what it is," Elizabeth paused to consider.

"Black improbabilities, certainly," Daggett sliced an end off the bread and spread it with butter.

"Impossibilities, you mean," Elizabeth fetched milk from the cooler and glanced at her husband. "That man simply could not be in two places at once."

"Seems he was," Daggett sprinkled sugar on the bread and took a bite. He chewed with pleasure.

"Have some pot roast," Elizabeth advised, "and tell me what the telegrams say," she added a jar of mustard and a dish of applesauce to Daggett's options.

XIX

"Why, young James," Edith smiled broadly and opened the screen door, "what can I do for you?"

"Good day, Miss Lewis," James Daniels grabbed his cap with both hands. He had tucked in his plaid shirt, his pants were freshly creased and his workboots clean, their soles free of dirt. Edith had seen young James the moment he arrived and very much wanted to interrogate him about the day before. Edith knew it was better, however, to curb her curiosity. Impatience and assertiveness in women were two things that never sat well outside of New York City. Not in Nebraska and not on Grand Manan. Besides, Willa should be part of any conversation she had with young James.

"Is Mr. Sharkey here?" Edith began again. "I didn't expect to see you on Sunday," she glanced past James toward the lane. "Are you going to deliver rocks today?"

"No, ma'am. Mr. Sharkey's likely at church. He doesn't like to work Sunday. Most Baptists don't."

It was one of the longest speeches Edith had heard from young James, who had been standing by the rock pile staring at the partially finished wall for several minutes.

"Actually, I came by alone," James cleared his throat, "to see you and Miss Cather."

"Miss Cather will be available shortly. Can it wait until then?"

Willa often broke her work schedule on Sundays, but after so many interruptions during this week, she had chosen to spend the morning in the attic. It was already after eleven, however, Edith noted, looking at her watch. Willa should be down soon.

"Yes, ma'am, I'll wait," James dropped his gaze to his feet. "I thought about coming earlier, Miss Lewis, but I held off. Everyone knows Miss Cather is not to be interfered with."

Edith smiled.

"You've made good progress," James nodded toward the wall. "You'll be needing more rocks soon."

"Yes, Mr. Sharkey said the same thing when he came by."

James glanced in Edith's direction.

"Yesterday," Edith decided to answer what James didn't ask. "He came by to tell us he couldn't deliver rocks without your help. You were unavailable."

"Mr. Sharkey came by."

"He said he didn't know where you were."

James studied the embankment with deep concentration, as though any moment the rocks might slide down or the wall topple over.

FOR the third time that morning, Daggett flattened the yellow half sheets out before him, running his fingers back and forth across their surfaces as though that would somehow bring more information from the inked words that ran in straight lines across them. Divining truth by touch, Daggett smiled at himself. On Sunday, too. But, of course, nothing unusual happened. What information these telegrams held he already possessed.

St. Andrews, St. Stephen, Montreal. Officials in all three Canadian towns knew Burt Isaacs. Runs with a tough crowd, that Isaacs does, according to the constable in St. Stephen. But no one in St. Andrews, St. Stephen, or Montreal had ever brought Isaacs up on charges. Haven't been able to catch him at anything yet, St. Andrews confessed.

Montreal, but only Montreal, had caught Jackson Knoll. At several things, mostly juvenile offenses from years ago, along with a recent assault charge. He had served time as a youngster, but Montreal hadn't been able to make the recent charge stick. They thought Knoll might be working as a middleman for bootleggers, but they had no certain proof. They did know that he was out of town a lot. Windsor, and Boston, and maybe Detroit. Daggett should check with Detroit.

No one had anything at all on Matthew Johnson. Nothing in St. Stephen, St. Andrews, or Montreal. Not even a record of his passing through customs. Daggett touched Johnson's name on each of the yellow half sheets, then spread out the next set.

Machias, Calais, Bangor. All had a great deal on Jack Watson. He had served time. Seven years for armed robbery, another three for extortion. But that was eight years ago. Since then, Jack Watson had been spotted in the company of bootleggers and went often to Montreal, but as far as anyone knew, Watson was shipping logs across the border, not booze.

And none of them, not one of them, had ever heard of John Thomas Bush, Daggett shook a match loose from his little tin box. But Boston and New Bedford had. And so might Detroit.

"Is that young James I hear?" Willa's voice called through the screen.

"Yes, ma'am," James snapped to attention. "How are you today, Miss Cather?"

"Just fine, James." The screen door squeaked and Willa joined Edith on the back stoop.

"James has been waiting for you to come down."

"I see," Willa rubbed her palms together. "Well, here I am, quite ready to get back to good, hard, physical labor."

"Not today, I'm afraid," Edith sighed.

"That's true," Willa patted Edith's arm just above her bandaged hand, "it will be quite a while before Miss Lewis can join us."

"The whole village heard about what happened," James turned to Edith, his bearing slightly more formal. "We were very sorry to hear about your hand, Miss Lewis. My mother said I should tell you, if you need any help . . . "

"Thank you, James. A few days and my hand will be as good as it used to be."

"We'll make out just fine, James. But do thank your mother for thinking of us."

"Yes, ma'am," James shifted his weight.

"Now," Willa looked around, "when are you bringing more rocks and where's Mr. Sharkey?"

"Mr. Sharkey's not here, Miss Cather," James squared his shoulders, "that's not why I came."

Willa waited, but James' silence extended. Willa chose to break it.

"Would you care to sit down, James?"

"Perhaps some lemonade," Edith offered.

"Yes, please," James agreed but said nothing more and did not move.

"How about the lawn chairs around front," Willa stepped off the porch.

"I'll join you in a moment," Edith disappeared inside.

"It's a perfect day," Edith could hear Willa rounding the cottage. "Just look at those blues . . . the turquoise . . . the aqua . . . the sky touching the sea," Willa would be punctuating her words with her hands. "With blues that pure, we must be at the very ends of the earth . . . where everything finally comes together."

Edith heard nothing from young James.

DAGGETT lit a match and drew on his pipe. Burt Isaacs worked for Jack Watson. Daggett blew a smoke ring and contemplated the wall before him. Jack Watson went frequently to Montreal. Jackson Knoll lived in Montreal and probably spent time regularly in

Boston and Detroit. Daggett blew a second ring, then spread out the last of the yellow half sheets.

Boston and New Bedford. Both supplied the lists of known rum runners Daggett had requested. Many of the same names appeared on both lists, but not one of them had any apparent connection to Burt Isaacs, Jack Watson, Matthew Johnson, or Jackson Knoll. Daggett looked carefully for Knoll, then blew another smoke ring. No one in Boston or New Bedford had heard of anyone like them running liquor into the United States from the province of New Brunswick either. New Bedford, in fact, had never heard of Grand Manan. Why run booze from there into the United States, New Bedford wanted to know. Seems a bit out of the way. Did Grand Manan produce liquor as well as herring, Boston inquired. Good point, Daggett conceded and tapped out his pipe.

On the other hand, New Bedford thought Daggett should contact federal agents in Detroit. Detroit's bootleggers were restless, the spot was too hot. Places like Grand Manan might suddenly look good. New Bedford was beginning to look good, they said. The list of known bootleggers hanging around their docks had just leapt into double digits. Daggett ran his fingers through his hair and paused to scratch the back of his head. He found the act comforting.

Facing the Bay

"Now," Willa watched young James settle into one of the Adirondacks, his right hand clasping a glass of lemonade, "tell us why you've come."

"Actually, I've been by several times since dawn," James' knuckles threatened to turn white from his grip upon the glass. He sipped at the lemonade and set the glass down on the Adirondack's wide arm. Finally, he folded his hands in his lap and left them there.

"This morning? You were here earlier today?" Edith hadn't noticed James earlier, though certainly he had been standing by the rock pile for several minutes before she went out to talk to him.

"Yes, ma'am, more than once. Only I didn't come up to the house," James shifted his concentration from his knees to look at Edith. "I've heard that Miss Cather works until noon and allows no disturbances, even after she comes away from her desk. I thought perhaps Sundays . . . "

"You were exactly right, James," Willa interjected.

"But what brings you?" Edith insisted.

"Well, I know you saw me," James seemed at once animated and still, his fingernails digging into his palms. Finally, he flexed his hands and placed them on the Adirondack's arms. He tried again, "You saw me yesterday."

"We did," Willa agreed.

"Yes," Edith nodded, "in your brilliant blue shirt."

During the brief pause that followed, James' eyes widened. "You saw him, too," he finally said.

"Him," Willa repeated as neither question nor statement. She was merely waiting.

When Daggett finished composing his telegrams to United States treasury agents in Detroit and police in Montreal, Boston, and New Bedford, he glanced at the clock. Nearly eleven-thirty. He reached for his pipe. The twists and turns in this case were beyond anything he had ever experienced. Daggett was certain he was on the right track, but not one lead was breaking his way. A corpse without papers. A meaningless button. A torch in the Chevrolet. An empty room searched.

Just twists and turns but no true direction. Just zig, he struck a match, and zag.

"Hɪᴍ, yes," James repeated, "you saw him, too." He glanced up sharply, "Didn't you?"

Edith appreciated Willa's restraint. She made no quick response. Without Willa, Edith feared she herself would give way to chatter. Yes, we saw him . . . he acted odd . . . we followed him . . . we saw you follow him . . . we don't know why . . . tell us why . . . tell us. But Willa never chattered. Willa waited. Willa listened. Through silence and through words, Willa waited and listened. Now she waited until James got around to supplying the vague pronoun "him" with an antecedent. Edith also waited and, like Willa, stayed as calm as she could.

Edith knew that Willa's apparent calm only seemed to run counter to the tremendous intellectual energy she possessed. Actually, that calm, that restraint, was central to Willa's creativity. That's why solitude was so essential . . . with solitude she could find the still, distant place, the cool seat at the center of things but not of them. A preserve too easily disturbed. Willa rarely rushed to presumption or prejudged or responded offhand. She once did—she had to—as a drama critic and later as a magazine editor. But she preferred to take time to hear . . . with an inner as well as an outer ear. And then to ask just the right questions. Because, Willa said, everything is always open to question. There are no sure things and at least two sides to every truth. Truth is never simple, she said. Sometimes in her novels, Willa once confessed, she made truth appear to be simple. But that was fiction, pure fiction, she laughed.

Edith wanted to laugh now, but that would be out of place. James was so serious, Willa so impassive. Edith took a long, slow breath and let it out at the same pace.

James took his time, too. Finally, the words came like a sigh, "Him . . . you know, the man from Swallowtail." With the words out, James seemed to grow somehow physically smaller, decompressed. He slumped in his chair, refolded his hands, and placed them in his lap.

"The man from Swallowtail," Willa repeated. "Yes, we saw him. Why were you following him, James?"

"I didn't say I was," James glanced up sharply. "Not at first, anyway."

"And once you did?"

"You saw me at Hole in the Wall, right? Where he cut inland? Well, I cut inland, too."

Both women nodded. James studied them for a moment.

"And at Eel Brook? We saw you there, too," Edith decided to take her turn.

"At Eel Brook," James stared at Edith. "How could you . . . ," he swung around and shaded his eyes and let his gaze run along the rocky shore all the way to Ashburton Head. Eel Brook lay between.

"Binoculars," Willa offered.

"We were watching several seals . . . three of them, I guess . . . play their way up the coast," Edith was fully part of this conversation now.

"Seals. Three seals," James seemed to want to make meaning of the words. Finally, he swung back around.

The women waited.

"I see," James finally broke the silence.

"Well, it doesn't matter," James broke the silence again, rubbing the grass with the bottom of his right boot. His head moved side to side.

"Well, I've been wanting to talk to you," James' voice picked up volume. "Both of you. You've been kind and, as my mother says, you know the world," his right hand waved vaguely toward the mainland.

Edith could see Willa's eyes kindle with compassion. They must be careful not to give too much warmth too soon. But Willa knew that.

"Eric said that you calmed him when he brought the body in," James turned to Willa and inspected her face. "Eric says you have sense. And Daggett says you write books. He called you wise."

Willa smiled in reply.

"Daggett said you know humankind," James flicked a glance in Edith's direction, "both of you."

Edith allowed herself a smile.

"I came here," an involuntary cough interrupted James. "I came here to tell you everything," he cleared his throat.

The women waited.

"You went to Eel Brook to see about rocks," Willa finally began for him. "Rocks to bring here," she motioned toward the wall at the back of the cottage. "You didn't say anything to Sharkey about it. You just went. You wanted to see what you could find."

"Right. Exactly right," James shifted in his chair and cleared his throat. "How did you . . . "

"I understand how things happen."

"Yes, I see. Well, like I said, I wasn't following anyone exactly. I thought it might be easier to get rocks from Eel Brook and carry them to Whale Cove by boat," he motioned with his hands, "than load them on the wagon and bring them up here. It was hard to get the wagon through the woods where we had been going."

"I'm sure it was," Willa's voice was gentle. "And the man from Swallowtail?" She paused. "I can never remember his name."

James stared at Willa, his eyes saying, Oh, Oh yes, I forgot that part, then he turned quickly toward Seven Days Work.

"Johnson," Edith spoke the name.

"Matthew Johnson," James said the full name and swung back to rest to his eyes again on Willa's.

"Matthew Johnson, of course. Thank you, James. And when you saw him, he was on the beach picking his way around boulders. He moved in odd ways. It was almost as though he were hiding or looking for something, or maybe he wanted to hide something. And," Willa paused again, "he was heading directly for the place where the man went off the cliff."

"You knew where that was?" Edith watched James closely.

James kept his eyes on Willa.

"Everybody knows."

"Is that why you followed him?"

"I thought he might have had something to do with it," James glanced at Edith, then dropped his eyes.

"They were both strangers. To the island, I mean," James looked up again. "Maybe they knew each other. That's what I thought. Anyway, you're right," he shrugged at last, "Matthew Johnson acted strange. He was moving real slow, head down, stopping, bending over. I thought he might have been searching for something."

"Something you wanted?"

James jerked his head toward Willa. His eyes widened.

"Well?"

"I don't know."

"Did he find anything?"

"He put something in his pocket."

Edith heard a sharp intake of breath and realized it was hers. She had also seen Mr. Johnson put something in his pocket, but at the time, it hadn't registered as important. She wished now they had written something about that on the note to Mark Daggett. They had told Daggett nothing at all about why they wanted him to stop by, she realized now. Nothing specific. They had felt rather silly about the whole thing. Doubly silly because they had lost sight of Mr. Johnson in the woods above North Head. Still . . .

"Do you know what it was he put in his pocket?"

Willa's question broke Edith's reverie.

James shook his head.

Edith raised her hand and held it close to her breast. It throbbed under the bandage.

"Do you want to say what happened next?"

"A light flashed from your cliff."

"Binoculars," Willa nodded.

"Picked up by the sun, glinting," James nodded. "Your binoculars, I guess."

"And then?"

"Johnson looked up. Not at you," James shook his head. "At the cliff," he nodded toward Seven Days Work. "He stared at the place where the man went off the cliff. Then he ran."

"Is that when you saw Constable Daggett?"

"Constable Daggett?" James visibly paled.

LEADS everywhere, but not one that was solid and not one that had broken his way, Daggett shook his head and laid his pipe on the desk. And none of the telegrams spread out before him pointed with certainty toward any one person. Not Burt Isaacs, not Jackson Knoll, not Matthew Johnson, not even Jack Watson. Worse, Daggett had nothing beyond a hunch from New Bedford to push for a link between John Thomas Bush and bootleggers. New Bedford seemed more interested in the disappearance of his girlfriend than in his connection to known criminals. And Feeney's assertion that Matthew Johnson had been on the S. S. Grand Manan when it docked simply made no sense at all.

Nothing did.

XX

"WHAT DID YOU do then, James," Willa continued to pursue her line of questions, "what did you do when the man began to run?"

James inhaled deeply, took a long swallow of lemonade from his glass and wiped his mouth with his hand. His hands were steady. His eyes returned to the beach below Seven Days Work and then to Eel Brook.

"I slipped into the woods and headed for Whale Cove."

"For Whale Cove? Why not North Head?"

"I thought I could match his speed."

"That was a long run," Edith's mind darted to their own fumbling rush once they saw the man run. Willa hadn't been wearing shoes, only the loose-fitting moccasins she liked to wear during her morning's work. And Edith had been hampered by the swaddling of bandages on her left hand. But once Willa changed into proper shoes, they had moved quickly.

"You were very fast," Willa observed.

"I know short cuts," James' smile tightened, "and Johnson slowed down."

Edith recalled Johnson's tennis whites flitting through the trees that rose above the shoreline on the trail to Hole in the Wall.

"I saw the two of you crossing the Cove," young James tipped up his glass and swallowed the last of his lemonade. His knuckles were white.

Willa nodded.

"You were following him, too."

"We were, yes."

"Why?"

DAGGETT pushed back from his desk, thinking he could smoke the pipe he had filled . . . or he could take a chance that Miss Cather was finished with her work for the day and drive over to Whale Cove . . . or he could meet Elizabeth and Jennifer coming out of church.

Daggett decided he could smoke his pipe any time, and Miss Cather and Miss Lewis would be there when he needed them. Those were two things of which he could be certain. Exactly when he would need Miss Cather and Miss Lewis, he had no way of knowing. Nor did he know what they might have to tell him. But whatever it was could not be terribly urgent. It had already kept through the night, it would keep a while longer.

Instead, he would fetch Elizabeth and Jennifer from church. Some things rightly deserved precedence. Then, while Elizabeth fixed Sunday dinner, he would drive over to speak to the ladies at Whale Cove. If he were careful about the ashes, he could smoke his pipe on the way.

"COME, James, you've wasted enough time," Willa declared. "Out with it."

Young James set his empty lemonade glass down on the Adirondack's arm and looked directly at Willa.

"You did not follow Matthew Johnson simply because he happened to be on the beach," Willa cocked an eyebrow and lowered her voice, "did you?"

James froze like a rabbit who's heard the twig snap. The pupils in his dark eyes flinched.

"And you did not just happen to be at Eel Brook looking for an alternative way to bring rocks here for our wall."

When Willa reached the word *rocks*, James began to breathe. He glanced at the cottage, then swung his body toward the coast, twisting sideways in the Adirondack until he faced altogether Seven Days Work and Ashburton Head. Eel Brook lay between.

Willa folded her arms.

"Actually, I *was* there looking for rocks and Johnson *did* just happen to be on the beach. But . . . well," James sighed, "you are right. I followed him because he was Matthew Johnson."

"You thought he killed John Thomas Bush?"

Edith harbored the suspicion herself. Why else would Matthew Johnson run the minute he saw Daggett?

"No, that's not what you thought, is it, James," Willa pushed harder, never taking her eyes from James' pale face.

"No."

THE Chevrolet coughed twice before the engine caught. Daggett settled back against the seat and admonished himself for not checking the spark plugs earlier in the day. Perhaps it wasn't the plugs. Perhaps it was the fuel mix, water in the line, the filter, the carburetor, the distributor, the starter. Daggett mentally moved through each part in its turn. Once he got Elizabeth and Jennifer home, he decided, he would have to take a look under the hood.

"No, unfortunately, no," Willa nodded agreement.

James tensed, wary.

"What's more," Willa continued with an intake of breath, "the day you first delivered rocks you were wearing a red shirt. Am I correct, James? Under your jacket?"

James wrapped his arms about his body.

Edith felt her own eyes grow large.

"And unless I miss my guess," Willa pressed harder, "you recently lost or misplaced that shirt. Perhaps you mislaid it in the woods or let it slip overboard when you were out fishing. After all, it had already lost a button on its sleeve. Am I right, James?"

James gripped his bottom lip in his teeth and made a single, sharp nod with his head. Then he sighed, a long, slow sigh. His hands released his ribs and cradled themselves on the arms of Adirondack.

"Young James?" It was all Edith could think to say.

DAGGETT rolled to a stop and cut the engine. Sunday peace. A light breeze, a warm sun, the waft of honeysuckle, the buzz of bees. Daggett loosened his collar.

Four cars lounged before the church, almost as many automobiles as North Head contained. With the Chevrolet silenced, he could hear the joyous notes of the recessional. Any moment now, Father Morgan would throw open the heavy wooden doors and place himself so that his parishioners, filing past on the church porch, would stop for a word or two.

Rising above North Head on the edge of town, the Anglican Church was impressive and protective. Its steeple, masonry, and brick set it apart from the rest of the island, where most of the buildings sported wooden clapboards or weathered shingles and nestled close to the earth.

The Anglican fathers had dared the elements with their church, placing it just beyond the town on a hill facing east. There it led the eye both upward and outward, looking east over Flagg Cove to the Bay of Fundy. Daggett squinted in that direction. Nova Scotia was somewhere over there, reaching down with its gentle arm to shelter Grand Manan from the fierce Atlantic, but so far east even the most powerful telescope failed to catch sight of its shores.

The rock of the church. The rock of the island. Bedrock, Daggett smiled to himself, settling more firmly in his seat. Strongholds, retreats. But storms came, he reminded himself, despite Nova Scotia. Too many storms. And no place on earth provided safe haven forever.

"YOU know then."

"I believe I do."

Young James fixed his eyes on Willa, his body newly taut, his breathing once again shallow. Willa's eyes were luminous and, for the moment, deeply blue.

"I've been frightened so long," James let the remaining air escape from his lungs. His body, decompressed, followed the contours of the Adirondack, lying against it inert like the Hindenburg without air.

"Oh," Edith reached over to cover his hand with her own. She patted the hand gently.

"Miserably frightened, yes, I'm sure you have been," Willa regarded the young man, her eyes thoughtful. "And for a long time, I'd wager. First of the man . . . of his finding you . . . and then of being found out about his death . . . which, I'll also wager, you did . . . and did not . . . cause."

It was fully one minute before James took a breath.

"Yes."

"And you've been in hiding ever since you came back from the mainland?"

"Pretty much. Yes."

"You came home first to hide from the man, and when he died, you began to hide from everyone else . . . "

"Yes."

"And you put on a false face, a mask . . . "

"Yes."

"And you were frightened."

"Terrified, yes."

XXI

WHENEVER ENDERBY CLEARED his throat, he lifted his hand as though he meant to assist the movement of his Adam's apple. He often cleared his throat in church. The gesture never failed to catch Janey Dawson's attention.

"Good day to you, Mr. Enderby," Janey rocked for a moment on the toes of her patent leather shoes and straightened the skirt of her best Sunday dress before stepping out into the aisle.

Janey Dawson was growing up. James Enderby approved, nodding a greeting to her parents, who had not yet risen from the pew. The counter in Enderby's bank had always been just beyond Janey's reach, but it would not be much longer, Enderby guessed, watching Janey drop the coins her father had just given her into the pocket on her dress. She was careful to inspect the pocket first to detect holes. Enderby appreciated her prudence.

"Good sermon today, didn't you think, Mr. Enderby?" Eric Dawson reached across his wife to shake Enderby's hand. Eric's sister and Mary Daniels stood just behind. Mary finished straightening the prayer books in the racks at the back of her pew before entering the aisle.

"Grand sermon," Enderby agreed. "It is always a good thing to be reminded of tolerance and universal love," he raised his hand again and coughed.

"Especially now," Eric glanced toward the back of the church, where Little John Winslow was pumping the priest's hand.

"No doubt congratulating Father Morgan on this morning's wisdom," Enderby followed Eric's gaze. "I do wonder at times whether a man like Little John has any idea what casting a stone means. He might very well think it has something to do with Miss Briggs making one of her pots."

"I doubt it," Eric chuckled, taking his wife's arm, "Little John doesn't know a thing about art . . . or the Bible."

"Mmmm," Enderby agreed, "and I doubt that today's sermon did much to enlighten him. I heard several snores emanating from the direction of Little John's pew," Enderby stepped back to make room for Mary Daniels.

"You must join us for Sunday noon, James Enderby," Mary Daniels took hold of his arm. "The Dawsons are coming, and you must too."

"That's very kind of you, fair lady," Enderby tucked Mary Daniels' hand into the crook of his arm.

"Good, then it's settled," Mary Daniels led the way toward the door.

"THIS simply can't be," Edith could remain silent no longer. Until this moment, she thought she knew exactly what was in Willa's mind. They finished each other's sentences, for heaven's sake. But this . . . well, this just wasn't right. Willa had to be mistaken.

"This young man would never do such a thing," when Edith finally got the words out, she patted James' hand with a firm sense of reassurance. She realized with a start that she actually felt self-righteous about the matter.

"Correct," Willa agreed with Edith but kept her eyes on James. "This young man," she declared, "would not and could not do such a thing."

"There, you see."

James dropped his head.

"But this young man did do such a thing," Willa cleared her

throat, "didn't he, James?" Willa's voice softened when she reached his name.

James folded and refolded his hands. They were deeply tanned.

"Didn't he, James?" Willa repeated the phrase.

"That was an evil man, Miss Cather," the words shot out of James. He inhaled sharply, then held his breath. His hands fell open and lay motionless on his knees.

"You didn't mean to do it," Edith had to feel her way. The novelist's gift for grasping character and plot had always been Willa's, she realized, not hers. She glanced at Willa for confirmation, "James couldn't mean it."

"Exactly," Willa sighed.

"He was going to kill me, Miss Lewis," James spoke the words quietly, but his hands gripped his knees. Then he freed them and began to rub his arms, elbow to shoulder, shoulder to elbow, as though the air held a chill. "He had a gun, Miss Lewis. I don't know where it came from. His pocket, I guess. He made me take him to Seven Days Work. He wanted me to jump. He must have hated me. He said he wanted the highest cliff. The most remote," James hesitated. His hands grasped again at his ribs.

"But you got the gun away," Edith began now to carry the scene forward on her own.

"Yes," James leaned into his words. "He stumbled, I grabbed hold of his arm. We fought. He fell. By the time he got up," James half rose in his chair, "his gun was in my hand."

"And, and you threw the gun over the cliff," Willa took up the narrative with a vehemence that surprised even Edith.

"He ran at me. I shouted," James nodded vigorously, "then there I was on the edge still holding the gun. He reached for it . . . and I threw it as far as I could," James flung out his arm and opened his hand.

213

"So," Willa nodded and completed the scene, "he went over the edge diving after his gun."

"WHERE is young James keeping himself today?" James Enderby patted Mary Daniels' hand, resting comfortably in the crook of his elbow. He was only being conversational but looked around expectantly. The young man was always putting away folding chairs or doing another of the chores he took upon himself. James was a good fellow. Enderby had always thought well of him. Most people did.

"I wish I knew."

The sharpness of Mary's reply surprised Enderby, but Mary wasn't really paying attention, he realized. She was nodding to Elizabeth Daggett in the next pew and adding a smile for Jennifer. But when she did turn back to Enderby, she seemed absent still.

"Wish you knew?"

"James rarely misses his breakfast, you know," Mary glanced up at Enderby, "but he never ate a bite this morning. And church, he never misses that," she looked around quickly, "but this morning he did."

"He must have had something very important to do then," Enderby patted her hand and they hurried to catch up with the Dawsons.

"THEN it was an accident," Edith reached the edge of her chair.

"Self-defense, surely," Willa pronounced.

"Not murder," Edith sank back, relieved. They did agree, then, all of them. She stared at James. He seemed composed, Willa serene.

"Thank God, you understand," James said the word softly. He too had dropped back into the lap of his Adirondack. It held him firm.

Edith heard and saw again the frightening details of that day.

They played in slow motion with a jerky stop-start, each frame freezing for momentary review. The sound of the waterfalls, the flash of red, the naughty spruce leaning back to touch the earth, the muffled shout, the gulls near the weir, the red shirt, its arm flung out. Then the body lunging, the body leaping, the body diving, the body reaching forward . . . toward a gun the red shirt flung out and Edith did not see. Now in her mind's eye Edith followed the trajectory of the gun's flight down to the sea, where, just as the waves were receding from the rocks, John Thomas Bush—his body tilted oddly throughout his decline—had also arrived.

Naughty Spruce

"GREETINGS and good day to you, my friend," Enderby reached past Mary Daniels to shake Daggett's hand. Enderby was always his heartiest on Sunday. "You should have been at the service. You'd have enjoyed the sermon."

Daggett grinned in reply, nodding to the Dawsons and Father Morgan. Daggett arrived at the front steps just as Enderby and

Mary Daniels came through the church door with Jenny Dawson. Eric and Lizzie Dawson were already there.

"I hear you gave an excellent sermon today, Father," Daggett caught sight of his wife and daughter standing near the altar talking with the Tinsleys.

"Tolerance," Eric Dawson picked up the cue, "Tolerance as opposed to Casting the First Stone. Appropriate topics for today, I'd say," Eric's grin broadened, his eyes following the receding figures of Little John Winslow and his family.

"Tolerance for everyone," Father Morgan admonished, catching the direction of Eric's glance.

"That's true," Eric relinquished his gaze.

"Surely not for murder," Enderby demurred. "Not tolerance for murderers."

"But one must be proven guilty," Mary Daniels reminded him, "before anyone reaches to lift the first stone. With murder, too, isn't that right, Father?"

"Exactly right, Mary."

"And true guilt, I suppose, involves evil . . . evil intent," Eric concluded. "That'll let Little John off."

"That's the sticking point, all right," Enderby conceded. "And how does one determine what is evil? Intentional evil. Isn't that how you phrased it?" Father Morgan's sermons were rarely so provocative.

"Mmmm, and how does one determine appropriate punishment or intentional justice." Father Morgan stopped short of returning to his sermon by nodding toward Daggett, "I suppose you could say that's why we Canadians have laws and the mounted police."

"Let's say that's why we have a just God," Daggett returned the compliment. "I just wish I could say that Canadian justice was certain and swift. But if I am the one who represents justice in this land," he shook his head ruefully, "then, at least in the case I'm pursuing right now, it's neither."

"The Lord takes care of our timing," Father Morgan asserted. "Man is meant to be uncertain and cautious, questioning and accepting. What humans need, you see, is empathy and patience."

"Patience and perseverance, you mean," Enderby broke the priest's solemnity with unexpected heartiness. "That's the Mounties for you. Dogged perseverance. And that's one of your better-known traits, too, Mark Daggett. No one on this island is much worried about swiftness or certain justice. Not with you around."

"WHAT I still don't understand," Edith finally confessed, "is why. Why did John Thomas Bush have a gun? Why did he want to kill you?"

James blanched.

"It's time you told the rest, James," Willa put a hand on his arm. "I guessed the first part right, but there is more, I know. An explanation, a reason."

With several long sighs, James began to put his story together.

"Bush thought I would tell what I knew... knew about him ... what he did ... what I saw him do." The words fell out of James' mouth like a crazy quilt, random pieces stitched with pauses. "I didn't tell ... I was just that scared ... and he knew I left there ... I ran as fast as I could ... from New Bedford ... I came here and I didn't talk ... didn't talk there, didn't talk here ... he didn't know where I was ... didn't even know my name or where I went ... everyone on the docks called me Jimmy, just Jimmy ... a Yank thing to do ... but he knew what I saw ... he'd seen me ... and when he caught sight of me here, here on Grand Manan, he came right after me ... wouldn't believe I'd stay quiet ... said the only way he'd believe me ... was dead."

Edith wanted to say, *Saw him do what?* and *How did he happen to come here?* But she didn't. She didn't say anything. She waited. And so did Willa.

"It was only chance he saw me," James began again slowly, between huge breaths, "just chance. Sharkey offered to drive me all the way home. Doesn't usually. And in one more day, I'd have been out to sea with Sam Jackson. Bush wouldn't have seen me then. Almost didn't anyway. He had barely arrived when Sharkey and I passed through town. Coming out of the bakery, he was. Had a little bag of scones or some such and stopped to talk to Miss Briggs. It was a big shock to see him standing there. I made myself as small as I could, hunched behind Sharkey. But he had me right off. I knew he had me. Soon as Sharkey dropped me off, I slipped away and went to wait on the dock. I figured he'd come there to look and he did. I told him I wouldn't tell. Swore it on my mother's soul. But he wouldn't believe me."

"Wouldn't tell what, James," Willa finally interjected, "say what you wouldn't tell."

"How could I know he'd find me," James seemed unable to stop the flow of words he had started. "Here, of all places, here on Grand Manan," the words marched forth, emphatic, even paced, as though his life depended on their orderly arrangement. "I'd seen him before on the docks at New Bedford, but I didn't know his name and he didn't know me. I never figured for a moment he'd find Grand Manan . . . find me on Grand Manan . . . "

The words stopped, almost of their own accord, and James let his gaze drift out across the water toward the weir. Two gulls lazed above. Farther out a whale rose and skimmed momentarily along the surface, then spouted.

"Tell us, James. Tell us what you saw. Tell us now."

"It *was* odd, you know," placing emphasis on the verb, Eric Dawson prepared to explain again. Daggett's response was so sudden, so dramatic, Eric thought perhaps Daggett had misunderstood. No one else was reacting that way. But there was Daggett, already six strides from the church, running full out for the Chevrolet.

"What on earth," Elizabeth Daggett called from the church door.

"Tell us again, Eric," James Enderby swung around to demand, "I'm not sure I . . ."

"It's just that yesterday I saw someone on Seven Days Work and someone else on the beach . . . pretty much at the same time . . . and in the very same spot where Mr. Bush went off the cliff. It took my breath away for a minute. There I was in the dory, in the very same place, rowing . . ."

"What on earth has gotten into my husband?" Elizabeth Daggett joined the small group, which had moved quickly to the grass just beyond the church steps. "Father, do you know?"

"That's exactly what we are trying to understand," the priest adopted his most reassuring tone.

"I hadn't expected to see him here in the first place," Elizabeth's frown drew vertical lines, one slightly longer than the other, between her eyes.

"The fellow on the beach was in white," Eric's voice maintained an even pace, "the one above in red, something red . . . then they were gone . . . the one on the beach running toward the Cove . . . the one above just gone. My heart stopped. I suppose he ran into the woods toward the road, but I don't know . . ."

"But why," Enderby demanded. "Why did they run?"

"I have no idea. It was just," Eric paused to review the scene, "they saw each other and then they were gone. And later, I guess I was already unloading nets for repair, I saw the same fellow in white dart out from between pilings to leap onto the deck of the

S. S. Grand Manan. Odd thing to do, but there was no harm. I don't think anyone else even noticed. They were just then lowering the gangplank, and a few minutes later he walked off across it."

The Chevrolet sputtered and jolted away.

"SORRY, Miss Cather," James shook himself like a dog and turned to face Willa. "It's hard to say it. A secret kept so long . . . so deep."

"It's all right, James, we understand," Willa reached over and took hold of his hand.

"James," Edith added, "you mustn't be ashamed or afraid. Not of us. And don't protect us. Very little shocks us and that man is gone. You have nothing to fear. We're here to help."

"I believe you are," James' voice was firm. "You're sure . . . "

Both women nodded.

"All right, then," James began. "I saw him hit a woman, John Thomas Bush. A blond woman. Her head snapped so," James flung his head to the right, "I think right then her neck broke . . . and blood gushed from her mouth . . . her nose . . . her eyes . . . ." James caught himself, "Sorry, you don't need to hear all that."

"It's all right, James," Willa's hand still covered his. "We don't want you to censor a thing. As Edith said, we're hardy souls, not much shocks us."

"Tell us what you saw, James. It's best to get it out . . . all of it . . . just get it out of you."

James gathered himself and moved back to the scene. "She was wearing a dress, a white dress . . . torn in places . . . and smudged . . . she had bruises . . . her arms, her cheek," James raised his hand to his face. "Even before I saw him hit her, she had bruises. She said *No* . . . once . . . loud . . . *No*. Then he hit her. Hit her so hard her head spun . . . and then her body followed. It jerked . . . lifeless . . . like a chicken runs when it's already dead."

XXII

"WHAT DO YOU mean, Johnson left the island?" Daggett's voice cracked.

"Harvey's right, Mr. Daggett," Geneva Andrews hurried from the dining room, drying her hands in her apron and crushing the tiny flowers in its patterned print. "Mrs. Johnson asked me to pack them a picnic. They left with the Jamesons not more than twenty minutes ago."

"Richard Dalhouse was going to take them off in his motor launch to look for puffins, they said."

"Puffins. Motor launch."

"That's right, out on Machias, they said," Geneva's hands wrapped themselves in her apron.

"Richard's got one of those new Evinrudes," Harvey shifted his weight behind the counter. "Lots of horsepower."

Daggett's mind jumped to Sam Jackson. His was one of the few boats that could catch them. But Jackson would be down island on Sunday at the Baptist Church. Eric Dawson, maybe. He was close at hand. He could get a boat. Or young James. Daggett almost leapt in the air. Young James could get Sam Jackson's boat.

Daggett spun on his heel and ran out of The Swallowtail before Geneva could straighten her apron.

THEY had been silent, it seemed to Edith, a very long time, during which she saw again and again the arm swing, the head spin, the blood spurt, and then . . . in slow motion . . . the man, John Thomas Bush in his dainty shoes and three-piece pin-striped suit,

221

reach down to fling the lifeless blond at his feet into the lap of a waiting trawler whose slime-covered nets cradled the young body so carelessly tossed. And what had he said while he pocketed his gun and straightened his tie and brushed at his sleeve with a white linen handkerchief, this man in the pin stripes, what had he said . . . *Now look what you made me do* . . . this John Thomas Bush, as he waved the boat off . . . *Now look what you made me do, you careless bitch* . . . this John Thomas Bush who turned on his heel . . . to see young James . . . hands slack, eyes wide . . . slip from the neighboring pier and into the quiet sea.

THE Chevrolet coughed and complained but flew past the docks and the bank and Rose Cottage and Tinsley's and Newton's and Jackson's, leaving enough dust in its wake to draw imprecations from Little John, who took several steps back toward the church until Anna's hand stopped him.

"Little John, we're on our way home. The constable would have stopped if he wanted to speak with you."

"But he just went the other way, and now here he is, coming back fast."

"I know."

"He has my gun," Little John tried again.

"So he does."

WILLA had it right all along, Edith narrowed her eyes. Willa had it right . . . *Now look what you made me do, you careless bitch* . . . the sentiments she gave Frank Shabata and Wick Cutter years ago . . . wife killers both . . . Willa had it right long before she knew about John Thomas Bush . . . *Look what you made me do* . . . and she had it right about Bush now.

And about young James. *He'd have shot me but I dove deep.* That's how James got away. *He'd have shot me so I dove deep.* Edith shook

222

herself. Her lungs hurt, her arms had turned to lead. She had been holding her breath, she realized, swimming hard in her mind.

James looked exhausted, too, slumped in the Adirondack. Edith inspected his hands, the strength of his arms . . . and saw again the other arm . . . the arm in the suit . . . swing again . . . and again the head spin . . . lifeless . . . careless.

"BUT that still doesn't explain Matthew Johnson," Willa's voice ended Edith's review.

"Why follow that man," Willa was frowning.

James took a full minute to reply. Then, reanimated, he glanced over toward Seven Days Work. "It's like I told you, I saw him poking around on the beach."

"He was there, so you followed him?" Willa chided.

"Not exactly," James shifted forward in his chair, "the truth is, I followed him because he was doing what I had come to do. Poke around for the things Daggett never found, the stuff that fell out of Bush's pockets when he went over the cliff. Not the gun. I knew the gun had to be there, but I wasn't looking for that. Johnson wasn't either. He saw it and left it. I watched him," James glanced at Edith, "I had binoculars, too."

"What did he want, then?" Willa's voice carried an edge. Impatience. Skepticism. Edith couldn't tell which, but she felt it, too.

"What we both wanted were names . . . names of the people who brought Bush to Grand Manan. I knew he had them on him . . . on a blue piece of paper he had slipped into his passport. He showed it to me, waved it at me. Said he was putting together some sort of big deal. Big bucks, he said, big connections. And he was the connector, putting big money with big muscle. He laughed at his own joke. I was nothing, he said, an incidental. He wasn't going to let me spoil his deal.

"He was putting his passport away when he sort of stumbled . . .

waving his hands . . . getting ready to put it in his pocket," James moved his hands in front his chest to mime, "one of those pockets on the inside of men's fancy suits. While he was doing that he took a step forward, looking at me and talking at the same time. The gun was in his left hand, the hand holding his lapel. . . . For the first time, the gun was aimed away from me . . . toward the sea . . . and then he stumbled . . . he stumbled just enough," James closed his eyes. He sat back in his chair.

This time Willa didn't hesitate, "The list, the list. Why was that so important?" She broke James free of the scene in his mind and sent him back to the beach, to Matthew Johnson, to the day before.

"Right," James cleared his throat and leaned forward. "What I figure is, Johnson was afraid Bush had his name written down somewhere and eventually someone would find it. He had to find that blue sheet and destroy it."

Edith broke in, "But why? Why would his name be there?"

"Money," Willa guessed, "he was the big money. Is that it?"

James nodded.

"I don't understand."

"Johnson came to Grand Manan to meet the big muscle and Bush was to introduce them," Willa tried an explanation.

"That's my guess," James agreed.

"But why would Matthew Johnson want to meet muscle?"

"Takes muscle and money," Willa ventured.

"What does?"

"Why don't you say exactly what you think they were doing," Willa turned to James.

"Bootlegging," James pronounced the word with a Canadian's elongated *oo*.

"BUT James can't take you out in Sam's boat."

"Bootlegging! Here!"

224

"Surely there's some mistake."

"James didn't come to church today."

"How on earth does bootlegging fit into this, Mark?"

"I think I know where James keeps Sam's keys."

"Bootlegging! Can't be. Not on Grand Manan."

"With those keys I could get you out in no time flat, Constable Daggett."

Mary Daniels' and Eric Dawson's were the only voices Daggett actually heard in the jumble of reactions from those still clustered on the sidewalk in front of the church. Sam Jackson's boat could catch the motor launch.

"Well," James Enderby pointed out to Father Morgan and Elizabeth and Jennifer Daggett as they watched the others speed off in the Chevrolet, "we might as well be at the bottom of the sea for all the more we know."

"Bootlegging on Grand Manan," Father Morgan scoffed and lifted his hand to his forehead, "I just can't believe it."

"Well," Elizabeth finally volunteered, "Mark doesn't usually act until he's sure of what he's doing."

XXIII

IT WASN'T UNTIL much later that everything finally came together. And not until the following evening, when everyone had the full story, that Grand Manan understood how close it had come to being dragged into the American underworld.

Jacobus had thrown open the whole of Whale Cove and the full crew of Cottage Girls were busying themselves in twilight celebration, clattering cups and saucers, pumping the handle on the ice cream freezer, icing and slicing freshly baked cakes, and handing out spoons and forks and plates and brightly colored napkins. The sky was shot through with pink and turquoise and lavender, and the sun hovered, gold and gargantuan, about to sink beyond the western edge of the sea.

The principals had not yet arrived, but at least half of North Head and several down islanders were already overflowing the main house and spilling out of its doors. Matt bounded among them, pausing only long enough to bark at Dottie Voorhees, striding toward the Reo, a freshly mended helmet tucked under her arm. Peter Coney and Sabra Jane Briggs, resplendent in red, strode beside her. They confronted a jabbering Little John, who was just coming in.

Coney jolted to a halt. "Let's begin the evening's remarks right here and now," she suddenly belted out, raising her right hand high.

Little John's mouth snapped shut. The crowd quieted and turned, expectant. Coney's hand drifted down to settle on Sabra Jane's red-shirted shoulder. When Coney prepared to speak again, Little John's mustache took a single, violent leap, then straightened itself out in an unbroken line.

"You may make your apology public now, Little John," Coney kept her tone casual. It was as though, simply and rather distractedly, she was calling a meeting to order to take care of trivial business, making official what had already been done.

But Little John would have none of it. His mustache held firm.

Coney tried again, "Now, Little John? Your apology?"

Little John puffed out his jowls until Anna caught his hand. He opened his lips but nothing came out.

"Now, Little John?" Coney's voice acquired an edge, "Your apology, please?"

"What a wonderful idea," Anna finally broke in. Her grip on Little John tightened almost imperceptibly. "What a wonderful opportunity. Why not seize the moment, dear, to tell everyone how sorry you are to have embarrassed Miss Briggs?"

Red crept upward from Little John's collar. He sucked in his cheeks. Anna held firm.

"Yes, all right," Little John glanced at his wife, "yes, I did . . . I did embarrass."

"And you're sorry," Anna nudged him on.

"Yes . . . that's right . . . I am."

Except for a sharp intake of breath from Eva McDaniels, who had halted just to the left of Little John's shoulder, no other sound ensued.

Finally, Sabra Jane cleared her throat and thrust out her hand.

Little John stared at the ground. Anna dropped his hand. Little John's floated by itself in midair but did not move forward. Seconds passed. Finally, with a little grunt, Little John pushed his fingers forward and clasped Sabra Jane's. Suddenly, his upper body began to bend, his hand lifted hers. He raised her fingers toward his lips.

Sabra Jane flinched and Anna grimaced. Old fashioned, the grimace said, and condescending. Little John caught himself, his eyes on his wife. Finally, he tried a few short up and down strokes, as if Sabra Jane's fingers were a handle and the pump fully primed.

Sabra Jane began to laugh. Little John reddened and then caught her laugh. He looked at his wife. She began to chuckle. Little John laughed and released Sabra Jane's fingers. He put his hands in his pockets. Sabra Jane shoved hers in the side slits of her breeches.

"Well, that's done," Peter Coney announced. "Let's begin the celebration."

"Hear, hear," James Enderby added from behind. The crowd raised a cheer.

"Good fellow," Sam Jackson clapped Little John on the back.

"That's the way, Little John," Roy Sharkey removed his cigar to shout, rolling his eyes heavenward.

At the far edge of the crowd, near an opening in the trees, Rob Feeney observed to those standing in the cake line nearby, "I suppose that means an end to this season's witch hunt."

"Naughty boy," Eloise Derby took Feeney's measure. "Perhaps you mean vixen hunt . . . with all those sly little broad jumps."

"Beg your pardon, Miss Derby?"

Eloise Derby struck the pose of Artemis in flight.

"Ah," Feeney nodded, "people do say she lopes."

"She lopes, others leap," Eloise Derby elevated her arms.

So Miss Derby was a tease, Feeney grinned. "How was I to know Matthew Johnson had been a track star at Yale," he raised his hands in mock surprise.

"Here, eat cake," Eloise Derby laughed and shoved a blue willow plate in Feeney's direction.

"Broad jumps, indeed," Feeney's voice rose, "the man's a veritable air ship. An Icarus," he spread out his arms, and Miss Derby placed the blue willow in the hand nearest hers. "The boat was that far from the dock," Rob waved both arms. "Ten, twelve, maybe fifteen feet from the dock," the cake clung to the blue willow, "and he made it both ways . . . off the boat and on again . . . made it without my ever seeing him do it."

Eloise Derby frowned and handed Rob a fork.

"SLOW down," Mary Daniels protested, "we'll get there soon enough."

Young James had insisted that before his mother did anything else, she had to meet Miss Cather and Miss Lewis and see the view from their cliff. The minute Daggett stopped the car, James leapt from his seat and whisked Jenny to his side. Lizzie and Janey Dawson joined them, but Mary Daniels took her time. She wanted to make sure Constable Daggett understood her full appreciation, both for her son's freedom and for the ride. Daggett said he did and put the Chevrolet in gear. With its new spark plug in place, the engine ran smooth. Daggett still had to pick up his wife and daughter and retrieve Eric Dawson from the docks.

It wasn't, James readily confessed, that his mother didn't know who Miss Cather and Miss Lewis were or hadn't seen their particular view. All of the villagers, after all, knew the women—Miss Cather, the famous recluse, and Miss Lewis, her protector. And the Red Trail crossed right before their cottage, so everyone knew the view.

It was instead that James had guessed that Miss Cather and Miss Lewis would refuse to join the celebration. Daggett had guessed as much, too, and said so in his office. That's why, the minute Daggett had given him leave, James grabbed Jenny by the hand and raced home. First he had to convince his mother she was the one who could change the ladies' minds, then he would see to it that she convinced the ladies. Daggett only promised a lift to Whale Cove. James and Mary Daniels could take it from there.

James wanted Miss Cather and Miss Lewis to be part of the celebration. He wanted everyone on the island to know how warm and wonderfully kind they had been. If it weren't for them, he would be in jail right now. He had withheld information. He had interfered with an investigation. He had tried to take the law into his own hands, Mark Daggett had declared.

Of course he had done all that, Miss Cather had pointed out James withheld information because he was on foreign soil where he knew virtually no one when he just happened to witness a violent murder by a powerful and influential criminal whose murderous intent—toward him—was eminently clear. And when James fled to Grand Manan, what was he to say to Mark Daggett? That while he was in the United States he had seen a young woman beaten to death by a well known and powerful criminal? That no other witnesses were likely to come forward? That no one would even be able to prove a murder had taken place? That the young woman's body would never be found?

And after John Thomas Bush appeared on Grand Manan, what was James to say? That a man James had never actually met and no one on the island had ever seen, within hours of his arrival, forced young James to take him to Seven Days Work where he expected James to jump off the cliff? That the resulting death was an accident and self-defense?

Would anybody believe any of this? Miss Cather was incredulous.

Of course, young James withheld information and tried at first to flee and then to conduct his own investigation, Miss Cather scoffed. If James had come forth sooner, his story would have made no sense at all and he might still have been in danger. Knowledge was what James needed, knowledge and proof. He didn't even know who else might be involved. And that's exactly what he was trying to find out when Miss Cather and Miss Lewis first spotted him at Eel Brook. When the time was right and they asked him what he had been doing, he told them. And then he told Daggett, Miss Cather assured Daggett. And what James said had allowed Mark Daggett to hold Matthew Johnson. Daggett had no reason to hold Johnson just for jumping on and off the S. S. Grand Manan. So Johnson had tricked Daggett and run when he saw Daggett on the beach. Nothing criminal in that. Quite right, Daggett finally conceded, quite right. And what more could the constable ask in terms of cooperation, Miss Cather wanted to know.

Miss Lewis said she thought James should be released. Where else would James go, she wanted to know. He wasn't likely to run off the island. Not now. Miss Cather said that if Daggett was reluctant, they would pay his bail. Daggett assured them he would release James without bail. Miss Cather had grinned broadly and Miss Lewis said she thought a celebration was in order. They would talk to Miss Jacobus.

That's why James thought Miss Cather and Miss Lewis should be part of the celebration. He wanted to make a speech. He wanted everyone to know the full story, to know what these women did. He wanted to give public thanks. Miss Cather and Miss Lewis would refuse him, he was certain of that, but they wouldn't refuse his mother. They could say no to him, but no one had ever said no to his mother.

Mary Daniels, however, was less keen about insisting the ladies come. She thought they should be able to preserve their privacy if that's what they wanted. Jenny Dawson took her side.

"Miss Cather already said it, James. What matters is not what they did but that you are free," Jenny squeezed his hand. They had already reached the bottom of the orchard. The cottage wasn't far beyond.

"You are free, the danger is past, the mystery is solved," Mary Daniels sighed her relief. "That's all that really matters."

"Right," Jenny dodged a low-hanging branch. "And besides, those women really didn't have much to do with that, James. You did," she patted his arm, "you and the constable."

231

"You're wrong there, Jenny," James chided. "Those women, the constable, and your brother Eric. That's who did it. Don't forget your brother in all this. Not only did he collect the body, he helped Daggett bring in the motor launch." James began to chuckle, "I just wish I could have been there."

"Puffins," Mary Daniels flung out her arms, "thousands of puffins . . . millions of puffins . . . and four people in a dingy," she began to giggle.

"Not my idea of desperate desperadoes," Jenny caught the joke and laughed at her own and James' seriousness, "or a dangerous situation."

"But Eric and the constable didn't know that," James felt he must defend their honor. "They couldn't know that until they got to Machias and saw the motor launch moored and Dickie Dalhouse rowing toward land. Even so," James ventured, "Johnson could still have been planning to force Dickie to take them to Eastport . . . or Lubec . . . or . . . well, anywhere," James flung his arms in the air. "He said he wasn't, of course. Daggett said he thought Johnson was enjoying the cat-and-mouse game so much, he just didn't want to call it off."

"Daggett doesn't take Johnson very seriously, does he? As a criminal, I mean," Jenny brushed away a low-hanging bough.

"Arrogant, that's what Mark Daggett called him, and I guess I agree," James paused to flick a mosquito from his forehead.

"Men like that never think about getting caught," his mother nodded, "and when they do, they think the law is just something for people like you and me."

"I never thought of it like that," Jenny glanced at her future mother-in-law.

The cottage lay just ahead, shadows stretching across the lawn.

"Anyway," James began to aim their conversation toward its conclusion, "I didn't do much to catch anyone. Eric did. I just told

Daggett what happened to me. And I might not have done that if Miss Cather and Miss Lewis hadn't forced me . . . hadn't figured it all out and listened and taken me directly to Daggett. Miss Cather had figured it out ahead, you know. My part anyway. But she thought I should have a chance to confess."

"Wise women, waiting for you to come to them."

"Yes, I guess so," James glanced at his mother. "Miss Cather said she knew I would, knew my character. Miss Lewis said she knew I would, too. It had just never occurred to her I had so much to tell. They hadn't talked it through yet, the two of them together, and Matthew Johnson was a total mystery to them."

"Some sleuths," Jenny giggled. "But you were the piece that didn't fit. That's what Constable Daggett called you, the piece that didn't fit."

"He had only one part of the puzzle," James responded seriously, "they had the other."

"A darned silly puzzle, if you ask me," Mary Daniels blurted out and pointed to the view ahead. Deep purple touched the horizon, spiked with lavender and pink. "All that fuss about liquor."

Without sunlight, a haze would soon settle down over Seven Days Work. James increased the pace.

XXIV

"Bootlegging on Grand Manan," Margaret Byington bellowed and wiped the table clean, "can you beat that. Just when we're beginning to enjoy the taste of champagne again, that could have caused a lot of trouble," she picked up a tray stacked with soiled tableware and carried it into the kitchen.

"Let's invite Hoover's Crime Commission to come for a visit, what do you say. They'll see how well behaved we are with liquor and how poorly off others are because of the ban," Ethelwyn Manning planted herself next to the swinging doors. She filled a tray with clean plates. The crowd was still pouring in.

"Let's, I say," Alice Jordan chuckled dryly, passing the cups along, "then Willa and Edith can swap their stories with old friends from Lincoln."

"That's right, I remember now," her sister nodded wisely, licking frosting from the back of her hand, "Dean Pound was a friend of theirs, wasn't he?"

"The way I heard it, his sister is the one Willa knew best. A lovely tennis champion, I believe," Manning added an elaborate wink.

"Is she the one who earned her doctorate in Germany?"

"She is," Alice Jordan gave Byington a sharp glance. "A Nineties' Modern Woman . . . socialite, scholar, and all-around athlete."

"A Nineties' example of Willa's janefoolery, to hear Edith tell it," Margaret Byington's deep laughter filled the room.

"Willa, too," Alice Jordan gave in and giggled behind her hand, "when she's in a mood to confess."

"So I understand," Manning confirmed, "though I've never heard her say it."

"There's a lot they never say," Margaret's humor began to turn droll, "and inviting the Hoover Commission to visit is about the only way the Commission . . . or anyone . . . will ever find out what Willa and Edith have been up to just now."

"Absolutely," Mary Jordan began to pump fresh water into the largest tea kettle.

"We must never tell a soul," Alice Jordan admonished.

"We never will," Margaret Byington crossed her heart.

"Mary Daniels is so proud of young James," Edith yawned and brushed crumbs from her lap, "it's a pleasure to see."

Mattie took the opportunity of the empty dining room to sidle closer to Edith's chair.

"It was absolutely the nicest thing in the world you could have done for Mary Daniels to have this celebration here tonight, Sallie Jacobus," Mark Daggett raised his empty cup.

"It was absolutely the nicest thing in the world you could have done to make it possible for her son to be here, Mark Daggett," Jacobus filled his cup with black coffee.

From across the table, Elizabeth Daggett smiled and added sugar to her cup.

"He still has to go through the hearing, of course," Daggett used a spoon to cool his coffee.

"Oh, but he should be fine with that," Edith sipped the last of her lemonade, "now that his secret's out and he knows the response. Such applause. Such cheering," she placed her glass exactly in front of her on the blue-checkered oilcloth, "and for Eric, too. Fine young men, both of them," she glanced up, "Willa said so, too. The island has a right to be proud."

"Of their constable, too," Jacobus poured the last of the pot into her own cup and returned Elizabeth Daggett's broad grin with one of her own.

The crowded dining room was empty at last, the main house and the grounds quiet. Only intermittent clattering came from the kitchen, one of the serving girls filling kettles in preparation for the early morning rounds of hot water. In her mind's eye, Edith could see young Kate who delivered their water each morning and hear Willa say, as she did without fail, I declare, that jug is bigger than the girl. Of course, the water wouldn't have much time to heat this evening. It was already past midnight. Edith stifled a yawn. Just about everyone had gone, including Willa. Daggett had delivered James, his mother, and the Dawsons to their doors and come back for Elizabeth and Jennifer, whose deep, sleeping sighs reached them from the sofa in front of the fireplace where she had tucked up her feet.

The islanders had reveled through the night, raising cheer after cheer when Daggett brought word that Jack Watson was under lock and key in Calais and officials in Montreal were questioning Jackson Knoll. St. Stephen had taken Burt Isaacs in tow. Telegrams had also come in from New Bedford, where several dockworkers had explaining to do, and friends of John Thomas Bush were being sought in Boston and Detroit. Bush himself, the telegrams said, was hardly missed. Even fellow gangsters feared the man and his temper. His real name, Detroit suggested, may have been Buschetti, Johnny Buschetti, a bad seed from Chicago who came back from the Great War a seasoned con artist and killer who was deadly with women. He had ties to Capone. Daggett planned to check with Chicago.

Edith and Willa had watched the evening's festivities from the edge of the orchard, where James made them comfortable. A compromise, Willa declared. They would see everything but talk to no one. And no one, James in particular, must say anything to or about them. And so, undisturbed, they had watched through the speeches and the fiddle playing and the dancing. Sabra Jane stopped by to talk. Daggett waved from a distance. No one else even seemed to be aware of their presence. Willa's delight when Emma Parker grabbed Jesse Martin for a few turns among the dancers had almost given them away, Edith chuckled to herself. Emma's gray curls bounced perfectly in time, but Jesse never quite got the step.

"Very likely no one will be tried for anything, you know," Daggett broke the silence.

"Self-defense is no crime in Canada," Elizabeth nodded.

"Neither is bootlegging," Daggett swallowed his coffee. It was agreeably warm.

"Shouldn't be elsewhere, either," Jacobus pushed back in her chair. "Too many people like their glass of wine," she waved her hand as though the dining room were still filled with her friends. "Most of us do. And none of this would have happened if it weren't for Prohibition."

"I wish that were entirely true," Elizabeth traced a line through blue squares on the oilcloth with the edge of her spoon, "but violence does go with drunkenness."

"It does," Daggett nodded, settling back in his chair, "but Jacobus is right too. Bush or Buschetti's kind of violence, whatever his name, well, that goes on with or without alcohol."

"True," Elizabeth conceded, "it's like a disease."

"Universal . . . endemic . . . epidemic," Edith extended the simile.

"Yes," Jacobus drew her own conclusion, "a plague upon men."

Daggett chuckled, and Elizabeth smiled.

"It's too bad about that young Mr. Johnson," Edith shifted to consider the lure of fast money. Jacobus' joke passed her by.

The three looked at her.

"Trying to catch up in that way with his wife's wealth, I mean," Edith tried to explain.

Jacobus cocked her head.

"It's hard for a couple when the money's not equal. Especially for men . . . for some men . . . "

"What's hard is earning respect, not money," Jacobus interjected, her voice acquiring an edge.

"Perhaps he has learned," Elizabeth smiled. "Mark says Matthew Johnson was truly shocked when he found out that Bush murdered a young woman and tried to kill James."

"He was, but he shouldn't have been. A man like Bush may dress like money and talk like wealth, but he's a man without breeding. Johnson would have known that if he'd had any real class himself," Daggett nudged his cup around on the oilcloth before him. When it reached the spot from where it started, he let it rest.

"Be careful, Mark, you'll sound like a snob and a eugenicist," Elizabeth scolded.

Daggett grinned. Elizabeth surprised him sometimes. Like now. She seemed perfectly comfortable with Miss Lewis and Jacobus. Comfortable enough to tease him.

"Putting class and breeding quite aside," Edith returned the conversation to the line of thinking she had been developing, "it's clear that the only gain from the sort of pact Mr. Johnson was about to strike with Mr. Bush is a great deal of pain. It was a devil's bargain. Mephistophelean."

"Right," Jacobus swung Edith's thought around to fit her own, "and Prohibition is the devil's tool box. Thou Shalt Not . . . "

"And *thou shalt not* means one has to try . . . whatever it is," Elizabeth nodded a faint *yes*, "I see what you mean."

"Fortunately for Johnson," Daggett reached for his pipe, "he never hesitated when it came to turning over the slip of paper and passport he found on the beach," Daggett paused to tap charred bits of tobacco into the ashtray before him, "never denied knowing John Thomas Bush . . . and never feigned ignorance when it came to explaining how he misled me." With the pipe emptied, Daggett tamped fresh tobacco and retrieved the little can of matches from his breast pocket. "He did try to mislead me, you know," he added between puffs as he relit the pipe.

"We certainly do," Edith said with emphasis, "and so did these . . . what were their names . . . the fellows who searched the room at Swallowtail and the cliff at Seven Days Work?" She paused to rub her sore hand, "They were looking for the same slip of paper, right?"

"That's my bet, anyway. And I'm guessing Jackson Knoll was the first one, Burt Isaacs the other. Knoll had easy access to Bush's room, Isaacs to the torch," Daggett paused to retamp his pipe and strike another match. "Odd sense of humor, that Isaacs," he mused through puffs of smoke, "leaving his torch in my car."

"Effective, though," Elizabeth glanced at her husband. "He managed to frighten me half to death and throw you off track," she turned to Edith, "to say nothing of what he did to you and Miss Cather."

"Added excitement to your evening, that's what he did," Jacobus chuckled. Mattie stirred, and Jacobus reached down to scratch her behind the ears.

"Lucky it wasn't Willa's hand, that's all I have to say," Edith glanced at her own bandaged left hand. "Such pain," Edith shook her head, "she's had enough of such pain, and it keeps her from writing."

"That's true," Jacobus agreed, "hard as this may be for Edith, the other's worse. Willa has been experiencing terrible pains in her hand," Jacobus explained to Elizabeth and Daggett. "Her thumb really." When Edith nodded, Jacobus stiffened everything from her wrist to her fingertips. "Had to keep her hand and part of her arm in a brace."

"Terrible, terrible pain and the dullness of immobility," Edith nodded. "It truly has been awful. Mine," she flexed her hand and grinned, "is nothing compared to that. And you're right, Cobus,

239

that experience certainly did add to the excitement of our evening . . . of our whole summer."

"But if you're right," Jacobus turned to address Daggett, "Burt Isaacs and Jackson Knoll must have been as mystified as everyone else. They didn't know who killed Bush, and they didn't know who Johnson was or how to find him. They only knew each other."

"Right," Daggett leaned forward and put his elbows on the table, "and until Johnson got his hands on that slip of paper, he had no idea who Jackson Knoll and Burt Isaacs were. But by the time he found it, he was more interested in keeping his own name out of the whole mess than he was in making contact with them."

"But then why . . . "

"Something he overheard Harvey Andrews say," Daggett anticipated Elizabeth's question, "made him think he might be able to find Knoll on Machias, so he decided it was worth a try. Imagine Johnson's surprise," Daggett began to laugh, "when Johnson found that the Machias Dickie Dalhouse took him to was an island populated only by puffins."

"Machias, Machias," Elizabeth caught the joke, "he wanted the town in Maine, but Dickie took him to the island."

"Exactly," Daggett leaned forward, his face sober again. "My theory," he pointed with the stem of his pipe to squares on the oilcloth, "is that only Bush knew all the players." Daggett touched one square with the stem of his pipe, then circled through the surrounding squares, "Johnson, Knoll, Watson, Isaacs." The pipe stem named off the squares, then stopped and backed up. "No, maybe Bush didn't know Watson and Isaacs," Daggett reconsidered, "maybe only Knoll knew them. Well," the pipe stem hesitated, "that's not entirely clear yet, but it doesn't matter. It's also not clear whether they intended to run liquor from Grand Manan," the pipe stem touched the center square, "or just use the island for their rendezvous."

The three women studied the squares in silence.

"In some ways a rendezvous makes sense," Elizabeth finally volunteered.

"Mmmm," Daggett thought it through, "we may never really know, but at any rate," the stem returned to square one, "Bush's job was to introduce Johnson and Knoll. Johnson was to put up the money, Knoll and Bush to arrange liquor and transportation. That takes a lot of money. Boats, trucks, guns, payoffs, ammunition, men, they all cost a lot. Knoll was to make arrangements in Canada, Bush in the United States. Knoll's was the easy part. He had to be secretive but liquor's legal in Canada, at least the production and transportation of it. Bush had all the rough stuff, and probably because of that, he couldn't look the part," Daggett chuckled. "Neither could, I suppose. Had to look classy, you know, Bush and Knoll, or they'd never have been able to hook a partner like Johnson," the pipe stem moved through the squares and back again. "Knoll might have been a little swaggery, as Harvey Andrews said, but presentable enough for Johnson, I guess."

"How did they hook him, anyway?"

Daggett looked up and grinned at Elizabeth. It was as though they were leaning over their own kitchen table, Elizabeth's questions falling right into place. He took a sip of coffee, cooling now.

"Johnson said he met Bush in Boston and saw him again in New Bedford. He said Bush impressed him. He had the right contacts . . . talk . . . manners . . . dress. All the right surface stuff," Daggett shook his head, "and, after all, Johnson's a fool."

"Naive," Jacobus glanced up, "that's not so bad."

"Yes, a true innocent," Edith placed her hands on the table.

"Naive, innocent, a fool. A man who wanted to win his wife's respect and didn't know how to do it," Daggett drained his cup. "He knew that what he was planning to do was illegal in his country, but he believed he could get away with it without real harm coming to anybody. Just a little irregularity, I believe he called it," Daggett coughed and took a moment to clear his throat.

"Not exactly high ethical standards," Jacobus agreed.

"And absolutely no judge of character," Daggett returned to his narrative. "Johnson had no idea, he said, that the man he chose to do business with would ever do anything so damning as murder. How could he realize that Bush was a killer, a man who killed women as if it were sport."

All three women at the table sat a little straighter. Mattie rose to her feet.

"And New Bedford thinks the young woman whose death James witnessed wasn't the only one Bush killed," Daggett sat back in his chair. "There may have been other girls, their telegram said. And in Boston. New York. Other girls. None of them heard from, none of them found."

"I can't understand a man like that," Edith pushed against a spot on the oilcloth with her fingernail.

"No one can," Daggett assured them.

"So James held the key to solving several crimes. Amazing," Sabra Jane sipped her tea and cast a glance toward the weir.

"Four murders at least," Edith held up four fingers on her good hand.

"All of the victims were young women," Willa settled deeper into her chair.

"And there were numerous dealings with gangsters and episodes of violence."

"That's not counting the solution to the death of John Thomas Bush or Buschetti or whatever his name really was. Or all they've learned about bootlegging and bootleggers," Willa pointed out.

"That's right," Edith agreed, "Mark Daggett says Matthew Johnson's testimony and the papers he found on the beach opened up a whole network of names. More than were on the blue sheet of paper. Bush had a little notebook tucked in with his passport. There already have been several arrests."

"But numbers don't matter as much as the fact that James is responsible for bringing an end to the misogynist's shady dealings and murderous career," Willa deepened her voice for melodramatic effect.

"The odd thing is, you know," Edith turned to face Sabra Jane, "that man seems to have murdered only women."

"At least that's all Daggett has been able to find out," Willa put her feet on the low wicker table they used for a hassock. "Of course, they are still investigating. Bush or Buschetti seems to have had several aliases."

Every morning brought new telegrams to Daggett's office and he brought them to show Willa and Edith. They served the best oatmeal cookies on the island, he declared.

"It is odd, though," Willa mused, "only women. But, then," she paused and went on, "misogyny is odd."

Edith and Sabra Jane agreed with silent nods. Willa moved her feet closer to Edith's. Their canvas shoes touched.

After a moment Sabra Jane chuckled and, placing her tea cup on the wicker table, rose to face the sea. "Now," she declared, "when we bring an end to misogyny, we'll really have done something."

"Yes."

Edith felt suddenly very tired and her hand hurt. An incoming tide lapped against the rocks below. Edith rested her head against her chair. All along the cliffs weathered spruce leaned in from the sea. Naughty children, willful children, Edith smiled and glanced at Willa. Naughty children with the wind in their hair, digging in their heels and reaching back to touch the land with their whole bodies. They would survive.

Beyond Sabra Jane lay the weir. Two gulls circled above. Edith watched their circles widen.

Their Circles Widen

Afterword

I FIRST VISITED Grand Manan, an island in the Bay of Fundy, in 1989. Willa Cather and Edith Lewis found Grand Manan in 1922, travelling by train to Campobello, Maine, where they caught a ferry to North Head, one of five fishing villages on the island and its main port. My partner Mary Ellen Capek and I reached the island the way most people do these days, taking a two-and-a-half-hour ferry ride from Blacks Harbour in New Brunswick, Canada. I had only a vague sense of where their cottage might have been on the cliffs overlooking Whale Cove. But within minutes of leaving the dock, we found ourselves taking the first drive to the right after the sign to Whale Cove Inn and bouncing down a single-track, rutted dirt road through the woods to where their cottage once stood.

Neglected after the beginning of World War II when Cather and Lewis felt it too dangerous to travel to the island, their cottage had collapsed. Before Lewis died in 1972, Cather's niece, Helen Cather Southwick, acquired the land and built a cottage replicating theirs on the same spot. When we arrived, that cottage was empty, its front windows blank, staring east through harsh sunlight toward a fishing weir circling into itself in the Bay below. There were no fishermen and no ships. The place was quiet, almost too quiet, but a trail passing through to the south proved magical, its tall pines and lush grass giving the shade and comfort Cather and Lewis must have experienced more than sixty years before. We sat a long while enjoying their presence and the sound of waves crashing on the rocks more than two hundred feet below.

Whale Cove Inn and Cottages had no vacancies that trip, so we stayed in the son's bedroom of a private home near Pettes Cove, on the way to Swallowtail Lighthouse. The room had a waterbed, a window facing the cove, and a hallway decorated with a black velour tapestry featuring a painted stag. Breakfast included strong tea and plenty of gossip about local islanders and the island's fishing industry but almost nothing about Whale Cove or Willa Cather. The next summer and the two that followed, we stayed in Orchardside at Whale Cove Inn. Located a bit farther south and closer to the Bay on the same trail we found that first day, Orchardside is an old guest cottage that Cather and Lewis shared with others during their early years on Grand Manan. It is divided into sections with two separate attic bedrooms, a small kitchen, and a living room made cozy by a fireplace and built-in bookcase. Cather and Lewis' quarters, downstairs on the north side, consisted of two rooms, one of which faced Whale Cove and held a small writing desk used, I was told, by Willa Cather.

The person who told me was the Whale Cove innkeeper, Kathleen Buckley, who had been a serving girl during the years Cather and Lewis were there. She explained that, for the first three summers, they stayed in Orchardside then built their own cottage in 1926. Other guests also built cottages on land bordering the property of Whale Cove Inn around the same time, Buckley said, all of whom continued to take meals and share in activities at the Inn. The same was true for Cather and Lewis.

It is through my conversations with Buckley, relatives of those other Whale Cove cottagers, and a local woman, Dora McLaughlin L'aventure (who as a teenager in the late 1950s and 1960s retrieved letters, manuscripts, and memorabilia from the deteriorating Cather and Lewis cottage) that I learned about Cather, Lewis, and the women who summered on Grand Manan. The Cottage Girls, the islanders called them. For many years, they reappeared every summer after 1900-1902, when Sally Jacobus, her cousin Sally Adams, Alice Coney, and Marie Felix bought the land, fixed up the house and barn, and invited friends to join them. They knew what they were doing. The first three completed their education at the Boston Normal School of Gymnastics in 1897; Marie Felix graduated from the Boston Cooking School in 1895, a year before its principal, Fannie Farmer, made it famous by publishing her cookbook. Their experiment quickly became Whale Cove Cottages, a summer colony. A women's summer colony. That was a surprise. Even more surprising, Whale Cove was eventually one of two women's summer colonies on the island.

Many places, especially in the Northeast, were well known as summer colonies, some for artists, some for religious gatherings, some for the elite who simply wanted to get out of the heat of their cities. Upstate New York was peppered with them, as were Maine, Massachusetts, Vermont, and New Hampshire, where Cather spent several weeks in 1926 at McDowell, a writer's colony in Peterborough. But a women's colony, a place where single women gathered again and again for several weeks, even months, each summer? That was unusual. And here there were two, Whale Cove at the north end of the island and The Anchorage at the south end.

The women who frequented these colonies were college-educated Americans well advanced in their careers as librarians, writers, teachers, nurses, social workers, and occasionally artists. Graduates of women's colleges such as Smith, Simmons, Mt. Holyoke, and Wellesley, they came from New York City, Boston, or elsewhere in New England; others came from the Midwest. Some had inherited money and so were independently wealthy with no need to work. But most did need to work. For them, Grand Manan was a well-earned summer vacation, a time away, a place to relax, read, hike along the cliffs, bird watch, play, indulge in conversation, and be themselves, unencumbered by the demands of their jobs or social obligations. Uninhibited. Free. And among friends.

This is the place and these are the people among whom Willa Cather and Edith Lewis chose to spend the better part of twenty summers. Cather found she could write there. If she needed to be left alone so she could stay in the book in her mind, even when she was not actively writing it, she could. They both enjoyed their cottage and the island's natural beauty. They could choose to spend time with others. Or not. Their cottage had no phone or electricity or indoor plumbing, but they were comfortably situated. They ate well, whether in the dining room of the main house—where they usually sat at the same table by themselves before joining others before the fireplace—or prepared a simple meal in their own cottage. They enjoyed an evening's stimulating conversation with friends. Or not. They had privacy when they chose and as much quiet as they liked. An ideal workplace for a writer.

The guest book at Whale Cove Cottages had long ago disappeared when I asked to see it, but Kathleen Buckley showed me the address book Sally Jacobus used during her last years at Whale Cove (she died in 1947, the same year Willa Cather died), and I began to see why Cather and Lewis were so comfortable there. Of the ninety-seven entries, at least ten were librarians from New York City, one of whom, Frances Overton, worked at the New York City Public Library and is thought to have told Cather about Whale Cove in the first place. But almost any of them could have.

Ethelwyn Manning was head librarian at the Frick Art Reference Library, established in 1920 by Helen Clay Frick, who took an active hand as director and whose name also appears in Jacobus' address book. According to Kathleen Buckley, Manning's "great friend"—a euphemism for life partner—was Katherine Schwartz, a children's librarian in New York City who made puppets and, reportedly, good whiskey sours. Other "great friends," Lucy Crissey and Phyllis Osteen, were also librarians. Lucy Crissey, like Florence Overton, worked at the New York Public Library and then for thirty years at Columbia's School of Library Science, eventually retiring as Assistant Dean.

Others flocked together in a variety of ways. Nan Peters and Henrietta Quigley, also "great friends," were part of the "Bird Girls." Along with Frances Covington, Ann McNaulty, and Etta Wedge, they took advantage of the island's trails to follow in the path of Audubon, whose early studies of birds on the island are still apparent in an extensive collection of stuffed birds at the Grand Manan Museum. Some, like Eloise Derby, who spent her winters in Paris and whose father developed Bar Harbor, had independent wealth. Several taught at private schools or universities; others, like Winifred Bromhall, wrote children's books and gained a certain amount of fame; still others like Margaret Byington were very well known.

Margaret Byington crossed paths with Cather and Lewis several times but probably did not meet them until Whale Cove. Byington earned her master's degree in sociology from Columbia University in 1902, the same year Edith Lewis graduated from Smith College and moved to New York City to begin her career as an editor. In 1906, the year Cather left Pittsburgh for New York City and an editorial job at *McClure's Magazine*, Byington moved to Pittsburgh and began a case study of poverty in Homestead, the town Henry Clay Frick built to serve his steel mills. She published the study in 1910 as a monograph entitled *Homestead, the Household of a Mill Town*. In 1910, *McClure's* was equally devoted to exposing social wrongs, and by then Lewis had joined Cather on the magazine's staff. If they had not met previously, Byington, Cather, and Lewis would certainly have known many people in common and shared similar interests.

In fact, the same is true for most of these women. Many were pro-suffrage Republicans (not the same party it is today), and some, but certainly not all, were pro prohibition. All were "Independent

Women." And in the first twenty years of the twentieth century, that designation meant something special. For Edith Lewis and several others at Whale Cove, the concept of "Independent Woman" was defined by Mary Augusta Jordan, a vivid personality in the Smith College English Department from 1884 to 1921. Jordan published well-received articles on "bachelor women" and women's colleges and designed a textbook explicitly for women entitled *Correct Writing and Speaking*. Hard work, rigorous attention to detail, and ambitious goals were only part of the task: women had to find their own voices. Edith Lewis, who was one of Jordan's students, graduating from Smith in 1902, found her voice as a professional editor, as Cather's personal editor, and as one of the top writers for the J. Walter Thompson Advertising Agency in New York City. And after she met Edith Lewis and finally stepped away from the exciting but all-consuming work of producing the monthly *McClure's Magazine,* Willa Cather certainly found hers, beginning with *O Pioneers!*

A younger set of Independent Women frequented The Anchorage, established by Sabra Jane Briggs on the southern end of the island a few years after she first visited Grand Manan in 1922. An extant registry for The Anchorage records forty-five women's names entered between 1938 and 1955, most returning year after year, often in pairs or with same group. They, too, were educated, professional women, but more of them hailed from the Midwest and, among those coming from New York, more were from Upstate or Brooklyn or from across the river in New Jersey than lived in Manhattan.

The number of entries in The Anchorage registry fell off during World War II, just as they did at Whale Cove, but unlike Whale Cove, which survived by hosting increasing numbers of tourists—many of them married couples—The Anchorage closed its doors when Sabra Jane Briggs retired. It is now a Canadian Provincial campground, open to the public. The Whale Cove Inn and Cottages still exists because, in addition to opening the Inn to the general public, Sally Jacobus and the Cottage Girls followed a unique strategy. Jacobus, who had no niece, left the Inn to Kathleen Buckley, the serving girl who had grown up on the island and worked at the Inn for years. The rest of the women who, like Cather and Lewis, built cottages surrounding the Inn, left their cottages to nieces. In time, with all of the nieces married and Whale Cove Inn open to the general public, the Inn survived, but the Cottage Girls and their summer colony simply slipped from view.

A final note about the writing: as fiction writers do, I exercised literary license. Occasionally I rearranged facts for the plot's convenience. Cather and Lewis really did build a stone wall behind their cottage, but it was actually constructed by Oscar Locke and Charles Green, the island carpenters who built their cottage. And none of these events actually happened in 1929. In February of that year, Alice Coney and her sister Grace were killed in an automobile collision at Winter Park, Florida, and for that summer Whale Cove Inn was managed by others. Sometimes what I saw on the island supplied ideas for the novel. Two small, aging watercolors in simple frames were propped on the fireplace mantel of what is now called "the Cather Cottage." "Oh," said Kathleen Buckley, who was showing me around, "Edith Lewis did those." At the time, I simply thought how wonderful then circled back later to take a closer look. The characters of Cather and Lewis I grounded in historical record, and I modeled the women of Whale Cove and The Anchorage on real people. I found a great deal of information on Ethelwyn Manning and Margaret Byington, for instance, but only a cheery little entry in the registry of The Anchorage for "Dot Viking Voorhees." The islanders, tourists, and others connected with the mystery are entirely my own creation.

Sue Hallgarth
Corrales, New Mexico

Acknowledgements

MY VIEWS OF Willa Cather and Edith Lewis came primarily from reading Cather's letters and Lewis' *Willa Cather Living*. My greatest debt is to them, to the late Kathleen Buckley, and to the many archives across this continent that hold Cather's and Lewis' correspondence—from the Huntington Library in California to the Houghton Library at Harvard, from the Cather Archives at the University of Nebraska-Lincoln to the University of New Brunswick–Fredericton and the Grand Manan Museum in New Brunswick, Canada. I am also grateful to members of the Cather and Lewis families, including the late Helen Cather Southwick, the late Katherine (Kay) Lewis Schulte, and the late Ruth Lewis Trainor. Thanks to the American Council of Learned Societies, Rutgers University, and Princeton University for giving me opportunities to pursue my research. And to those Cather scholars who went before: Sue Rosowski, Bernice Slote, and Virginia Faulkner.

I am also grateful for the generous advice, encouragement, and informative research of writers and scholars Cecil Dawkins, Melissa Homestead, Bill Howarth, Anne Kaufman, the late Rosemary Keefe, Betty Littleton, Lynn Miller, Susanne and Jake Page, Hilda Raz, and Ruth Rudner; Cather Foundation board members Lucia Woods Lindley and the late Mildred Bennett; those who know Grand Manan well—Laura Buckley, Jaune Evans, Sabra Jane Johnson, Ted Jones, and Dora McLaughlin L'aventure; and supportive readers and friends—Herb Altheimer, Libby Atkins, Tim Backes, Linda and Gloria Bailey-Davies, Sandra Becker, Barb Bracken, Linda Branstetter, Charlotte Bunch, Doris Burkemper, Roxanna Carrillo, Jeanne Englemann, Jennifer Gardner, Dorothy Haecker, Lucy and Rob Hays, Dorothy Helly, Clifford Hill, Sheila Kaplan, Ginny Kerr, Jeff Lucker, Ruth Mandel, Sally McGrath, Lynda Miller, David Muench, Dale Nordyke, Kathleen O'Malley, Leslie Peirce, Patti Peterson, Ronnie Riner, Linda Roe, Cynthia Secor, the late Janet Spector, Adrian Tinsley, Martha Trolin, Linda Vanzi, Jenn Verhoog, Gwen Walker, and Kate Woodward.

Thanks to those who helped with the production of this book—Mary Bisbee-Beek, Ann Weinstock, Sara DeHaan, and Charlie Capek—and to others who provided timely and essential advice: Randall Beek, Lisa Graziano, Beth Hadas, and Michelle Huff. A final thanks to my partner Mary Ellen Capek: without her, this book simply would not be.

Cecil Broad
7 Days Wk